PLAGUE

A God Blood Novel

MATTHEW JAMES

ALSO BY MATTHEW JAMES

THE HANK BOYD ADVENTURES
Blood and Sand
Mayan Darkness

THE GOD BLOOD NOVELS
Plague

STANDALONE NOVELS
Dead Moon (2016)

PRAISE FOR "PLAGUE"

"PLAGUE is a monstrously thrilling read! If you like thrills, chills, and nonstop action, then Matthew James may just be your next favorite author!"

–John Sneeden, Bestselling author of THE SIGNAL

"PLAGUE erupts from the pages in a steroid-filled tornado of terror and shock!"

—SUSPENSE MAGAZINE

"It doesn't take long for this action-packed story to kick into gear and keep the pages racing faster than a terrified gazelle on the Serengeti... A triumphant series opener that will leave readers chomping for the next installment!"

—Richard Bard, Bestselling author of BRAINRUSH

PRAISE FOR "THE HANK BOYD ADVENTURES"

"Matthew James, and the Hank Boyd series have been added to my must read list!"

–J.M. LeDuc, Bestselling author of SIN

"BLOOD AND SAND takes readers on a spellbindingly treacherous journey that also manages to have fun along the way."

–Rick Chesler, Bestselling author of
HOTEL MEGALODON

"The next Hank Boyd Adventure can't come soon enough!"
–David McAfee, Bestselling author of 33 A.D.

ACKNOWLEDGMENTS

This is the part of the book where I thank a few people who have helped and/or inspired me along the way. While this is still true, and there are many, I'd really like to take this time and thank my readers. Without your interest this section wouldn't exist and I'm truly humbled by that.

I'd also like to express my gratitude towards the person or persons responsible for recommending my work to you—even if it was a website that may have done it. I'd like to thank the luck (or maybe fate) that was involved when you saw an advertisement for my work somewhere out in cyberspace.

Here's to a long and happy friendship!

To the men and women fighting for our freedom, I salute you. Thank you dearly for defending my rights and mine and my family's lives.

PLAGUE

A God Blood Novel

PROLOGUE

Egypt, 1944

Erwin Johannes Eugen Rommel, Field Marshal for the Nazi's *Deutsches Afrikakorps,* stood watch as his men marched their recently captured prisoners through the force's makeshift camp. Known throughout the world as the *Wustenfuchs*—the Desert Fox—Rommel was an expert in desert warfare. The nickname was a testament to that.

"Mien Herr," a voice said behind him, announcing the arrival of one of his troops. Rommel turned, accepting the salute without verbally acknowledging the man. His cool and calm demeanor was renown, even in the desert's oppressive heat.

"Die erfasst werden festgenommen," the soldier continued, explaining that the recently captured had been successfully detained.

Rommel nodded his approval, turning back to his post on the small hill overseeing his men. He liked to watch from afar and marvel at his troop's efficiency and might. They would not give in, not with him leading them. He glanced over towards the prisoners, his face as stoic as ever. He had strict orders from the *Fuhrer* to eliminate all captives immediately, but he didn't believe in such treatment. Yes, Rommel was a Nazi, but he was a soldier first, and was respected by even his enemies for that reason.

"Mien Herr?"

Rommel didn't acknowledge the other man again. He just wanted to be left in peace. He looked up into the dimming sky, the sun almost touching the horizon now. Closing his eyes, Rommel dreamed of being back home with Lucie and the children, riding his motorcycle. He had it since he was a young boy and enjoyed every moment spent rocketing through his hometown's winding streets.

He could feel the warmth on his sunburnt face and welcomed the inevitable coolness that the approaching sunset brought. He dreaded every sunrise, knowing the cruel heat would soon soak his clothes in sweat and—

"Generalfeldmarschall?"

He turned at the sound of the soldier's interruption. The use of his official rank threw him off. It wasn't required out here, a respect he gave to his men. A simple *Sir* was all that was needed when addressing him. No, it was the questioning tone in the young man's voice, and when Rommel turned, he saw the soldier wasn't looking at him, he was looking past him.

The Desert Fox, peered north and saw something that shouldn't have been there. Barreling through the flattened section of sand, was a convoy of trucks, heading south. They were headed to his camp's front door.

He was momentarily perplexed as to why another wave of German forces would be headed this way. They were holed up fine here and had plenty of supplies for another year if needed. It felt like overkill to send *this* much more support.

At least a dozen large covered trucks, lined up like chicks following their mother, pulled up to the northern gate. From this distance, he could barely see the driver and the gateman conversing. But after talking for only seconds, the guard quickly lifted the entrance's long wooden arm, letting them pass.

He knew this wasn't right and he needed to find out what was happening. This was *his* command and he was becoming more and more furious as the seconds ticked by. Not knowing what was going on was unacceptable.

"Bekommen das auto!" Rommel barked to the young soldier, ordering him to bring around transportation. The private hurried off, finding the first vehicle he could, a Krupp 6x4.

It screeched to a halt beside Rommel as he hurriedly climbed into the six-wheeled truck's front passenger seat. The back was a flatbed, perfect for carrying munitions or other equipment, but it was currently empty, having been unloaded earlier that morning. It was one of at least a dozen or so models they had at their disposal here, at the heart of his Afrika Korps' outpost.

The "blocking force's" mission was to shore up the already established Italian defenses in northern Africa. They would supply them with reinforcements against the Allied forces, consisting of both men and machine, mostly Panzer tanks.

"Schnell!" Rommel ordered, as the other man floored the pedal, sending twin rooster tails of sand into the sky. They quickly accelerated, careening towards the approaching *herd* of elephant-sized vehicles.

Thirty seconds later, Rommel ordered the vehicle stopped, dead center in the road, hindering the army of Opel Blitz 3-ton cargo trucks from moving any farther.

The convoy didn't slow.

The young soldier grabbed at the driver's side door's handle, about to launch himself from the Krupp, but stopped, seeing his commanding officer go to stand. If he fled and Rommel didn't he'd be seen as a coward, leaving his senior officer behind to die.

Now beyond enraged, Rommel stood on the seat, raising his hand in protest, shouting for the lead truck's driver to stop. He *would* restore order. They *would* stop, or be tried and convicted for his death.

Finally, reacting after seeing Rommel for who he was, the driver hit the brakes, stopping the large truck from bulldozing them. The transport vehicle skidded to a halt, coming to a complete stop not ten feet from the general and the now shaking driver.

Wide eyed after almost running over Rommel, the Opel's driver threw the truck into park, and leapt out of the driver's side door. He ran up to the field marshal, a look of remorseful fright in his eyes. He almost singlehandedly turned one of the most feared and respected men in all the German military into paste.

"I entschuldigen," the man said apologetically, saluting Rommel. He then went on to explain what he and the other trucks were doing out here and the obvious hurry they were in.

After hearing the broad version of the driver's instructions, Rommel still didn't fathom why the Fuhrer would send a group all the way out here, especially since they weren't here as reinforcements. That was now apparent. They were here for some other reason...

Rommel was about to ask as such, when a passenger climbed out and marched over to him, joining him and the driver. Turning his attention to the newcomer, Rommel noticed two things. First, the man was clean cut and had a hardened look in his eyes. It was a look that could only come from fighting on the front lines, but the freshly shaved face was a sign that he hadn't recently. Secondly, the symbol on his chest gave Rommel a sinking feeling in the pit of his stomach. *Both* men wore the emblem of the Schutzstaffel—the Armanen runes of Himmler's SS.

The twin lightning bolts told him this was no

ordinary visit. *"Was—"* Rommel was about to question, but the second man cut him off, handing him an envelope.

He quickly took it and reached into his pocket. He procured a small pocket knife, unfolding it, sliding the blade under the pasted flap, tearing it open. He hurriedly read the script. It was addressed directly to him and was not to be opened or read by anyone else. This didn't mean anything though, he was the general after all, and he got plenty of classified documents all the time, mostly communiques from the offices of the Fuhrer—only... This particular dispatch *wasn't* from the Fuhrer... It was from Himmler himself.

After rereading the body of the message twice, Rommel still didn't understand why the SS's commander would send this to him. The Afrika Korps and the Schutzstaffel, while both parts of the Nazi's military arm, weren't exactly in communication with each other on a regular basis. Their *jobs* were completely different. His was war. Theirs' was... His thoughts immediately went to Himmler. Was he up to something—something the Fuhrer didn't know about?

It's then Rommel noticed a third man exiting the truck's cab. He was of average height like himself, but carried himself differently. This man was no ordinary soldier—if one at all.

The third man stepped up to Rommel, face hidden by a wide brimmed fedora. He was about to reprimand the man for not removing it and introducing himself, but the visitor did eventually take it off, finally revealing his face to him.

Normally unscathed by everything the world brought to his door step, Rommel's face went white. He couldn't believe who was standing in front of him. It was a man who was responsible for countless deaths, many by his hand.

Rommel looked into the sinister eyes of Auschwitz's *Angel of Death* himself, Dr. Josef Mengele.

DISCOVERY

"If we can teach people about wildlife they will be touched. Share my wildlife with me. Because humans want to save things that they love."

~Steve Irwin

"Nothing is more important to human society than preserving its natural capital. Nature does not need people. People need nature."

~Harrison Ford

1

Iraq, 2007

"Damnit, don't!" he grumbled in a shouted whisper, staring through the scope of his sniper rifle. "Don't do it, kid."

The driver was already dead, a bullet had just torn through his chest in a spout of blood and gore. Their job was to take out these particular weapons dealers and then incinerate the truck and its contents. They just couldn't prepare for the ages of two of the smugglers.

"The bloody wankers are just kids, Captain," another man said. "What do we do?"

Captain Logan Reed of Australia's elite, Special Air Service, looked down from their perch atop a cliff. He watched as one of the two *boys* bent over to reacquire the recently felled AK-47. The SAS was the Australian

Army's Special Forces division, and was world renown for their abilities—abilities that Logan had honed to a T over the last seven years of service. He was one of the best—if not the best—at what he did... Elimination.

Sweating heavily now, Logan readjusted his aim, firing at the only other clear threat in his sights, another middle-aged man. This one held a Rocket Propelled Grenade (RPG) launcher. The powerful rifle bucked silently, the round coughing like a man with a sore throat. It was in reality a whispered, *thwap*, silenced by a state-of-the-art sound suppresser attached to his rifle's barrel. The bullet hit the man dead center in his chest, knocking him off his feet, splattering the white truck's siding with the known terrorist's blood. Any higher and the larger caliber round would have taken the man's head clean off. Now that the *real* threat was over with, Logan was ready to let the kids walk away.

"What are they? Thirteen?" one of the other operators asked. Even Logan was still bewildered at the age of some of the *men* this part of the world used as soldiers.

"Fourteen at most," Logan replied through gritted teeth as the other boy ambled over to the fallen man's RPG.

For God's sake.

Logan breathed in and then out...hard, steadying his nerves if only a little and pulled the trigger of his Barrett M82 .50 caliber sniper rifle again. The round found its target, the passenger side window of the truck. He fired it straight between the two teens, hoping a closer shot would scare them off.

But it didn't.

The second kid, maybe even younger than the first, shouldered the RPG, looking for the source of the gunfire. He didn't find it, but his buddy did, letting loose a few rounds unsuccessfully towards Logan's SAS fire team. They were safely concealed from bullets though.

But not the RPG, he thought.

Their luck was about to run out.

It's then the younger child turned his attention towards them, aiming the RPG in their general direction, towards the outcrop of rocks that concealed Logan's team.

"Um... Captain? If that kid gets off a lucky shot, we're boned. What's the call?"

Logan knew his teammate was right and he knew what they had to do. He repositioned the scope in front of his right eye and breathed in heavily again. He wasn't what you would call a religious person, but even Logan found himself praying to whoever was listening for forgiveness. What he was about to do would surely block him from any kind of entry into Saint Peter's Pearly Gates, but maybe asking for forgiveness would help, if only a little.

"On my mark."

A single tear started to drip from his eye. If it did, it would surely blur his vision. He quickly blinked it away and reacquired the boy with the more dangerous weapon. It wouldn't have mattered if the salty liquid found his eye though, they weren't that far away, and he was a really, really good shot. His sight could be partially impaired due to injury, or in this case salinity, and he'd still hit his target.

"Three..." he said, beginning the countdown with a shaky voice. He again saw the boy pointing up towards their roost, his aim finally steadying a little more. They obviously had very little, if any, practice with the awkward armament.

"Two..." Logan's forehead started sweating profusely now, even more than the last couple of hours while they waited for the transport truck to show. The desert heat had nothing on this current situation.

"One..."

As he squeezed the trigger to his M82, Logan knew he had just given an order that would haunt him for the rest of his life.

* * * * *

That was almost ten years ago and dozens of useless therapy sessions later. Logan saw four different psychiatrists including a specialist who dealt with a lot of soldiers returning from active combat completely mentally screwed...like him. But they all wanted to drug him and make him feel like a Woodstock patron. He didn't need meds, Logan just wanted to know *what* was wrong with him and the proper way to deal with it.

He was eventually diagnosed with Post Traumatic Stress Disorder—or PTSD—which was unfortunately a very common condition with soldiers still overseas and also those coming home. It was a debilitating psychological condition and affected those who suffered from it differently. Some were just severely depressed, but others became psychotic, and some even became suicidal.

Logan liked to think of himself as somewhere inbetween them all. He had some pretty messed up nightmares, like jumping from very tall buildings, but hadn't actively tried to end his own life. Even being on the better side of the *PTSD Bridge*, Logan still wasn't the same man he was before he ordered those kids dead.

After the Iraqi incident, Logan couldn't forgive himself. A lot of the men returning home were dealing with similar issues, having seen friends and innocent civilians die, but he believed himself to be solely responsible for the deaths to two teenagers, personally handing out the kill order.

He had instructed his team to hit them with everything...and they did. The SAS didn't screw around when it came to any type of terror cell, even one that used children on the front lines, or as brainwashed delivery boys in this particular case.

The men in charge back home in Australia called it 'collateral damage,' feeling none of the remorse Logan felt. After the words were spoken, Logan had to be restrained by a fellow soldier, his number two, Gray Fitzpatrick, or 'Fitz' to anyone who knew him. Logan would later tell one of his shrinks of the vision he had of ripping his commander's throat out and chucking the bloodied mess out the window.

More meds were recommended.

The next day Logan resigned from the army, stating that he no longer believed in what they fought for. But that was a lie, Logan cared more than anyone what his country stood for. He just couldn't face the facts that he was too scared and heartbroken to go back out into the field.

What if I had to do it again? he asked himself. He decided that the best way to prevent it from happening again was to not be involved in it anymore. But again, he knew better. If it wasn't him leading a team into a shitstorm, then it would just be someone else doing it. Someone less qualified most likely.

He lived off his savings for a year and was eventually contacted by a long, *long* distance number.

The hell? Logan thought, seeing the strange number. He'd gotten used to seeing odd numbers calling him lately. He'd been late paying several bills and had even stopped paying some others altogether.

He almost didn't answer it, but something inside him told him to do so. "Logan?" The voice on the other end asked when he silently answered. "You there, baby brother?"

"Yeah..." he said, sighing at the way his older sister, Cassidy Jo Reed—or CJ as she preferred—greeted him. It was her way of teasing him after all these years, even though she knew he wasn't exactly someone that *should* be messed with. It's what made it so fun for her. Logan was a very dangerous person and she knew it.

"What's going on sis?" he asked, getting to the point. He really wanted to get back to the 12-pack he had on ice. Drinking was the only medicine he believed in. He didn't necessarily abuse it, but it was the only thing that calmed him down when things got dicey mentally.

"Well, actually," she said. "I have a job for you."

"A job?" Logan replied, coughing, choking on his lager. "You...(*cough*)...called me about a job...in Africa?"

There was silence on the other end and Logan thought he lost the call. Sat phones did that sometimes, like the one his sister was calling from, but CJ was still there.

"A *big* job," she said, emphasizing the *bigness* of it.

"How big?" he asked, skeptical.

"Huge. The current game warden, Charlie, is set to retire and he asked me for a recommendation. He specifically requested if I knew someone with a background that would help keep the bastard poachers out here on the plains in check. A real and I quote, *go getter.*"

"What'd you tell him?" Logan replied, honestly a little curious.

"I said, *shit yeah I do, he'd be perfect.*"

Logan sat up, scratching his beard that he recently started to grow. He figured it really didn't matter how clean shaved he was anymore. It's not like he had anyone to impress that would give a damn.

"So let me get this straight," he said, standing. He began to pace as he continued. "You want me to leave Melbourne and move out to Tanzania and take over as the game warden of the Serengeti National Park?" He breathed. "You do realize I don't even know what the hell a game warden actually does?"

CJ just snorted a laugh, but calmed after a couple of loud guffaws. "Logan, slow down, you're overthinking this. Charlie is still six-months out from calling it a career and will be here to walk you through the paces of the gig."

Logan calmed at hearing the current warden would still be around for a little while. But still...

"Look, CJ, I—" He didn't get to finish.

"We need to know by tomorrow morning."

"Tomorrow?" Logan asked. *Bang!* "Ow, damnit!" He hopped around his apartment holding his busted toe, having just kicked the edge of his coffee table.

"Um, Logan?" CJ asked, listening to her brother empty his dictionary of curses into the phone. "You okay?"

Logan relaxed, flexing his toes. "I'm fine, but damnit that hurt!" He regained his composure a little more. "So...tomorrow, huh?"

"Yep," CJ said, laughing a little. "There are other internal candidates, but none of them are good enough. The only one capable is a real jagoff—name's Quinn—a real beast. Physically I mean, not mentally. The man's dumb as a box of rocks inside a bull's body."

"So what you're saying is... I'd be doing you a favor?" Logan asked, a smile creeping onto his face. "Is that it?" He could tell by the way she talked about it there was something uncomfortable between CJ and this Quinn fellow. *It seems CJ may have gotten a little frisky with a coworker recently.*

"Sort of..." CJ replied, sheepishly. "But it'd also be a fresh start for you and something you could be *constructive* with."

He knew what *constructive* meant. She was speaking to his abilities as a soldier, a leader, and a man of action. A man that could get the job done.

"Ugh," he groaned, scratching his chin again. "Shit, CJ... Okay look, tell the ole' codger to give me a week to pack and get there."

"So you're in?" CJ asked, her voice rising an octave with excitement. "Seriously?"

Logan stopped pacing and turned to the closet door off his bedroom. Inside was *everything* he brought with him from the SAS and then some. He could have started a small war with what he had collected over the years.

He gave the dead bolted door a smirk. "I'm in."

2

Tanzania, Present Day

"Georges! We've found them!"

Georges Boluva, leader of the *expedition*, stubbed out his cigarette and hurried over to the dig. When he arrived he smiled at what he saw. They had struck their professions version of gold. Twin tusks stuck out of the dry dirt like those of the skyscrapers he'd read about. If they had time to extract them...

We are going to be rich, he thought, smiling wide, revealing his stained yellowing teeth. He could already feel the money bulging in the empty pockets of his worn, faded jeans.

He turned and shouted orders to the others. "Clear off the rest of it! I want it fully uncovered and ready to move by night fall!"

No one argued with the seemingly impossible task

of raising and extracting the ivory in that short of time. They all knew the consequences of their actions here today if the Aussie caught them. It had been hell for people like him and his men to make a living in these parts since the newest warden had taken over. Rumors had it that he was a former soldier back in his homeland.

It doesn't matter, Georges thought, shoving another cigarette in his mouth, lighting it. *The Serengeti is a very big place. We 'should' be fine. Not even the great 'mlezi' could see everything.*

Should...

The word frightened him more than anything, but the reputation the *walezi* had was warranted. The *Guardians*, as they were called by the locals, had done a spectacular job to some, reducing the number of deaths caused by man by almost half since taking over nearly a decade ago.

Georges looked back down to the massive skull staring back at him, its hollow, lifeless eyes burning holes into him. It made him smile though. These were already dead and by the looks of them, they'd been here for quite a while. He and his men couldn't be charged with the killing of these creatures. Something else had slayed them. Something Georges' grandfather had told him about before dying when he was a boy.

There had been a legend of an ivory stockpile dating back to World War Two, but no one had been able to find it. Most had been looking for it in Northern Africa, where the Nazis were known to have ventured, eventually setting up various bases of operations. Egypt was the most popular locale to search.

"We just need to go where no one has looked yet," Georges had said to the men now with him. "The *stories* suggest they may have gone even farther south than originally recorded."

And so they went south, back to his grandfather's home in Tanzania. They had searched for months, asking every local tribesman they could find about the mythical treasure trove. It's only until recently that they had found any hard evidence that the burial even existed. But did it still hold its wealth...or had someone claimed it already?

They had stumbled upon a group of men making their way west to Lake Victoria to fish. One of them was easily in his eighties and confirmed that his own father had seen a line of trucks push through these parts in the 1940's. The Nazi's were supposedly headed to where the park now sits.

"Have you looked for it?" Georges asked the old man.

The elder man shook his head. "Never—for it is cursed."

"Cursed?" Georges asked, skeptical.

"By a demon," the old man said. "Brought to these lands by the Germans."

Georges thanked the man for the information and went on his way. He specifically remembered the look of fright in the old man's eyes that day as he looked up from the bull elephant's vacant stare. A faint breeze tickled his neck in the waning hours of daylight, causing his skin to break out into goosebumps.

Damn ghost stories, Georges thought, looking down at his arm. He then again peered into the animal's empty eye sockets, second guessing himself for writing off the legend as myth so easily. Legends had a way of holding some truth.

He stepped up to the edge of the large pit, surveying his men's work. Three large bulls, tusks and all, had been uncovered, along with a variety of other animals. None of them interested him like the elephants did. He and his men were here for one thing and one thing only. Ivory.

A scream quickly snapped him out of his thoughts as he saw two of the diggers scampering back, frightened by something in the mass grave. Their wide-eyes held pure terror in them.

"What is it?" Georges asked as the men climbed out of the burial. "What did you find?"

Daudi was the first to speak. "We found bodies, Georges."

"Of course there are bodies, Daudi," Georges replied, laughing. "What did you think you would—"

"Not those," Daudi interrupted. "Those…"

The frightened man pointed back down into the pit, towards the bodies of the other animals. Next to what may have been an extremely large cat of some kind, was a boot.

A boot? Georges thought. *Why is there a boot in my dig—*

He realized what it must be. He leapt down into the site and carefully stepped over an excessively large, half buried cat, kneeling where his two scared comrades had fled from. He dug into the earth with his bare hands and found a pant leg. He then moved up and brushed aside more dirt, revealing a belt buckle.

Filled with an anxious nervousness, Georges quickly cleared the body, finding an all too recognizable emblem on the man's sleeve—one that was easily recognizable around the world.

"It can't be..."

He reached for the soldier's insignia and pulled. The corpse's entire left arm came away with the movement, making Georges fall backwards and wince as something scraped against his hand. On his back, he leaned up and inspected the wound, finding only a superficial cut. It was nothing he had to worry about as long as he cleaned it out immediately.

The webbing between his thumb and forefinger came away with a droplet of blood. He quickly stuck it in his mouth, stopping the bleeding instantly and winced. It tasted like metal, and dirt, and something he couldn't identify. He spat the grit to the earth beneath him and started to stand.

Ugh, he thought, regretting his quick instinct to clot the bleeding with his mouth. The taste was truly awful.

"Georges," called Daudi, "you okay?"

He went to wave off his friends, but stopped as he saw something strange happening to the nail of his thumb. At first it slowly darkened, like he hit it hard, bruising the underside. Then, it quickly turned black as if about to fall off, but it didn't. It started to grow, forming into a point at the end.

What?

He then experienced a horrible pain in his other fingers, like someone was pulling all of the nails of his right hand out at once. He screamed in agony, howling into the hot, dry air.

As he wailed, his teeth began to ache, like they too were being pried from his body. Blood flowed down his chin and onto his shirt as the agony continued, sending Georges into a comatose-like state. He fell, blacking out from the pain, but caught himself before he struck the ground.

What? he thought, but his question quickly vanished. Another sensation took root, taking the place of his worries, and it was infinitely more powerful. Hunger.

Daudi and the other man, Jengo, rushed to his aid, but stopped when Georges sat back on his knees and looked up to greet them. They just stayed there, mouths agape, at the sight in front of them.

Meeting their fear filled gaze, Georges smiled, kneeling in the dust of the dead, revealing his still forming fanged filled mouth. The teeth were as black as night, like his finger nails, and his eyes were quickly changing—turning the color of blood.

The only thing Daudi and Jengo could think of was that the demonic presence that *obviously* haunted this place took over the other man's body and—

Georges attacked before either man could verbally question him. He slashed and ripped at them with his newly formed claws and dagger-like teeth.

Neither man stood a chance.

Once both men were dead, Georges cocked his head to the side and grinned. He could hear the others coming to investigate the noise.

He would kill the others.

And then feed.

3

"Sir!" A man yelled from the corner of the command center, his voice laced with a Swahili accent. "We have reports of poachers in the plains. Jan is en route but only has one other man with him."

Logan turned. "Who's with Jan, Mo?"

The local man, Molambwe Monembu, also known as 'Mo,' stood, retrieving a Mossberg 590A1 tactical shotgun from the weapons supply rack. His station, which was mostly compound security, was surrounded by screens and computer monitors. He faced north through the tinted glass windows of the third floor Observation Deck.

The rest of the third floor was built like a *huge* studio apartment. It was one massive room with no partitions, minus the cubical-like desks arranged around its interior. Logan's workstation was in the center of the room, *surrounded* by a dozen weapons racks and supply closets. Not only was he the leader of his team, but he was also its weapons expert...for obvious reasons. Instead of making his men maintain their own weapons, Logan charged himself with doing it. It was a *hobby* of sorts and the intricate tinkering helped him with his PTSD.

It was normal and monotonous work to him and kept his mind busy and off the alternative. *His* perfect therapy. He ditched the twelve-packs after coming to Africa. An active duty soldier—of any kind—needed to be in both peak physical and mental condition at all times. Alcohol squelched both, but he was also human, and did like to indulge in the occasional adult beverage during his off hours.

"It's Fitz, sir," Mo replied, loading the weapon. "He said to send in the cavalry."

Logan's eyes went wide at the prospect of Fitz, the man he'd known for fifteen years, calling for help. The two men were close from their days in the SAS, and when he came calling about a job after he retired, Logan immediately hired him as his new second in command. *Just like the old days,* Logan thought.

Like Logan, Fitz was never the same after they took out the truck full of munitions and its four sellers...including the two teens. It was his and Logan's bullets that finished the job and neither one of them fully recovered. Fitz held it together better than Logan did, enough so, to stay in the army, that is. The other man, like Logan, still had the occasional nightmare, spurred from the horrible memory of that day.

"Alright, Mo, saddle up. Get Saami and Pandu and

make for the roof. We're taking Kipanga for a ride."

Mo's face lit up when Logan mentioned their new*ish* transport helicopter, a retired military Blackhawk. *Kipanga*, meaning *hawk* in Swahili, was a recent edition to the SDF. Mo had emphatically asked to be its pilot too, having experience in the air.

The Serengeti Defense Force, or SDF, was Logan's pride and joy. He formed the paramilitary group two years after establishing himself as game warden. The ten-man crew quickly became the most feared unit in all the Serengeti National Park, having been retrained and handpicked by Capt. Logan Reed himself.

Besides CJ, Mo was his first recruit. He was a pilot from across the northern border in Kenya, and was a natural for the team. He steadfastly believed in the conservation and protection of the animals in the park so much, that he'd been arrested several times for buzzing *hunting parties* with his small prop plane. He eventually crashed the plane and was subsequently arrested again. It would be the last time he'd be incarcerated though. CJ begged her brother to help Mo, respecting the local man's drive and over-the-top compassion. Logan abided by CJ's request, trusting her judgment of the man, bailing him out of jail on the condition that he'd come to work for him.

"Absolutely," Mo had said, climbing into Logan's secondhand jeep after just meeting him. Eventually, Mo had recommended two more Kenyans, Saami and Pandu, join them. He trusted them with his life and Logan needed the men. But soon, Logan came to trust the men too. Neither one were pilots, like Mo, but were in fact, expert trackers.

Now hunched over a computer, Logan ran through a series of photos coming in from Fitz and Jan in the field. They were running recon in the area after a local tribesman reported seeing two trucks speeding through the plains earlier in the morning.

Logan looked up from the computer, scanning the inside of the Bullpen's command center, thinking.

Inside the circular high-tech building were three levels of the best that money could buy. That was the other thing Logan provided with his skills. Several unnamed multi-million-dollar conservationist companies heard of his exploits when he took over and wanted to help.

Through anonymous donations, adding up to the low millions, Logan built the *Bullpen*, named after the African *bull* elephant, or more specifically, Irwin.

Irwin was born the day Logan left the army and he saw it as good luck. He named him after his favorite celebrity growing up, the Aussie icon, the Crocodile Hunter. The love and respect Steve Irwin gave the animals and people of the various countries he traversed had always stuck with Logan. After hearing of Steve's unfortunate death while scuba diving, a piece of every Aussie died, Logan included. It was in his honor that he named the *real* king of the Serengeti.

"Logan?" asked a voice from behind. Logan knew it was CJ, especially since she was the only woman on the team.

"Hmm?" he mumbled, finishing up the slide of photos. They showed two sets of fresh tracks heading out to part of the plains that a lot of things, both human and animal, didn't venture. It was a random *dead zone* in the otherwise full-of-life park.

"You ready?"

He turned and found CJ dressed for war. She had on the standard SDF attire. She wore a snug fitting tan BDU, Battle Dress Uniform, complete with Kevlar vest. Stitched into the left breast was their logo, a simple African bull elephant head, its eyes blazing red. Logan made the logo and wanted it to instill a deep fear in anyone who opposed it. CJ recommended the eye color. She said, "It looks more menacing like that."

Her strawberry-blonde hair flowed in layers over her shoulders accenting her sharp green eyes—a family trait. A lot of the Reeds had those same green eyes, including Logan. If she wasn't in her early forties—and his sister—Logan may have appreciated the way the uniform fit her. He was never embarrassed thinking of his sister as a beautiful woman. He was proud to call her his sibling.

CJ barely looked to be in her mid-thirties let alone forty-two. Logan looked older than her and he was, in truth, four years younger. They both had good genes. Their parents were proof. Kenneth and Judy Reed were currently in their late-sixties, but could pass for people ten years younger. Their father still had a full head of hair, with only the hint of greying around the temples, whereas Logan had the sign of aging in his beard.

CJ said the greying made him look dignified.

Logan thought it made him look old.

The biggest difference with his and CJ's gear was that she didn't carry an assault rifle or shotgun. She wasn't a soldier and, quite frankly, was a terrible shot. She did however carry their standard issue sidearm, a Glock 23 .40 caliber pistol. They all did. It was the most durable weapon on the market and could withstand the sand and everyday grime of the African plains better than any of the weapons they tested and subsequently carried.

Of which, he thought, thinking about the handgun. *She's a great shot.* CJ always had jittery hands growing up, and couldn't aim a rifle for shit because of it. But a pistol? She could hit a gnat's ass.

"Coming along?" Logan asked, grabbing his custom made FN SCAR assault rifle from the weapon's rack. He would have preferred his M82 though. He had two of them sitting in the primary weapon's rack, just in case, but he hadn't needed either in some time. He very rarely needed to hit a target from long range anymore, moving or otherwise, since they *acquired* Kipanga. They could get up close and personal very, very quickly now.

CJ smiled. "You know I am." She then drew her weapon, checking it over like he had taught her. "I've been meaning to have Mo take me around for a sweep of the area. Might as well kill two birds and come with."

"Could be dangerous," Logan said.

"I seriously doubt that," CJ said, snorting out a laugh and grinning from ear-to-ear, laying it on thick. "You guys are just *too* good for that."

Never turning away from praise, Logan just shrugged. "True enough."

He checked over his beloved CQC, Close Quarters Combat rifle, slapping in a fresh mag. Then, like a warrior on the battlefield Logan grabbed three extra, slipping them into their assigned pockets on his vest.

He looked up into CJ's weary face. She didn't like it when he went all Rambo and overkilled the ammo. But Logan just smiled his perfected shit-eating-grin.

"Let's go have some fun."

4

Kipanga soared northeast, away from the setting sun, towards Fitz and Jan's signal. It would take nearly thirty minutes by air to reach the two SDF troops, so there was time to kill.

Logan sat up front with Mo scanning the surrounding land, lost in thought. He remembered riding around this very expanse of land with Charlie Whitten, his predecessor, while he gave him his first tour of the surrounding area.

"The Serengeti is 12,000 square miles of protected land," the South African said, motioning to the general landscape with one hand, while steering the rusted Jeep with the other. "It sustains over seventy large mammal and five hundred bird species—give or take a couple. And that's not even counting all the other little critters crawling or slithering around out here. I doubt there has ever been a true census ever taken. At least, not in the last thirty-plus years since I've been here. It would be almost impossible to do it."

Logan just sat in the front passenger seat, marveling at the sight. Off to his right was a herd of wildebeest. There had to be at least a couple hundred of them— maybe more. They moved like a school of fish, bobbing and weaving through an invisible current, moving as one.

The two men had also passed a family of African bush elephants twenty minutes ago along their left side, about three hundred yards off. Charlie mentioned that the larger animals were used to him and his men buzzing around and didn't mind their presence. Unless they got too close, that is.

Note to self, Logan thought. *Don't sneak up on a six-ton bull and his mates.* The Jeep barely weighed a third of that.

"The *Loxodonta africana* is currently the largest land animal in the world and is loved and respected by everyone who lives and works in this part of the world. Even the poachers," Charlie had said when passing the herd. "But they love them for far different reasons."

Ivory smuggling was still a lucrative business venture in these parts and fetched a price of nearly six hundred American dollars per pound. There was literally no other *job* that paid as well.

Logan shifted his weight in Kipanga's reupholstered co-pilots seat, clearly uncomfortable with the thought of all the killing and maiming the elephant population had gone through. Unfortunately, most of it had happened in the last few decades. The economy had taken a dump world-wide and work was tough everywhere, especially in Africa.

Bullets were still relatively affordable though. He knew if the cost of ammo were to sky rocket one day it would put everyone out of business. Even his men would find it hard to justify the use of the ammunition. *So would the poachers.*

Either way, his park's kill rate had been cut in half since he developed the SDF, but there were still deaths, most they never knew about. Generally, they would find the body of a dead creature, baking in the sun, long dead, its bones picked clean by the various scavengers populating the area. The Serengeti was just too big to fully protect.

Even with their poaching rates dropping significantly, the death toll of the African elephant, as a whole, continued to decrease. He didn't care how, but Logan was damn sure going to make the bastards hunting them down work for it. It's why he called in a favor and had Kipanga delivered.

It happened over night. Two Blackhawks arrived and only one left. There were no 'hellos' and no 'thank yous,' just the delivery of their saving grace. It had taken a lot of work, but they had their new ride and it immediately paid dividends. A rusted-out truck couldn't flee the scene anymore. Not easily, anyways.

He and CJ, along with the Kenyans, Mo, Saami, and Pandu, flew at full speed towards Fitz and Jan's last reported location, weapons hot and ready to go. They left Kel, Adnan, and Dada back at the Bullpen to watch over things.

Kel was Mo's right-hand-man with base security and preferred to stay put if he could, especially when Mo had to do his pilot thing. Kel had a strong heart...but a weak stomach. Dada was very laid back and would do whatever was asked of him. He was truly the utility man of the team. He had talents sprinkled into everything, but excelled at mechanics and general repair. He'd become the unofficial handyman of the team a few years back, and loved it.

And then there was Adnan... He was what you would call the "nerd" of the group. He was the SDF I.T. guru and basically hated going outside in the heat. He preferred the control room on the third floor or the server room/bomb shelter at basement level. Air conditioning and electronics were his true loves. Heat and dirt... Well, let's just say, he despised them as much as the poachers.

Regardless, their home was in good hands, Logan thought. He had triple checked everyone's backgrounds and personally interviewed each of them twice, looking for inconsistencies. "Military paranoia at its finest," he had said when CJ asked him about his hiring process.

Plus, he wanted to do the people who financed them the due diligence to make sure he weeded out the crazies and put together the best-of-the-best. He had one consistent theme with his recruits. Conservation. Everyone in the SDF was a nut when it came to protecting the various species that called the Serengeti home.

"Mentally stable nutjobs?" Fitz asked, laughing. "Like us?" Logan actually smiled a little at that whenever he thought of it. *Like us.*

Logan also laughed inwardly at the notion that he was probably the *least* passionate about conservation, but that was a good thing to him. He really did love and respect the animals here, so if he found people that loved them *more* than him...

The newest member of the Serengeti Defense Force was Jan Gruber, a German. *Yan,* as it's pronounced, was actually a recommendation by Fitz. He had met the man a few years back, before joining Logan in Africa. Jan was on holiday in Australia right when Fitz retired from active service and the two of them randomly met in a local dive bar. Apparently, the big man loved the opera and was fulfilling something on his bucket list, seeing the shell-shaped Sydney Opera House.

Jan was in his mid-forties at the time and he himself recently retired from the German Army. The two men instantly bonded and stayed in touch, even after Fitz left for Africa. Now fifty, Jan was built like a tank and was easily the most physically gifted of the team. Even at his age, Jan could out lift and out run anyone in SDF. He was even a relative of the legendary World War Two Nazi General, Erwin Rommel.

The first thing he told Logan when he was interviewed was that he had never and would never believe in anything his great-uncle represented. He did, however, respect the man's might in the field.

"As did his enemies," Logan said.

"You know your history, Herr Reed," Jan said, smiling. He was pleased that Logan knew his history.

"Yes, I do," Logan replied, "and its Logan."

"Ten minutes out," Mo said through the soundproof headphones. "Get ready to drop in five."

Logan sat up, fully back into reality, and began to sweat. *What on Earth was there out here for these two to call in reinforcements?* He turned and looked back into the body of the aircraft, finding CJ's worried eyes. Apparently, she felt the same thing. *I guess we're about to find out...*

Unbuckling his seatbelt, Logan climbed in back with the rest of his team. He clipped on to the support bar above his head, attaching a heavy-duty carabiner clip to his waist via a custom rappelling harness. They didn't land Kipanga, not without clearing the area first. They would then throw a line from the aircraft to the ground below and rappel from thirty feet up. Only when the area was secure would they call in Mo. Losing the chopper was not an option, so they took these calls with the thought that the *hawk* could get destroyed or stolen, leaving them to rot in the African sun.

Or get eaten by something at night...

5

"Go, go, go!" Logan yelled, as the two side doors flew open. Immediately after the first *GO* was shouted, rappelling lines were cast out into the night sky, followed by leaping bodies. Logan and CJ, one after the other, jumped from the left side door, as the Kenyans, Saami and Pandu, leapt from the right side.

Logan and Saami landed first, disengaged their lines, and fanned out, weapons up and ready. CJ and Pandu joined them, having just arrived and unclipped. Mo then pulled up on the collective, banking the Blackhawk off to the south where it would wait, circling five hundred feet up, waiting for Logan's all clear.

They were still a mile out and would hoof it the rest of the way there. Seeing nothing, Logan slowly stood from his crouch, finger hovering over the trigger of his SCAR, ready for anything. The others stood, following their leader. He then took a step north, towards their rendezvous point with their people in the field.

"Okay," Logan whispered. "Go green and move out."

As one, all four of them flipped down their night vision devices and went *green.* The world around them instantly bloomed to life, causing the surrounding landscape to glow in various shades of green. After adjusting to the new color spectrum, they all broke out into a sprint, something that was made more bearable as the minutes went by. The sun had fully set halfway into their helicopter ride, making their run a little more tolerable. The ground was still hot as hell, but it would slowly cool as the night wore on.

Ten minutes later, they arrived at a large kopje. *Koppies*, as they were referred to, were large rock formations found mostly in southern Africa. The Serengeti was technically in the southern region of the continent, but at its northern end in Tanzania.

Logan stopped as an out-of-place, but familiar, birdcall sounded over the airways. Then, he saw it. Parked at the base of the thirty-foot koppie was a Land Rover belonging to Fitz and Jan.

As Logan's team moved in, two men stepped out from behind a large bush to the right of the flat black vehicle. They were dressed identically to him and the others, also sporting similar night vision gear.

He stopped, getting right to the point. "What's the situation?"

"Ugly, boss," Fitz said in his usual casual demeanor.

"It's on the other side of the rocks." He motioned to the three story tall pile.

"What is?" CJ asked, stepping forward.

"The bodies," Jan said in his thick German accent. "It is not for the faint of heart."

"Wait," Logan said. "I'm confused. There aren't any poachers? No one alive?"

Both Fitz and Jan shook their heads no, which perplexed Logan even more. Why sound the alarm with everyone gone or dead?

"So why are we here?" CJ asked, on the same thought waves as her brother.

The two men looked to each other and shrugged. "Honestly," Fitz said. "I'm completely in the dark—no pun intended—on what to do here. Some of the bodies look fresh. Some don't."

Logan just nodded. He didn't expect his men to know what to do in every circumstance. That was his job. He trained his mind and body to handle every situation that could be thrown at him. *Well,* he thought. *Almost all of 'em.* They did the right thing calling it in.

"Was it an execution?" Logan asked, as Jan turned, leading them around the right side of the large koppie, shotgun wedged tightly to his broad shoulder.

"No," the big man said. "It is a burial of some kind—looks like they were working for quite a while."

"So—"

"Look mate," Fitz interrupted. "Just look for yourself and tell us what *you* think it is. I personally, have no bloody clue."

What the hell could have gotten two former soldiers so spooked out here? Logan thought, scanning the terrain.

As they rounded the last of the boulders, the scene came into full view. It was definitely a pit of some kind—maybe thirty-by-thirty and another ten deep.

Logan cautiously and quietly walked up to the edge of the pit and stopped. *What the...*

He had no idea what to make of it. Inside was a mass grave, but it wasn't animals or people... It was both. Multiple species were represented here, some missing limbs. Some their heads.

"CJ," Logan said quietly, still trying to take it all in.

He could hear the crunch of her boots as she approached. "Oh, God."

Logan glanced through his night vision goggles at his sister, seeing a gloved hand to her mouth. He wasn't sure if she was just reacting to the sight, or actually trying to hold back her vomit.

Probably both, he thought.

"What do we have?" he asked, trying to get down to business. He knew what some of them were down there, but she was truly the expert. The PhD after her name said as much.

"Well," she said, calming her nerves, "we have *Loxodonta africana*—the African elephant. There are also *Pathera leo* and *Panthera pardus*—the lion and the leopard. I also see a few *Crocuta crocuta*—the spotted hyena. Plus, a couple of different genus of gazelle and of course...those blokes there."

Logan looked down, following the outstretched

arm of his sister. She pointed below their feet, at the base of the animal pile where the five *fresh* bodies lay.

"Who are they?" she asked, stepping back.

Fitz and Jan took her place, one on either side of Logan. "Poachers most likely," Fitz said, "but I'm not exactly sure *why* they are in the hole with the rest of the dead."

"No bullets," Jan said, pointing out the obvious.

"Look," Logan said, motioning to three of the dead poachers. These were gathered around a long and girthy tusk of what Logan knew to be a bull. A chainsaw lay at their feet.

"It can't be..."

The two Aussie men snapped their attention to the right, straight at Jan, who stepped back in shock. They had never seen him with a look of abject horror on his face before. Logan didn't even think the man was ever scared.

He is now.

"What is it, mate?" Fitz asked, trying to place a hand on his shoulder.

The bigger man flinched, but stopped when a smaller, gentler hand caught his arm. CJ stepped up beside him, rejoining the three men at the edge of the grave. The two had become close over the last year and neither held back their feelings for the other anymore.

Logan wasn't exactly sure if they were technically an *item.* It didn't matter either way as he approved in her choice. Jan was a strong person, both mentally and physically, and would take care of CJ—not that she couldn't handle what life threw at her by herself.

"What is it, Herr Gruber?" Logan asked, getting Jan's attention, focusing the man.

Jan stepped forward, blowing out a heavy breath. "It's the men in there with the animals."

Logan looked back down into the pit at the dead poachers, confused. *That's what got this guy all worked up?*

But before he could voice as much, Jan continued. "Look past the newly dead—to the old."

Eyebrows creased, Logan did as instructed and paid no attention to the five poachers. He glanced at the first man, noticing the bullet hole in his head. *What the hell?* This one was *obviously* older than the others, but besides the unnerving execution-style bullet wound, he only saw shredded rags.

Clothing.

Logan then moved on to the next and instantly saw it, embroidered into the man's uniform. Everyone on the planet that wasn't just born yesterday would be able to recognize the emblem.

"Bollocks."

CJ and Fitz followed suit and found the body that Logan had seen and instantly froze in the still warm nighttime air. As one, they all shuddered at the symbol's meaning.

"Is that...?" CJ asked, her voice trailing off. She knew what it was, but didn't want to believe it.

"A swastika," Logan said, confirming her fears.

"It's worse than *just* the swastika."

Everyone turned to Jan.

"Look at the *other* symbol my friends."

"Ah, shit," Fitz said, seeing the easily recognizable double lightning bolt.

"It's not just the Nazis," Jan said, breathing heavily. "It's Himmler's SS... The Schutzstaffel made it to Tanzania."

6

"The SS made it down here?" Logan asked. His knowledge of World War Two was fairly deep, but he didn't know the finer details. He'd studied general *World War History* while in the service on his down time. He figured if he was in the business of preventing wars, he should, at the very least, learn about them.

"No, they didn't," Jan said, shaking his head as he turned away from the pit, leading the others away from the foreboding place. If he had hair, it would have whipped back-and-forth with as hard as he shook it. "Not that I know of, anyways."

"What of your family? Was there ever an account of them traveling this far south?" Logan asked.

"There were some...ghost stories," Jan replied. "I have heard tales that never made it to the tabloids, but we were made to believe them as the stuff of myth or folklore."

"Anything about the SS having business in Tanzania?" Fitz asked, gripping his combat shotgun tighter.

The sound of shifting dirt caught everyone's attention as a breeze kicked up the dirt surrounding the dig. Then as quickly as it came, it stopped, returning the site to its previously quiet state.

"Not officially, no," Jan said, "but there were rumors and hearsay about a convoy of Nazi transport trucks arriving at Rommel's Egypt base unannounced. It was said he was ordered by the offices of Hitler via transcript to not record their visit in any log books on penalty of death."

Logan knew that the news of a Nazi SS team making it down to southern Africa would change the way we viewed some of the war. He also knew it would bring a number of unwanted visitors. Which begged the question...

"What do we do with this?" he asked the group. "It's not like we can just cover this up, or forget we ever found it."

"Either way," Jan added, "we are going to have every fanatic on the subject traipsing all over our park. Nature is best left alone. We know that. We don't need hundreds—maybe thousands—of people coming to see this site, destroying the various habitats."

"Or endangering themselves to some pretty nasty buggers out here," CJ added, motioning to the land around them—the whole of Africa.

The sound of shifting wind and dirt struck the

group again, this time eliciting a yelp from CJ, who was nearest to the pit.

"I think that came from down there," she said, pointing down into the burial. The trembling of her finger as she pointed definitely gave Logan a reason to believe her. Yes, CJ was quick to startle, but the woman didn't *scare* easily.

"Nah," Fitz said, "they're dead, mum. Was probably just the wind picking up and whipping through the brush—"

The sound started again, this time getting everyone's attention...towards the excavation. Something was definitely moving down there.

"You think one of the poachers is alive?" CJ asked, Glock already clutched in her hand.

"Could be," Logan said, "but they sure looked down-for-the-count to me when we checked."

Then, what sounded like a muffled moan sang out from the bottom of the pit, getting a response out of Pandu. The Kenyan, Saami's twin in every way—minus the lower tone of his voice—edged towards the rim of the crypt, rifle slightly shaking, but ready.

"Logan, sir," Pandu said in heavily accented English. He paused, looking straight down into the seventy-year-old tomb. "Something moves—"

As the man said, "moves," a clawed hand sporting black dagger-like talons, reached up and out of the grave, stabbing into Pandu's gut. Before he could scream out in pain, the hand gripped his pierced stomach and yanked, sending the bleeding SDF member into the shadows below.

"Pandu!" Saami shouted, seeing his brother attacked and taken. He rushed to the lip, weapon raised, and screamed. "Oh my God! They're killing him!" He then released a barrage of gunfire into the darkness as his brother wailed in agony.

Just as he was about to send his third three-round burst, another hand, this one coated in what could only be his brother's blood, wrapped around his ankle and squeezed. The audible sound of the man's bones breaking was horrifying and his shouts of pain worse, as he too was dragged down into the burial.

They're? Logan thought to himself, recalling Saami's horrified words. *There's more than one. But how many?*

"The fuck?" Fitz yelled, leveling his Mossberg at the opening twenty feet in front of them. "What the hell is going on Logan?"

Logan froze, unable to move. He had no idea how to react. He was more than qualified to take on just about anything this world had to offer. But this...this was something different.

For what seemed like minutes, but was really more like seconds, the only thing the SDF members could hear was the tearing of fabric, the snapping of bones, and the chewing of flesh.

"Back up," Logan whispered. "Slowly."

What was left of the initial team backpedaled as one, making it another twenty feet. Then, a hand emerged from the hole, covered in even more blood than before. It did, indeed, sport a set of menacing black finger nails. Logan then saw a form behind the hand rise. Followed by another. And another. And another. Six in all.

Six? Wait... There should have only been five, he thought, terrified. There had only been a couple times in his life when he was genuinely frightened, but this topped them all.

"Hey, boss," Fitz said, his voice quivering in fright. "Lose the green."

He glanced over and saw that Fitz, along with CJ and Jan, had ditched the night vision equipment. They were just standing there, staring towards where Saami and Pandu had been undoubtedly killed.

Following the advice of his trusted friend, Logan flipped the goggles up, and stopped. The only thing he could feel, besides his shaking hands and trembling legs, were the six sets of glowing blood-red eyes burning holes into him. The things that just killed two of his men in a matter of seconds peered up and over the rim of the grave, eyeing what he believed to be their next meal. He'd seen a predator's hungry look before.

This was much worse.

And then the owners of those devilish eyes attacked.

7

"Fire!" Logan yelled as he flipped down his night vision goggles. He opened up on the closest *man* with two quick three-round bursts, all six bullets finding their mark dead center in its chest. The man-thing stumbled and fell, but still stirred.

Damn, he thought. *How the hell do we kill them?*

A single round, popped from CJ's Glock, striking the man that Logan felled in the forehead. The poacher's head snapped back and he fell limp. Dead.

Logan, Fitz, and Jan got the hint.

Headshots.

All three men, carefully aimed their weapons. Logan fired another controlled burst into one of the four remaining men's heads, busting it open like one of Gallagher's watermelons.

Fitz and Jan both carried shotguns, which they boomed across the Serengeti from pointblank range.

The other crazed poachers fell in a heap of blood and gore, silencing the night air.

"Backs on me," Logan ordered. The three remaining members of the SDF team backed up into Logan, essentially creating a four-man compass of flying lead. If anything tried to spring a sudden attack, one of them would see it coming and alert the others.

"Was that all of 'em?" Fitz asked, scanning north.

"Should have been," CJ replied, "but who knows if there were others who weren't in the pit to begin with. They could be roaming the plains for all we know."

"It's not," Logan said, never taking his eyes off the pit. He knew he would never be able to get the vision of the six sets of demonic eyes out of his nightmares.

"What?" CJ asked, voice shaking.

They didn't see it.

"There were six of them," Logan replied. "Only five attacked us. Which means—"

"Which means..." Fitz said, finishing Logan's assessment. "Either the sixth is *dead* dead or he buggered off while we were busy with these blokes."

"Quiet," Jan said, firmly.

"What is it?" Logan asked in a whisper.

"Listen," Jan replied, his voice barely audible. He had a single finger pointed to his ear.

After a moment, they heard it. There was a faint shuffling sound, like someone—or in this case *something*—moving further off in the distance, away from the burial.

Damnit, Logan thought, keying his ear piece.

"Mo?" he said. "Come in for immediate EVAC. We have men down."

There was a long pause over the airways before Mo replied. "Yes, sir. On my way."

Logan looked up towards the koppie and had an idea. "I'm going up there to see if I can spot our friend. Watch my back—and your own—until Mo gets here."

Before anyone could argue, Logan ran for the thirty-foot rock formation. The boulders were small enough to scale, but large enough to hold his weight. A few of the inner rocks looked like they weighed a couple thousand pounds at minimum. On any other day—or *night*—he would have enjoyed the climb and the koppie's natural beauty, but not now. This was no ordinary night.

Halfway up, he could hear Mo coming in from his holding pattern somewhere in the nighttime sky. He was certainly making good time. *Like always.*

Reaching up, Logan found his last handhold. He then clasped the top edge of the rock, finding a seam, and pulled. As he hoisted himself up, the rock beneath his feet shifted, loosening. Scrambling for purchase, Logan shoved with his legs, rolling onto the top of the koppie.

He landed with a bang of what sounded like metal. He froze, unsure of what just happened. Now, lying on his back, Logan knocked the top of the *stone* rock formation with his elbow, duplicating the metallic *bong* of bone on metal.

"What the..." he said to himself, getting to his knees. Through his night vision, he could see what appeared to be stone, but as he knocked on it again, this time with his knuckles, it banged like you were pounding on the hood of your car.

He keyed his earbud. "CJ to me. Double time it."

"On my way," CJ replied, never asking why. It's only when she was halfway up that she asked. "What is it, Logan? Did you find the other...thing...that killed Saami and Pandu."

He was so engrossed with his find that he completely forgot to look for the sixth poacher. He quickly scanned the area, finding nothing.

Shit, he thought. *Another time.*

CJ hopped up to the six-by-six upper most rock, landing with a gong. She paused, looking utterly confused. Then, she looked down at her feet and stomped, prompting another report from the obviously metal *rock.*

"Um, that's not supposed to sound like that," CJ said, eyebrow raised to the heavens.

Logan stomped on it one more time, putting his 185-pound frame into it. The rock where he was standing didn't sound as empty.

"Trade spots with me," he said, motioning to CJ.

She complied and they carefully switched spots.

He stomped again, dead center, and the rock resonated, sounding almost...

"It sounds hollow," CJ said, like she read his mind.

"Lights," Logan said softly. They both lifted their night vision devices and turned on their ultra-bright LED flashlights.

"Damnit," CJ cursed, blinking hard, trying to force

her eyes to readjust quicker to the brightness. After two more heavy blinks, she looked down and saw Logan fiddling with the edge of what looked like an opening of some kind.

"Is that what I think it is?" CJ asked.

Logan unsheathed his knife, a M9 Bayonet, and dug it into the crack between the stone and metal. He pushed and scraped until he dug into a crevice between the two. Once the blade tip was deep enough he asked CJ to move down a section and he pulled.

The six-by-six rock revealed a four-by-four hatch, as it popped free. The lid was heavy and Logan needed his sister's help to fully open it. They shoved together, opening the hatch, locking into place.

He couldn't help but smile. But then it faded as Mo came in low and fast, kicking up the dirt surrounding the dig.

Keying his earbud again, Logan spoke, "Jan you're with me and CJ. Fitz, go with Mo and see if you can spot the bastard that ran off. If you see him land the Blackhawk on his fucking head and take him out. I wanna' see a stain on the bottom of that bird when you get back."

After getting a round of "yes sirs," Logan peered down into the hole he just discovered and noticed two things. First, it wasn't a hole. It was the shaft to a hidden underground structure of some kind, complete with ladder. And secondly, he saw an emblem he knew all too well engraved into the underside of the lid. Twin lightning bolts.

"It's the same," he said more to himself, hearing Jan

come up from behind.

"The same as what?" The big German was so caught off guard by what he saw he almost fell backwards off the koppie.

"The SS," Jan said bewildered, CJ gripping his collar. "This can't be good."

8

He wandered through the dark, unable to see more than a few feet in front of himself. The moon, which normally provided enough light to see by, was behind dense cloud cover, only revealing itself a few seconds at a time. So, instead of relying on his sight, he relied on his other senses, particularly his sense of smell.

Georges Boluva, was born in Zambia, across Tanzania's southern border, near the capital of Lusaka. He grew up a poacher's son, so naturally he took to the family business. It's all he knew. It was the only *steady* job around now-a-day.

But now, he didn't remember any of that, and if he could, he wouldn't have cared. All he was concerned with now was his next kill...his next meal. He knew he hadn't always been as blood thirsty as he was now, but again... He didn't care. This felt right. It felt normal.

He looked down at his hands, seeing the elongated

obsidian colored talons on his fingers. He smiled at the prospect of using them again. *Up close, and personal.*

A sound like a creature stirring caught his attention as he meandered through the darkness. He quickly stopped unsure of the direction in which to go, but quickly heard the noise again off to his left. It was followed by a low growl, emanating from a creature he knew very well. A lion.

Fueled by the bloodlust that now consumed him, Georges charged into the dark, claws outstretched. He flexed his fingers as he neared, ready to hack and slash anything that he came across in the low light.

He stopped a few hundred feet later and smiled a sickly, fang filled grin. These too were new...and he liked them. It helped him tear the throat out of one of the men that got too close. The men with the guns.

Movement caught his red tinted gaze as the cloud cover opened enough for him to see the family of lions fifty feet away from him. He stopped and licked his lips. He could smell the blood that pumped though the beast's heart, feeding the rest of the animal's body with the life giving liquid. It was intoxicating, like that of a woman's sweet perfume. He could see it too, through the crimson that engulfed his vision. The pulsating of major arteries was there just underneath the skin.

A roar broke him out of his stupor—and just in time too. For what he saw would give the *normal* man pause and then fear. A male—a big one—was pounding through the open plain, quickly cutting the distance between the two predators.

He smiled again. He was no *normal* human.

Not anymore.

He is not the predator, Georges thought. *He is the prey.*

He lunged, raking his razor sharp nails across the animal's snout. It roared again in fury and in what sounded like pain, but Georges knew from experience—even though he couldn't remember how he gained such knowledge—that the big cat was far from defeated. It would fight to the death.

So will I.

Georges went on the offensive, catching the lion off guard. He thrust out his left hand, using his newly formed claws like a set of daggers, and caught the lion in the throat. As he attacked, the male swiped at him, dragging its own large claws through his flesh.

But it did not hurt. It barely bled at all. The only sign of injury were the slash marks themselves and what little blood did spill. The liquid was bright red and dripped from the various veins that now bulged from his black skin.

The lion wheezed, its breathing compromised, a few of the two-inch-long talons had found their mark, puncturing the lion's esophagus. With its oxygen supply quickly depleted, the male backed away, confused and dying, but Georges advanced, stalking his prey.

You are prey.

Then, as quick as a lightning flash, Georges lunged, teeth bared.

9

The clanging of boots on metal echoed through the vertical shaft, increasing the tension Logan felt in his temples. The resonating sound felt like a jackhammer was going to town on the inside of his skull.

"How much further?" CJ asked from above. He had gone in first, shortly after dropping three glow sticks down the entryway. They landed with a soft clapping noise fifty feet later—twenty feet *below* ground level of the plains outside.

Fitz had indeed met up with Mo and the two men immediately took to the sky, searching for the lone poacher. The one that got away. They needed answers and he—it—was the only thing that could provide them. So for now, the pit was off limits, just in case some sort of World War Two era contagion was down there.

That's what Logan was betting on, anyways. He saw what the men had turned into. He would never forget it either.

The blood-red, glowing eyes.

The dagger-like claws.

The ferocious behavior.

Something was definitely down there and they needed to figure out what it was. If this place is what Jan thought it was, then they would have their answers soon enough. That is...if the Nazis left anything behind when they bugged out.

Let's hope they did, Logan thought as his foot struck solid ground, startling him. He was so lost in thought that he hadn't even realized he had finished the fifty-foot climb. He turned and through the green tinted haze, saw a hall stretching away in the opposite direction of the mass grave now above them.

Taking up position just outside the short hallway, Logan aimed his SCAR down the corridor, and waited for CJ and Jan to join him.

A few seconds later he heard CJ land and then the heavier Jan after her. Both took up positions next to Logan, waiting for him to make the first move.

"Alright," Logan said. "Jan, take point. CJ you're next. I'll take up the rear."

"Logan?" CJ asked, about to complain. Normally he would have taken point.

"It's fine," he said, staring down the hall. "I'm out of my element right now and Jan can read German. Plus, he has the better weapon for clearing tight spaces like this."

Jan hefted his Mossberg tactical shotgun, a staple for them when out in the grasslands. They used steel slugs instead of your standard shell too. Slugs were good for taking down large predators or disabling engine blocks. The latter of which was standard practice for them. Ruining a poacher's vehicle was an important step to stopping them. They were much easier to find when forced to flee on foot and replacing the damaged vehicle would take time and money. Money was something they didn't generally have unless they poached something valuable—which goes back to the trucks and their importance. No transportation means no hunting.

Logan looked up towards the entrance and thought about the cat and mouse game Mo and Fitz must be dealing with right now. Even with all the advanced equipment they had on board Kipanga, it wasn't a sure thing they'd find the escapee. But it *was* possible now. If it was a year or two ago it would have been completely absurd to even try.

"Let's move," Logan ordered, voice just over a whisper. The others understood the need for stealth and answered in their own hushed tones.

From what he could see from the rear of the pack, there was an intersection about forty feet ahead and a door directly in front of them.

Jan lead them silently forward and stopped before entering the conjunction. He then leaned against the wall and quickly peeked out in both directions, right then left. After returning to the *safety* of the coverage the corner provided, he signaled for them to continue. They did, stopping in front of the door at the top of the T, the one Logan had seen just moments before.

Logan saw that the metal door had a name plate on it and, of course, it was in German. He saw Jan tilt his head to the side, thinking.

"We don't want to go in there," he said, turning back to Logan.

"Why?" he asked looking at the label. It read, *Waschraum.* "What's it say?"

"It's a restroom," Jan said with a grin. "Unless you have to go that bad?"

Logan could hear CJ snickering behind him as he shook his head. *Great, with everything going on...the first thing we find is a seventy-year-old shitter.*

"Fine," Logan said, "keep moving."

Back to business, Jan leveled his Mossberg and headed left.

He stopped twenty feet farther down the hall at another metal door. This one was on the corridor's left hand side and read, *Gehause.* Jan cautiously tried the door's handle, turning it until the bolt popped and the door swung open.

Swiftly, Logan and Jan took either side of the door, weapons ready. Holding up his fingers, Logan silently counted from three-to-one. When they hit one, both men spun and aimed through the doorway. What they saw gave them pause.

It, indeed, was a *Gehause,* the housing for the people who called this place home. They saw bunks and central tables, all of which were still covered with the belongings of whoever had lived here.

"It's like we've stepped into a Nazi-era time capsule."

Logan just nodded, agreeing with his sister's evaluation of the German barracks. On the left you had bunks stacked two high. There was at least a dozen of them.

But who's to say this is the only room like this down here? Logan thought, continuing to scan the room. *How large was the force stationed here?*

On the right side of the barracks you had more beds, but these were singles with no second tier above them. It screamed of an upper echelon. The bed sheets were even more elegant looking than the bunks had. The mattresses appeared to be softer too.

"The more privileged would have slept here," Jan explained, giving air quotes to the word, *privileged.* "The higher ranking officers and science types."

"Science?"

It's then Logan noticed a coat laying on the first bed to the right. A *lab* coat. Jan must have seen it upon entering and deduced what Logan now did. They stepped farther in, CJ moving towards the communal tables at the center of large room. He and Jan turned to the bed with the coat.

CJ found playing cards and half a pack of cigarettes on one table and a plate with long rotted food on another. Military jackets were strung occasionally on hooks next to what was probably their owner's bunks.

"Weapons," she said, seeing a variety of them leaning against the walls and lying atop several of the mattresses.

"Leave them," Logan said. "We have better and don't have the right ammo for relics like those."

"I didn't mean we should take them," CJ said. "I was going to comment that they were still here at all."

Logan agreed with her logic and instantly regretted jumping down her throat, but this place made him...nervous. He glanced over and saw multiple rifles, coated in seven decades' worth of dust. *What soldier would leave and not take anything with him— especially when you are stationed out in the middle of nowhere in Africa.* He then remembered the dead Nazis buried with the animals topside. *Maybe they didn't leave after all...*

Turning back, he picked up the coat, inspecting it, finding a name and an unfamiliar logo on the chest pocket. Tapping Jan on the shoulder, he got the man's attention off CJ and back to the task at hand, startling him.

Jan spun, noticing Logan staring at him through his goggles. "Sorry," the bigger man said. Logan couldn't tell if he was blushing, but he was pretty sure the man was.

"It's fine and so is she," Logan said in a hushed tone, a matter of fact. "She's strong."

Jan just nodded.

"Take a look at this," Logan said, holding up the embroidered coat. "You ever see this before?"

Jan took the coat and shook his head, brushing away the coat of dust from the logo. "No idea. But it wouldn't surprise me at all to learn of a secret scientific sect within the larger Nazi party."

"What do you mean?" Logan asked.

"Look."

Logan saw it instantly. The swastika was obvious, but the symbol it was accompanying was what threw him off. Surrounding the "hooked cross" was a helix. The universal symbol representing a DNA strand.

"What about the text underneath the symbols? What does it say?"

Jan stared down at it and for a moment looked like he was going to refuse to speak it aloud, mouthing the words to himself first. But he found his resolve and said, "It says, *Wohn Tod.*" He then looked back up to Logan. "It means, *Living Death.*"

10

"You see anything, Mo?" Fitz asked over the chopper's headphones. He'd been scanning the surrounding landscape for the last few minutes, finding nothing. In any normal circumstance they would have found the guy already. He thought back to what he witnessed, instantly recalling how *not* normal this night had been so far. Pandu and Saami were dead, torn apart by these... He didn't even know what to call them. What the things had done didn't describe anything human to him.

"No," Mo replied, "but we should be coming up to the lion's den shortly. We are just a minute or two out. I will light it up when we get there and circle around."

Fitz knew what he meant. Over the years they mapped out where a lot of the major predator's territories were, trying to avoid them whenever they could. CJ would mark them on a map and have Adnan upload it into a database, sort of like a GPS system. It worked wonders in the air.

"You think the bloke went *towards* the lions?" Fitz asked, in his heavy outback accent. Unlike Logan, who grew up in the city, Gray Fitzpatrick grew up in the 'backwoods' of Australia. They compared each other to Americans who grew up in the *south* versus say... Florida.

"If he did," Mo said, "the lions would take care of him and whatever is left of his body would be easy to spot. Either way, it's worth a shot to look."

Fitz nodded his agreement. "You mean *if* there's anything left."

Mo just shrugged continuing to scan the plains below.

"We should be coming up on them now. Flipping on exterior lights."

They both turned off their night vision devices as Fitz looked out his window. The world below their feet bloomed to life in the soft glow of the Blackhawk's lights. They outfitted Kipanga with a specially made "soft glow" system. It was basically a dimmer switch, but on a grander scale. The animals of this region got frightened easily by the intense light that a standard spotlight would give off. So depending on the time of day, they could turn down the light's intensity.

"Damn," Fitz said, seeing the terrain. There was blood...a lot of it. And bodies... Well, pieces of them.

Seeing the carnage for himself, he didn't have to ask. Mo was already landing the helo as he stared in horror at the brutal sight in front of them. It was unlike anything they had ever witnessed before.

As the landing skids touched down, Fitz realized something. There was too much blood to belong to one human being, and the bodies...they were covered in a golden-brown fur, not skin.

These are the lions, Fitz thought as a shiver rolled up and down his spine. *What on Earth could do this to a pride of lions?*

"Leave the chopper running and follow me," Fitz said, grabbing his Mossberg. Mo did as asked and reached for his identical weapon—when movement just outside of the range of the Blackhawk's lights caught his attention.

"Fitz," Mo said, snatching the Aussie's arm before he exited the helicopter. "You see that?"

The look in Fitz's eyes said he did.

They looked at each other and nodded in unison. Both men were officially terrified, remembering what happened to Saami and Pandu just minutes ago.

They exited Kipanga together, twin shotguns pointed forward, and started towards the moving shadow ahead. It slid in-and-out of focus like a specter against a pitch-black backdrop.

Halfway to where they saw...whatever it was...moving, they paused, hearing a soft mewing from behind one of the large Acacia trees that spotted the Serengeti. Normally, you would see a family of a dozen or so lions lounging about beneath it, trying to avoid the ruthless heat emanating from the summer sun. They were known to sleep twenty hours at a time.

"What the—" Fitz whispered as a shape stepped out

from behind the tree trunk.

It was, sort of, a lion, the largest male, but it was torn to pieces... *But alive?* There was no way this thing could be alive with the wounds it obviously suffered at the hands of...

Could it be? Fitz thought, remembering who they were really after.

Half of the skin on the lion's face was gone, including its right ear. The skull was in plain view as it stepped closer, looking like the Terminator with battle damage. Then, it roared loudly, noticing the two men for the first time. Its attention had been past them, to the Blackhawk.

Fitz and Mo had heard a lion's roar up close and personal a few times, but nothing like this. The low baritone bellow was accompanied by a high-pitched shrieking, like it had an eagle or some other bird of prey stuck in its throat. But that wasn't the worst of it. The most horrible part was when the lion started to change.

The SDF men stared in awe as the *king of the jungle* shivered. It was more like intense muscle spasms really, but they weren't what kept the men's attention. It was the golden fur... The golden fur that began to turn black.

The lion roared again, screaming into the night as its blood-stained coat faded to black, almost camouflaging it against the nighttime setting. The only reason they could see it was because of its eyes.

"They're red," Fitz said, hands shaking, "just like the bloody poachers back at the pit." In all the years he served his country killing terrorists, he'd never been this afraid.

As the ghost-lion approached, its fangs also enlarged, like those of a saber-tooth. They continued to grow until they were around a foot long, sharpening to points at the tips. With each inch they made a cracking sound, like bone was being broken over and over again. Each snap made the two men flinch.

"It's a *hai wafu*," Mo said, his voice trembling, slipping into his native Swahili.

Fitz had been in Africa long enough to pick up on some of the region's most common language. Mo had taught him most of it—Logan too, who was fluent.

Hai wafu, Fitz thought. *Living dead.*

"Great... Frickin' zombies."

11

"Let's keep moving," Logan said, moving towards the door. They had swept the room for anything they could use to identify this place. While they didn't have any concrete evidence to the *exact* use it held, Jan had come up with the obvious.

"I think this a secret Nazi bunker," he said as he moved about the sleeping quarters. "The bodies in the pit above, suggest a murder of some sort as well."

"What of the poachers?" CJ asked.

"No idea, but I have my suspicions," Jan replied.

"Which are?" Logan asked.

"First off, the logo stitched into the lab coat shows us the symbol for DNA. I think it's safe to assume that this place was used for some sort of experimentation."

Logan and CJ nodded, silently agreeing.

"Secondly," Jan continued, "I think some sort of virus may have been uncovered when our friends dug up the dead. It's possible that the contagion was still active after all these years, lying dormant until disturbed."

The two Aussies nodded again.

Logan then stepped back out into the main hall. The eerie glow from within his device cast shadows everywhere, giving the illusion of something moving further down the hall, back the way they came. He turned left, taking the lead, continuing their search. He stopped after another twenty feet in front of another metal door. It too had a name tag.

"Personlich?" Logan read, turning to Jan. The towering German stepped up and confirmed the word, translating it.

"It means, *Private*," he said, reaching for the door handle. "Like a *'Keep Out,'* or *'Do Not Disturb'* sign."

He turned the handle and pushed, but nothing happened. The door was definitely unlocked, but it didn't budge.

"It's stuck," Jan said. He then shouldered the door, shoving hard. The door gave a couple of inches, resisting against some unseen object, blocking it from opening the rest of the way.

He leaned, peering into the small crack between the door and its frame. "It looks like another bedroom, only it's much more nicely decorated." He stood. "Maybe it's that of an officer or some other higher ranking official?"

"There's only one way to find out," Logan said, stepping up. "Together on three."

They softly counted down and on *three* both men

drove their combined girth into the door. It gave between the might of the two soldiers, shoving the dresser that was used to block it out of the way. The dank room was revealed...and so was the body it contained.

"Ugh," CJ said, looking around her brother and seeing the long dead, decomposed body. It was sitting in what passed for an office chair during that era, its empty, lifeless eyes staring back at her.

The space was definitely another bedroom and very dapperly appointed, unlike the shared quarters next door. It also held a makeshift office, complete with desk and typewriter.

Logan pushed the dresser aside, stepping in first. He slung his rifle over his shoulder and examined the square room. It was roughly ten-by-fifteen and was easily searched for dangers. There weren't exactly a lot of places to hide. Jan and CJ stepped in next. Jan stopped, staying near the open door, just in case, shotgun pointed out its opening.

The right side of the room held a single bed along with a trunk at its foot. CJ stepped over to it and lifted the heavy lid. Inside were multiple sets of clothes, mostly undisturbed by age and dust. She quickly searched through it, but found nothing of importance.

"You see anything, Logan?" she asked, turning.

Logan stepped up to the left wall, which was floor to ceiling with books. Most were titled in German, but a few were in English. They had titles featuring words like *Biology* and *Chemistry* and *Anatomy.*

"Looks like they were definitely into some sort of

experimentation just based on the subject matter of these books," Logan said, shuffling to his right, continuing to read. "But most of the titles are in German. Jan, can you come over here and—"

Logan's foot struck something as he side-stepped again, spilling him towards the floor. He was halfway down when something arrested his fall. Leaning sideways, he looked up at what *caught* him, finding only the dead eyes of the man who had called this place home.

"Great..." he said, lifting his dust covered elbow out of the person's withered crotch. "That's just great."

Using the deceased man's thigh for a boost, Logan stood and noticed something. The Nazi had a hole in his temple. "This man was shot," Logan said, looking back to the others. "Right temple."

CJ and Jan quickly came over to inspect the body. "Suicide?" CJ asked, looking to the two war veterans for confirmation.

"Don't look at me," Jan said. "I was in demolitions. I wouldn't know what to look for when it comes to—"

"How 'bout that?" Logan interrupted, reaching for the man's right arm. As he pulled on the dried out appendage, something else came with it, still clutched in the dead man's hand. A gun.

"It's a Luger P-08," Jan explained. "Standard issue Nazi-era pistol."

"Well that explains the bullet hole in his head," Logan remarked.

"But why?" CJ asked.

Both men shrugged, but Logan noticed something

else. He looked over the seventy-year-old corpse's shoulder and saw that the typewriter still had a sheet of paper in its platen. He leaned around the body and carefully plucked the paper from the roller, careful not to damage it any more than *Father Time* had. He stepped away looking it over.

More German, Logan mused.

"Jan?" Logan asked. "Would you mind?"

The German gently took the offered paper and read it aloud, translating the letterhead.

7, May 1945

On this day I have heard of our forces surrender back home and I am saddened. We will no doubt have to leave our work here behind sooner than expected. If only we had more time, but unfortunately we do not. There are reports coming in that Allied forces are incoming. I will do my best to deter them and send out false trails. If we cannot discourage them, the Wohn Tod will be no more.

"The Wohn Tod?" CJ asked. "The scientific group?"

Jan nodded. "The *Living Death.*" He looked back down and continued reading.

The Gott Blut only needs some fine-tuning, maybe another month, before it is ready. But if my advisors are correct—and I hope they are not—it may be closer to another year before we get what we truly want. We are so close. I can feel it. Once finished, the Wohn

Tod—not the Fuhrer and his band of fools—will be the ones to rule the Fatherland. We are the future of Germany, not them.

"What the hell is he talking about?" Logan asked, goosebumps enveloping his body. "Who the hell were these people?"

Jan shrugged. "Sounds like they were, indeed, some secret cult within the Nazi party, and apparently even Hitler himself didn't know they existed. It wouldn't be the first time a government had another entity within it vying for control."

Logan didn't know if Jan was speaking from experience, or if it was just a belief, but he had to agree.

"What's *Gott Blut?*" CJ asked, getting them back on point.

"It means, *God Blood,*" Jan said, translating the German text.

"God Blood?" Logan asked. "From what you've read, it sounds like they tried to develop some sort of elixir or something."

"Yes," Jan agreed, scanning more of the text. "And they were fairly close from what this says. It goes on to summarize that they were trying to enhance the soldier's abilities and invulnerabilities, making them nearly invincible on the frontlines, but they never got to fully test it in live battle."

"Super soldiers?" Logan asked, eyebrow raised. "So it *was* an elixir of some kind."

"Sounds like it," Jan agreed, continuing his recap of

the letter's body. "Listen to this... The only thing that could stop these *Unterblichen*—means 'Immortals'—would be the destruction of the brain. Disconnect the *power supply* and they will fall."

"Like the poachers?" CJ asked.

"The only thing that stopped them were headshots," Logan added.

"It continues stating that the earliest version of the *serum*—if that's what it was—had a negative effect on the brain," Jan summarized. "The damage done during the initial testing was irreversible and left the subjects primal and violent, craving flesh and blood like one of the predators of the region."

"Subjects? Do you think that's what's in the grave?" CJ asked, thinking aloud, nervously rubbing her arms. "I mean the animals and the people, you think those were failed experiments?"

"Most likely, yes," Jan said, agreeing with her assessment.

Real life zombies, Logan thought, not believing what he was hearing, but knowing it to be true. The description of their behavior coincided with your run-of-the-mill undead type.

"Also..." Jan said, continuing. "There is a mention of light sensitivity. Not quite sure if it's referring to sight or skin, though. The letter doesn't go deep into that particular research, just the traits of the...subjects."

The three of them stood there, lost in thought for a few moments, trying to figure out what to do next. But what could they do?

"Is there anymore?" CJ asked, shuffling her feet

back and forth. Logan thought she either had to pee or she was scared shitless.

Probably the latter.

"Yes," Jan said, "there is."

The only regret I have over this endeavor of mine is that I will not be around to guide it to its end, and that is unfortunate for anyone who comes across the current state of the Gott Blut... Like myself. I have barricaded myself in my room, the plague has spread quickly down here.

Be warned, the Gott Blut has the power to give great strength and near god-like invisibility, but at a cost. The side-effects our subjects are experiencing is something we have yet to decipher. It's as if some primordial part of their very being is unlocking itself. Very troubling. The mammals of this land have responded poorly to our tests. Pray you don't get in their way.

"It's signed too," Jan said, his voice cracking as he looked down to the dead Nazi wearing one of the lab coats. He gestured to the corpse, sweat trailing down his temples. "I know who this is."

"Who?" Both the Reeds asked together.

"This letter was written by the worst of them." He then dropped the transcript to the dust covered floor.

"The dead man," Jan said, swallowing hard. "It's Dr. Mengele—the butcher of Auschwitz."

12

"Mengele? Josef Mengele?" Logan asked, shocked. "But I thought he escaped capture and lived out his days in South America?" That's, at least, what was written in the history books Logan had studied.

"Me too," Jan agreed, "but it seems we—the world—have been deceived. He obviously came here instead."

"And never left," CJ added. She then crouched in front of the corpse. "So this is the man who was responsible for the atrocities in Auschwitz?"

"Appears so," Jan replied.

"He committed some of the worst crimes against humanity ever recorded, experimenting on young and old, man and woman." Logan said, recalling what he knew about the *Angel of Death*. "He even *tested* on twins, seeing if he could cause one of them pain, while torturing the other. Most were kids."

"He was on a level with, General Shiro Ishii and

Unit 731 with his measures," Jan added, a look of disdain on his face.

"Unit 731?" CJ asked. "They were the Japanese equivalent, right?"

Both men nodded.

"Most agree they were *worse* than the Nazis though," Logan explained. "They specialized in chemical and biological warfare, testing the weapons on human subjects. They operated like the Nazis, using anyone who fit the bill. Even their own people were fair game."

"While the Nazis death toll reached insurmountable heights, Unit 731 was still feared more," Jan added. "They even performed surgeries on their captives without anesthesia, keeping them awake so not to risk decomposition to the organs they retrieved."

"Oh, God," CJ said, looking sick. "That's horrible."

"Yes," Logan agreed, again looking to Mengele's corpse. "Yes, it is."

"Can we leave now?" CJ asked, motioning to the door.

Logan just nodded, heading for the door. "But," he said, looking left, peeking around the corner. He then started to look to the right, "we need to search the rest of this place first and—"

He was tackled by an unseen force, taken to the ground. The wraith was fast, leaping from the shadows. Whatever it was, it was strong and moved silently, like a phantom.

"Saami, no!" CJ screamed, watching the man take

Logan down. She also watched as Jan—who was following her brother closely—stumbled back into the room, banging his head against the bedside trunk. The German crumpled to the ground, unconscious, unable to help.

Pinned to the ground by the much smaller man, Logan could barely move. The strength his friend now possessed was incredible—impossible to develop in such a short time period. It's like the man's muscle density had doubled, turning his physicality into what most ape species around the world possessed.

Unless, he thought, recalling what Mengele's letter said about the God Blood. It gave its subjects super-human strength and a vicious disposition.

Saami snapped his teeth at Logan's face, leaning into the Aussie hard. The teeth were jet black, like his finger nails. The fangs reached a length of at least an inch and were razor sharp. Saami leaned in harder, pushing closer and closer, aiming right for Logan's exposed neck. He wanted to end this quickly and he wanted it messy.

The only reason Saami hadn't sunk them into Logan's flesh, was because, while getting tackled to the ground, Logan got his left arm up, in between the two *men.* He held the Saami-thing at bay, pinning his forearm under the dead-man's chin, acting as a barricade.

And he *was* dead. This wasn't his friend anymore. This was something else entirely...

Saami's face was a gore-fest of clawed hanging flesh. His nose was completely gone and so was most of the skin on what used to be his bald, shaved head. The majority of it was exposed bone and dried blood.

And the eyes. They too were blood-red and glowing. Logan couldn't see the color of them in his green-tinted night vision, but he could easily see them radiating bright white. It was easy to assume that they matched those of the poachers from before.

If the man had any wits left in that brain of his, Logan thought, glancing at the man's hands. *He would just use those claws and slice me to ribbons.* But Logan wasn't going to mention that. The primal aggression that Saami was displaying was the only reason Logan was still alive after all.

Which means I have the advantage. I can still think logically.

Logan knew he could hold off Saami for a little while longer, using his chest and arm muscles to neutralize some of his former friend's new found strength. He just needed Saami to keep doing what he was doing and not change tactics. Thankfully, it looked like any and all strategic thoughts were gone. It was just primordial lust for his life.

Slowly and cautiously, Logan reached to his chest, feeling for what he needed. Finding it, he shoved with all his might, lifting Saami up a few inches. He gripped his Bayonet, the same combat knife he'd used while a member of the SAS, and slid it quickly and silently from its sheath attached to his chest armor.

"Sorry, mate," Logan said, apologizing to what used to be his friend.

Then, he relaxed and let Saami's weight, and gravity

itself, take over. With a slurp, the seven-inch blade sunk into the Kenyan's flesh. It slipped in, like a hot knife through butter, puncturing Saami's left lung and what should have been his heart in the process, burying itself to the hilt.

But Saami didn't stop, he didn't even respond to the lethal attack. He just pressed his assault harder, still going for Logan's jugular.

"Shoot!" Logan yelled, starting to panic. "Somebody shoot the bastard!"

"I can't!" he heard CJ yell. "You're too close!"

Then his night vision goggles went flying, effectively blinding him in the pitch black of the underground bunker. The only visuals he had was CJ's green glowing lenses and Saami's devilish red eyes.

Shit. Logan thought, not being able to see anything. But he could. He knew exactly where his enemy was and he knew what to do next. He needed to be careful, though. These things were obviously contagious. It's how Saami got infected in the first place.

Looks like I'm going to have to do this my way then, Logan thought. He just needed an opening to do so.

It's then Saami gave him one.

The dead man lunged at Logan, but not before he reared up, trying to add more force to the savage onslaught. This would be Logan's only chance.

He reacted immediately, yanking the tactical knife from Saami's chest. As the creature dove forward, undoubtedly aiming for Logan's throat again, he drove the bayonet skyward, aiming just below the set of eyes. The blade found its mark, piercing the underside of

Saami's chin where it buried itself halfway in.

Now free of the thing's weight, Logan snapped his right leg up and blindly kicked. His booted foot, found the base of the knife's hilt and drove it the rest of the way in.

With an audible crack, the steel blade punched through the bottom of Saami's skull, entering his brain. The fight instantly went out of the man-beast's eyes, as the body—disconnected like a puppet's strings being cut—fell to Logan's side. Dead...again.

"Logan!" CJ yelled, rushing to her brother's side. "Are you okay?"

"I guess you could say that," he answered, finding his goggles. He reset them and laid back, laughing at the absurdity of what just happened. "My friend—who happened to be a recently turned undead monster— tried to eat my face." Jan appeared over Logan, hand outstretched, rubbing his head with his other hand. The Aussie took it and was pulled to his feet. "Besides that..." he said, dusting himself off. "I'm good, just another day at the—"

A growl emanated from the direction they'd originally come from, startling the three into action. As the pounding of footsteps approached from around the corner, Logan, CJ, and Jan swung their respective weapons down the hallway—just as another form entered and turned their way. A form they recognized.

"Pandu..." CJ said, recognizing the twin brother of Saami. "No..."

Hearing CJ's sorrow-filled, mouse-like voice in the still tunnel, the hellish form of Pandu bared his fangs and charged, claws spread. He too had the same crazed look emanating from his demonic gaze.

When he was halfway to the group, they fired. As they opened up on what used to be their friend and comrade, each one of them bit their lips, doing their best to hold back the tears that threatened to blur their vision.

Logan could feel the presence of Saami's lifeless body near his feet as he again pulled the trigger. He knew the man's brother would soon follow his lead.

Sorry, mate.

13

The lion's body fell limp, its head missing. It took three shots from each man to finally re-kill the beast. The damned thing was fast—too fast. It had cheetah-like quickness, but in the bulk of a male lion's body.

Fitz and Mo, carefully inched closer to the carcass, weary of the creature, not trusting that it was *fully* dead. Neither man wore their night vision devices because of Kipanga's exterior lights. That meant they were actually *seeing* this thing for what it was, and it made Fitz long for more ammo. They still had plenty of slugs left in their shotguns though, but they didn't have any extra on *them*. It was all in the helicopter. If any more of these things showed up, they'd need to hightail it back to the Blackhawk pronto.

"Logan, come in," Fitz said, keying his earpiece. "Damnit, boss. Please respond. Over." He kicked at the dirt, frustration setting in. "Bollocks. I'm not getting through."

"You think something may have happened back at the burial?" Mo asked, thumbing behind him, pointing back in the direction they came.

"Not sure, mate. Maybe?" Fitz replied, turning to Mo. "But we need to get in contact with someone. Ima' try the Bullpen and... Down!"

As Fitz turned, he saw a blur of motion over Mo's shoulder, coming from behind Kipanga. It was smaller than the male, but had the same black fur and an identical set of fiery red eyes.

Mo ducked as Fitz let loose two quick shots from his Mossberg, felling the smaller lion, a female. "Damnit, these buggers are quick."

"And ferocious!" Mo yelled, clearly having problems hearing anything from the close quarters concussions at the hands of the 12-gauge.

He stood, shaking his head, trying to clear the ringing, but stopped. "Um...Fitz..."

Fitz looked and saw fear in the other man's eyes. He was looking back towards the Acacia tree. He turned, joining Mo's gaze, and backpedaled.

There were four more sets of glowing eyes staring back at them through the darkness of the night sky. Each one of them had the same menacing, carnivorous stare as the two they'd just slain.

"Shit, Mo. Run. Run now!" Fitz said, yelling to the pilot.

One of the creatures advanced, leaping into the low light of the helo's front lamps. The two men didn't need any more encouragement than that. They ran like hell itself was chasing them—which wasn't too far from the truth.

"Don't stop, mate. Get this bird off the ground fast!" Fitz stopped, spun on a dime and let loose the rest of his shotgun's ammo. He clipped one of the advancing females in the shoulder and another one, a juvenile male, in the flank. Both beasts were knocked off balance, tumbling to the dirt, but neither were dead.

He could hear the rotors behind him powering up quickly, and decided now was as good of a time as any to do what he had planned. Fitz reached into a pocket on his hip and procured a black cylinder filled with a pyrotechnic metal-oxidant mix of magnesium, and an ammonium perchlorate. These components put together made up your standard issue M84 stun grenade.

He turned and held up the flashbang for Mo to see, warning him, before pulling the pin and releasing the safety lever. He chucked the explosive device towards the tree and bolted for Kipanga's passenger door.

As he climbed in, he shut his eyes, and opened his mouth, a tactic he learned while in the army. It helped reduce the pressure the concussive force of the explosion caused. A fact he was sure an animal *wouldn't* know.

Halfway into his seat, a blinding light blinked to life along with a boom. If he'd had his eyes open, he'd be blind for up to a minute from the effects of the white hot blast. Without being able to cover his ears, his hearing was shot, but it'd have to do. He could live with a little ringing for a few hours.

"Up!" he yelled, unable to hear his own voice. "Hit the lights!"

Moments later, the Blackhawk rose and the exterior lights were amped up to their full brightness... The scene below them was unbelievable.

The four remaining lions—while technically dead—were still quite alive. Disoriented, but moving. With the lights at full power, he could also see the ground and the battle that had been fought recently.

Blood covered everything. He hadn't noticed how bad it was until now. The entire section of grass and dirt looked like the floor of an unkept slaughterhouse. He knew his boots had to be covered as well and couldn't wait to hose them off when they got back.

Shit, I'll probably just toss 'em and get another pair from my room.

The lions writhed on the ground, but were slowly coming to. As they rose higher, Fitz held out his hand telling Mo to stop. "Wait, I need to see something."

Mo obliged and leveled out the aircraft eighty feet off the ground. As the two men looked down back towards the plain, they noticed something. The lions weren't retreating. If anything they were more interested in the fleeing aircraft than ever.

Like a curious house cat.

"Okay, Mo," he said, "take us back to the others. We need to figure out what the hell is going on."

The Blackhawk began to turn and Fitz immediately saw something he didn't like. "Aw, shit."

"What is it?" Mo asked, concentrating on his duties. "What do you see?"

"You don't want to know, mate," Fitz said, his voice full of despair.

"Gray?" Mo asked, using Fitz's first name.

"It's the lions," Fitz said, turning back to Mo. "They're following us."

14

"Damnit, Logan. I really think we should leave. We need to warn someone."

Logan agreed with part of what his sister said, but he didn't approve of leaving. Yes, they had just rekilled two of their friends who had turned into some sort of genetically altered undead versions of themselves, but they needed to continue their search of Mengele's facility. They needed to figure out a way to stop it.

If there is a way to stop it, Logan thought as he led CJ and Jan around the next corner. Jan suggested that he guard their backs, since his shotgun was the best defense in the tight corridors. They agreed that if they were attacked again, it would most likely come from behind.

"It's closer to the entry shaft too," Jan had said. "I suspect these creatures hunt by scent and sound and not by sight."

"How do you know that?" CJ asked.

"Because," Jan replied, "Pandu didn't attack until he heard you speak."

CJ just nodded her head, but looked like she was going to say something.

"It's fine CJ," Logan said, placing his hand on her shoulder. "You didn't know. It isn't your fault. He would have found us eventually."

He stepped away. "But I agree with Jan. We can see in the dark because of these," he said, tapping on his night vision goggles, "Pandu couldn't. It's pitch-black down here and the human eye doesn't have spectacular low-light capabilities."

"As long as the virus doesn't eventually improve that..." CJ said, worried.

"Let's hope not," Logan said. "Also," he continued, looking at Jan, "how's the head?"

Jan just shrugged. "The chest was a bruiser. Knocked me out cold when I went down."

They walked in silence for a few seconds, but something nagged at Jan.

"What of the others?" he asked.

"Others?" CJ replied.

"Mengele's letter," Logan explained, understanding Jan's line of questioning. "It mentioned *mammalian* subjects. If it were only human experimentation, I'd assume he would have just said as much. But he didn't. He specifically said *mammals.*"

"Which means we are screwed if anything else out there gets infected," CJ added, pointing up to the land above their heads. "There are some nasty buggers out there who specialize in nocturnal hunting."

Logan and Jan nodded their heads. They understood what she was implying, everyone in the SDF did. One of CJ's main duties was to keep everyone up to date on the ever changing information that came in on the various species, primarily the predators. She was in essence the team's educator and teacher.

"I'd be most worried about the leopard's to be honest," CJ said. "They were already the masters of stealth. If they somehow get a hold of this virus—or whatever the hell it is—we could be in for some serious problems and a very long night."

"Considering the sun just fell, what, 90 minutes ago?" Logan said, looking to his watch. "That gives us approximately eight-and-a-half hours left of limited visibility topside."

"So standing around here and discussing the sun's summer habits is more than likely a huge waste of time," CJ added with a smirk. She then turned to Jan. "Right?" The big German shrugged and looked to Logan.

Logan just shook his head, smiling at his sister. *At least she's trying to make the most of it.* But he could still sense she was terrified, like him. If this had been a *normal* problem, he'd be his *normal* self. But now...

CJ then turned back towards Logan, motioning for him to continue. "Well then... Onward, baby brother."

"You'd better watch it with that shit you old bag or I'm bound to feed you to the leopards," Logan smiled, "dead or not."

She slugged him in the shoulder, instantly

regretting it. CJ just stood there shaking her hand, muttering curses under her breath.

Both men laughed, hard, but quickly stopped after getting a hate filled, venomous look from the much smaller woman.

Logan silently turned and continued forward, deeper into the seventy-year-old bunker. He had a sneaking suspicion that what they had found out so far would only be the tip of the iceberg.

Fifty feet later, Logan saw an aberration on the left. It wasn't a doorway, but it wasn't a hall either. He inched closer and peeked around the corner, recognizing what it was.

"Stairs," he said, with dread in his voice. "There's another level underneath us."

"What are you thinking?" Jan asked quietly, looking back down the hall behind them, shotgun up.

"Knowing a group like the Nazis," Logan replied, "or any other secret organization, the real juicy stuff will be down there."

"Ugh," CJ said with revolt, "please don't say *juicy* right now."

"Right," Logan said, apologetically. "Sorry..."

Jan looked over his shoulder to Logan. "I seriously doubt it's a good idea to split up too."

CJ immediately shook her head *no*. She'd have no part in separating from the two men.

And Logan had to agree. "You're right. We stay together."

"Plus," CJ added, "It's not like we have the best weaponry for this current problem." She specifically motioned to her lighter hitting Glock. "If we all had those..." she said, pointing to Jan's shotgun.

"We'd be deaf," Logan quickly said. "You're fine. Just keep aiming for their heads." He then shook his head, not believing what he was about to say. "Zombies can't survive without their brains."

After an awkward moment of silence, both CJ and Jan burst out laughing at the absurdness of the thought.

"Really?" she said. "Are we really going to refer to these things as *zombies*?"

Logan just silently threw up his hands with a *'don't shoot the messenger'* kind of look on his face.

"*Nachzehrer*," Jan whispered quietly. "We can call them the *Nach* if you'd like?"

"Nachzee-what?" CJ asked.

"The Nachzehrer was an old German folklore similar to that of vampires and zombies," Jan explained. "*Nach,* means *afterwards,* and *zehrer,* means *devourer.* 'Dead eaters' or 'eaters of the dead,' depending on the translation used."

Fitting, Logan thought. *The Nach—or the dead eaters—definitely sounded like what they were dealing with.*

"The Nach..." Logan said, trying out the name, pronouncing it, *knock.*

"It's better than calling these bastards zombies and feeling like a moron."

Both men laughed at CJ's comment, again releasing some of the built up tension, but also agreeing. They had laughed a few times, but Logan knew it wasn't on purpose. Sometimes you just had to laugh at the ridiculousness of what life tossed at you.

"Very good then," Logan said, squeezing CJ's shoulder. "Shall we?"

She nodded and brought up her Glock, doing her best to squelch her rising fear. "Always."

"Down we go," Logan muttered, looking at the set of stairs.

"And where we stop," CJ added.

Logan moved to the first step.

"Nobody knows..."

He stopped, his foot hovering over the stair. Both him and CJ glanced back to Jan who had a 'my bad' expression on his face.

"Let's hope not." Logan said, descending the first step, leading his team deeper into the unknown.

15

He could smell them off in the distance some five hundred yards ahead. There were quite a few of them too, plenty of sustenance. The pride was quick work. Once the large male was down, the others tried and failed to avenge him.

But these were different. These were smaller and much more numerous.

Sniffing the air, Georges smiled a sickly grin. He could almost taste his next meal.

And then he heard them. It was soft, but there. The cackling of the animals off in the distance helped him zero in on their location. *Northwest,* he thought.

They would be in a group numbering anywhere from ten to fourteen and would be led by a matriarch, larger than the rest.

Shaking his head from the knowledge running through his head, he was thrown off by it. *Where?* he thought, trying to recall where he learned that.

He looked down at his blood-stained hands. The talons had grown another couple of inches after his encounter with the lions and so had the fingers themselves. It seemed that with every feeding something grew, and the more he fed the stronger he became. *This is good,* he thought, flexing his now prodigious arm muscles. They had almost doubled in girth and strength since he...

Georges squinted, thinking. He couldn't remember what he was like before this. All he could do was remember his first name and waking up being this way. But something in the back of his mind itched, telling him there was more to his past.

Another bout of what sounded like laughter erupted from deeper into the darkness. He strode towards it and stopped, feeling something bothersome around his foot.

He looked down and saw it. Whatever it was covered his foot, preventing the bottom of it from touching the ground beneath. *Why?* He no longer understood the use for the protection. His toe nails had pierced the uncomfortable material long ago. He didn't need them.

One by one, Georges flipped off the annoyances and spread his toes, feeling the dirt between them. *Better.*

He then examined the rest of his body and felt the same irritation he had before. He recalled waking with all this...clothing—that's what it was called. His body was covered in it, but he couldn't remember what it was for.

He made quick work of the itchy fabric entangling his chest and arms with two quick slashes. Each one of the strikes cut into his own flesh, but he didn't mind. He felt no pain and he only bled a miniscule amount.

He grinned again, but this time it was the sight of his naked form. Muscle rippled underneath his jet black skin, teaming with veins—veins that glowed red beneath his skin. If he was his prey, he would be frightened as well. He remembered the looks on the human's faces when he and the others emerged from the pit. Not only was he camouflaged within the darkness... He *was* the darkness.

He blinked and noticed something else had changed. He lifted his hands in front of his face and saw four of them. He tilted his head to the side, confused. He didn't have four arms. Then something in his mind's eye told him to focus on the two he knew he had. So he listened and concentrated as his vision slowly normalized.

He blinked again, feeling the other set of eyes for the first time. He now sported four of them instead of two and his night vision had enhanced some as well. His peripheral vision had widened as well, allowing him to see almost 180 degrees from side-to-side. Georges actual eyesight got better too, being able to see just that little bit better, and farther, in the pitch black of the African night. He grinned. *This just keeps getting better.*

The scent of his prey hit him again and he sniffed, drawing the final inhalation in deep. They were just ahead and waiting for him. By the agitated sounds of their calls, Georges knew that they recognized something was close, but they had no idea what was coming.

Me, he thought, flexing his arms again.

He squatted, bending his legs, and dug his front claws into the ground. It didn't feel as awkward as he figured it might. It almost felt natural.

Launching himself forward, the form that was once the poacher, Georges Boluva, sprinted on all fours. From a distance he would have looked like some demon-man hybrid, pounding through the night like a feral beast.

And that's what he was. He was in every sense of the term, a *super* predator.

16

"Don't land!" Fitz yelled as the wind whipped through the rear hold of the Blackhawk. "I'll drop a line to the top of the koppie and try and find Logan and the others! You go back to the 'Pen' and get help and restock! Bring every heavy-hitting piece we have. We'll take the Land Rover back if we have too."

Mo nodded as Fitz clipped on and leapt from the open side door, armed with his Mossberg shotgun and *plenty* of spare slugs. Fitz hoped he could find his friends before the remaining lions did. He and Mo had barely gotten away alive.

He landed quickly, straddling the entry point to what Logan thought was some sort of World War Two era Nazi military bunker. He could plainly see the twin lightning bolts of the Nazi's SS, but had never heard of them reaching this far south. The northern countries were under Axis rule once upon a time, but not here.

"Doesn't matter," he said to himself. "I need to find the others and figure out what the hell is going on."

Signaling to Mo that he made it safely, Fitz detached the drop line and started his descent. As his boots clanged against the metal ladder, he thought back to the dumbfounded reactions the men back home had.

"You find something out in the bush and smoke it?" Kel asked, laughing at Fitz and Mo. "You guys fog out Kipanga?"

Kel and Dada laughed hard, but Adnan held back. The desperation in Fitz's voice was unnerving. Not once in the four years he'd known the man had he ever seen the ex-Special Forces soldier nervous, let alone afraid.

"Shut the fuck up you wankers!" Fitz cursed, shouting over the radio. "Or so help me, I'll feed you to the lot of 'em!"

Adnan quietly walked over to another station and pushed the talk button, commandeering the conversation. "Fitz, this is Adnan. Say again, please. What happened?"

Kel and Dada gave Adnan an annoyed look, but they let him speak. Both men just leaned back and listened, waiting for something else to laugh at.

"Adnan," Fitz said, his tone calming down slightly. "We have men down and Logan, CJ, and Jan are MIA. Mo is going to come and get Kel and Dada. They need to be ready in thirty for pick up. Dress heavy. I repeat. Dress...heavy." He breathed heavily and continued. "Adnan, stay put and keep the Bullpen operational. Lock down everything until we get back."

Kel and Dada stiffened.

"Men down?" Adnan asked, shocked. "Gray? What—"

"It's the twins," Fitz interrupted. "They're gone."

The room went silent, the three remaining men at HQ were stunned at the loss of Saami and Pandu.

Adnan pushed the receiver again, speaking. "What happened?"

"Hell if I know," the Aussie answered. "Jan and I arrived at the site and eventually met up with the others. As we went to engage the target—the poachers—something...strange...happened."

"Happened?" Adnan asked.

"Yeah, mate. It was frickin' weird. We found them down in a hole. Dead. Only not."

"Wait," Adnan said, "I'm confused."

"You and me both," Fitz said, continuing. "We found a burial dating back to World War Two. It had bodies in it too, both man and animal."

"Men?" Adnan asked. "What men?"

"Nazi assholes," Fitz replied. "SS to be exact."

Adnan was shocked and still unsure of what to make of everything. He remembered studying about the Nazis in school at the University of Dar es Salaam, in eastern Tanzania. He couldn't recall ever reading about them coming here.

He was getting a degree in software engineering with a minor in history, when he met a spunky Aussie named CJ Reed. She was there to lecture students majoring in the various environmentalist programs. After her visit, they stayed in touch, and she offered Adnan a job six months later when he graduated. Now, he was the I.T. guru for the most state-of-the-art anti-poaching outfit in the world. He was also the youngest on staff by quite a bit.

Not exactly what I had in mind, Adnan thought at the time. *But a job is a job.*

But now, he loved it. The Serengeti Defense Force actually made a difference in his beloved homeland and he wanted to do what he could to help.

"What killed them?" Adnan asked, snapping back into the now. "What killed Saami and Pandu?"

Fitz breathed in heavily again before answering. "It was the poachers. They tore them apart."

"The poachers?" Kel asked, finally speaking up since he and Dada were put in their places.

"No, mate," Fitz said. "It *was* the bloody poachers. *Was.* They aren't poachers anymore."

The airways went silent for a tick, only light static could be heard.

Adnan swallowed hard, unsure of what to ask next. But after another few seconds, he asked the only question that made sense. "What are they now?"

The three men could actually hear Fitz laugh, but it was short lived. "Monsters, mate. They're damned monsters."

Fitz's earpiece crackled to life, almost spilling him down the rest of the entrance shaft. It would have been a nasty fall, having another twenty or so feet to climb. Mo's voice came to life in his ear, but it was hard to hear him through the interference the metal shaft was creating.

"Say again, Mo," Fitz said, activating his comms

system.

"They...here...hurry," Mo replied, the words came out choppy, cutting in and out.

Fitz's eyes went wide as he looked up and saw a shadow slowly appear over the opening above his head. Quickly, he slid the rest of the way down, grasping the sides of the ladder and dropping. He landed hard, but in control.

He turned and fled, down a narrow, concrete corridor, popping out a few seconds later in front of a metal door with a sign written in German. *Waschraum?* He looked right and then left and saw them. Two *fresh* bodies lying on the ground.

"Ah, shit," he said, recognizing what was left of Pandu. Another booted foot could be seen farther into the darkness, but he had no qualms on who it belonged to. *Saami...*

"Damn. Damn. Damn."

A clang of metal from behind, started his feet moving. He went right, not knowing what lay ahead of him down this hallway. He'd have to wing it and figure out where the hell he was going while trying not to die.

17

"What do you think is down here?" CJ asked, following her brother closely. She stepped up next to him and stopped, seeing another sign in German.

"It says, *Holding*," Jan said, pointing to the right. "And *Labs*." He then gestured to the left. There were arrows as well, indicating which way was which on the metal sign. It was bolted to the wall directly across from the bottom of the staircase.

Silently, Logan approached the T-junction and stepped right, towards the 'Holding' section of the underground facility. He didn't like the sound of either of the options, but he also understood that they didn't really have a choice. One way or another they would search both.

"I'd assume this was where they held their captives," Logan said, answering CJ's question. "Most likely animals and soldiers, but I wouldn't put it past them to test on locals either."

"The Nazi's didn't discriminate against their subjects," Jan added. "Anyone who opposed them and was caught would eventually make it down here if Mengele ordered it."

Logan knew Jan was right. The Nazi's—especially the SS—were bad news. They held every other race at an almost inhuman standard, like a family dog, or livestock. He remembered some of the horrifying things that he had learned in school and also what Jan had recently told him.

Despicable, Logan thought. *People were people. You don't have to like everyone, but we're still the same. Down to the very last strand of DNA.*

DNA.

He stopped and turned to Jan, thinking about the Wohn Tod logo they'd seen upstairs. The swastika and the helix. "What was their endgame?"

Jan abruptly stopped, almost running into Logan, at the suddenness of the question. "What?"

Logan continued. "The Wohn Tod—what was their endgame—their mission?"

As Jan contemplated his answer, CJ called from down the hall, another twenty feet further.

"Guys," she said, standing in front of what looked like a set of metal bars, "you need to see this."

Logan and Jan both looked towards her and continued over, finishing their discussion.

"The Wohn Tod were obviously looking for some sort of super-serum or elixir," Jan deduced, walking in stride with Logan. "From what Mengele's letter said, it looked like they were close too, but they apparently hit a snag. DNA is a fickle...thing..."

He trailed off when he stepped up next to CJ, having the air sucked out of his lungs. They were in front of a set of bars, belonging to a jail cell. A *large* jail cell.

But it wasn't the cell itself that caused the three SDF members to squirm under their uniforms. It was the body inside the makeshift prison. The dead body, long since departed of life, was huge and at one time or another...human.

"Oh, God..." CJ remarked, the sight finally sinking in. For a moment, she'd just be staring at it, but now her brain finally caught up, fully processing the sight.

The mostly decomposed body was seated, strapped down in a chair that resembled one used for examinations in a dentist's office. Its wrists, all *four* of them, were lashed to the arm rests, as were its two legs. Due to its severe decomposition, it was hard to determine its girth, most of the muscle and other tissues having been gone for some time. But the bone structure was enough. It was truly a monster in every sense of the word.

Its mouth lay agape, revealing teeth like a lion's, except for the fangs, they looked almost serpentine. They were small for the creature's overall physical size, but no doubt they were sharp and just as deadly.

The eyes were something else altogether too. First off, there were four of them, all situated across its forehead. He could picture this thing looking like Data from Star Trek at a distance. *Especially if they glowed red like the Nach did here. If they did, their night vision capabilities would have been subpar,* or so Logan thought. *Unless the extra set of eyes made up for it...*

"It must have been left behind when the Nazi's abandoned the facility," Jan said, staring at the creature in front of them. "It was most likely alive too."

"What makes you say that?" CJ asked, swallowing down her vomit. Her skin had already started to darken some, having turned a ghostly white at first seeing the behemoth.

"If it wasn't," Jan replied, "why would they have secured it like a prisoner?"

Logan unfortunately agreed with Jan, but it didn't make him feel better about anything. Either way, there was a dead monster fifteen feet in front of them, seated in a giant recliner.

Giant.

"How big do think it was?" Logan asked, stepping closer to the barred door. "If it was standing I mean—how tall?

Jan and CJ joined him, CJ grabbing the bars with both hands.

"Well," Jan started, "as of right now it's eye level with us and its legs are fully bent in a 90 degree angle. So if you estimate the length of the legs and add that to our own heights you'd get—"

"Nine feet," CJ said, finishing off Jan's math. "Maybe ten."

"Bollocks," Logan said softly in disbelief. "Could you imagine what this thing looked like alive?"

Both Jan and CJ shook their heads no. Logan wasn't sure if they *couldn't* imagine it or if they didn't *want* to.

"Probably had the girth and musculature of an oversized Silverback," CJ stated, breathing out heavily, reverting back into 'professional Zoologist' for only a second.

Logan could take it a step farther with his child-like imagination. While CJ's description was apt, she lacked the boyhood thought process he had. Then again... Logan was basing everything he knew on things that he'd seen on television or in a movie. This was the real thing, not the imagination of some over-caffeinated fiction author.

The creature before them was, indeed, huge, but the skeletal structure was all wrong to look like a gorilla. Its arms, while large, were spindly for its overall size. *Like a spider's.* Its neck and midsection were elongated a little too, giving it a classic alien profile. Imagine a four-armed, ten-foot tall NBA player with above average muscle tone and a ravenous appetite and you'd have what Logan pictured in his mind's eye.

"You see the hands?" Jan asked, pointing through the bars. "The fingernails mostly."

"Damnit," Logan said, realizing where he'd seen them before. "They're the same." The talons were definitely similar to one's he'd seen before, but these hands only held three digits—a thumb and two fingers. The other's held five, like a human's.

They were human.

Jan nodded in silence, but CJ just turned facing the two men, not understanding. "The same...as what?"

Logan looked down at his shorter sister and swallowed. "Saami and Pandu—"

"And the poachers," Jan added.

"And the poachers," Logan agreed. "They all had similar black claws, only they weren't *this* big."

18

He hunted on all fours, a predator stalking his latest prey. The last female, the largest of the group, sat not twenty feet away, nursing what he knew to be a mortal wound. Soon she would succumb to death, but it would be slow and agonizing...for them both.

Not quick enough, he thought, snapping at the suddenness of the voice speaking into his ear. After the last transformation, he no longer remembered who he was before the initial change, and therefore didn't understand the simple concept of *inner thought.* His mind was becoming one hundred percent primal—wholly animalistic—with every new adaptation.

His name even escaped him now as did the majority of his memory of his past life. The only thing that filled his primitive mind was images of demons and devils. It's like he had seen them in real life before, but not *real*. It's like they were projected onto a large white sheet inside a large room.

Devil, he thought as the horrific images flashed through his mind. *Shetani...* The word came and went as quick as the breeze did.

Shetani, he thought again, concentrating on the word, turning back to his dying quarry. *Devil...*

The spotted animal no longer laughed into the night sky. She only moaned, licking her wounds, dying. But he knew better. She still had some fight left in her.

The jet black demon smoothly and slowly approached the matriarch hyena. He no longer needed to implore his expert stealth. This one wouldn't be going anywhere.

Shetani now stood eight feet tall and his sizable frame blotted out the moonlight when it showed itself. The shadows made him look like the cloaked Grim Reaper himself—and that's what he was. Death in the flesh.

Stretching his arms out wide, Shetani attempted to intimidate his foe, but glanced down to his right wrist. He saw the puncture wounds from the injury sustained by the powerful jaws of the female. She had even punctured a few of the luminous veins just under his thick armor-like skin.

Normally, she would have been able to crush bones, delivering a bite at over a thousand pounds per square inch—one of the strongest in the animal kingdom—but Shetani's limbs were thicker and tougher. They could stand up to the crushing force of her premolars with very little effort.

Why he knew such things about the mammal eluded him, but Shetani enjoyed the facts none-the-less. He would use such information to his advantage.

Circling the bleeding animal, he sized her up for one last attack, but stopped and roared in pain as something in his back pulsed with pain. Shetani glanced over his shoulder and saw something solid protruding from where the shoulder blade should have been. Now, instead of the flat, plate-like bone, there was a knob...

The bone continued to grow, pushing and stretching the skin further, until finally piercing it with a quick gout of blood. But, just as quickly as the wound started to bleed, it stopped, the large laceration cauterizing around the still advancing bone. It continued to slip out of Shetani's skin, advancing higher.

Once it and its twin, which was currently following suit on the other side, grew to five feet in length, they cracked in unison and bent. Thick sinews and what could only be musculature then formed, wrapping themselves around the bare-bones of the new *appendages*.

He roared in agony as the searing hot pain continued, causing its entire body to quake. They grew faster now, draining him of strength and energy. He could even feel himself losing weight and mass from other body parts in order to feed the new growth.

But, Shetani knew it was a good change—a needed

change. So far the other changes had been for the better... Why not these? They had made him into a supreme killer.

The tips of the five-foot-long bones broke, splintering. The portion between the two sections, thickened. Then, each bone formed what looked like another knob on their ends. Tendon and muscle grew next, covering the freshly formed joint. As the second half grew, it curved away, becoming...

Shetani smiled when he realized what they were, but as the growth slowed, he realized he wouldn't be using them for their higher function just yet. He would need to feed again and regain his strength.

Convenient...

Shetani tried to move the newest additions to his body, but all that did was cause him more pain. They weren't ready. So, like his brain's involuntary command over his arms, he subconsciously told them to flex and rest against his back. They listened, operating like they were part of his original body.

As the discomfort subsided, he looked up to the wounded animal. He bent his large legs—and just as he was about to pounce—the hyena chirped, but this time it wasn't in anger or fright...it was in...recognition. Then, something strange happened. The one-hundred-fifty-pound female, the largest in the region, tilted her head as if in thought, her eyes slowly turning a deep shade of red. Seconds later, they grew brighter, glowing in the darkened sky.

The hyena stood, completely forgetting about the large bite marks across her left flank. They had stopped bleeding upon her eyes changing color. She had been bitten when she locked onto her attacker's arm.

Instead of engaging the much larger adversary, she turned and fled, cackling the whole way until she finally disappeared deeper into the Serengeti.

Shetani just stood there dumbfounded, wondering why she didn't try to attack him again. Confused, but satisfied with the latest events, he stretched his larger, better form, and howled into the night. This wasn't a cry of agony, though. This was a shout of triumph.

He could have pursued the hyena, but something in the back of his mind told him to wait for a *fresher* meal. Something about the lack of blood the female offered him was a turnoff. It wasn't appetizing to him in the least.

So he would wait.

He looked straight up, his hypersensitive hearing had picked up something back in the direction he came, miles back. The droning of machinery maybe, but in the air. *In the air?*

He shook his head violently at the irritation, like something was cupped over his ears, but then uncupping itself rapidly. A *whup*, *whup*, *whup* sound.

Shetani reached his massive hands and covered his—they were gone! He no longer had ears. Then again, he couldn't remember if he ever did. He had no recollection of having them. All that was there now was a set of small holes, one on each side of his head.

He shook his head at the annoyance again. It would need to be dealt with.

Turning, Shetani backseated his insatiable hunger for the time being, and decided to investigate this new threat.

19

Fitz ran as fast as he could down the hall of the bunker. Well, as fast as he could without making a racket. He knew his footfalls would sound like gunshots in the quiet, empty space to those pursuing him.

If they hear me, then I can guarantee gunshots, he thought as he passed a door on his right labeled in German.

He skidded to a halt and backtracked, opening the door, quickly peering inside. There were rows and rows of what looked like canned goods and rotted out boxes.

A Nazi storehouse.

The skittering of what must have been the lion's nails on the hard floor advertised their presence in the still, clammy air. Fitz turned and ran again, but stopped at another door, again on his right.

He swung it open with a bang, the hinges working just fine after all these years. *Damn,* he thought. He listened for more movement, but heard none. The lions were probably trying to decide which way he went.

Hopefully the gore I saw down the other way will confuse them a little.

Another bang echoed down the hall as a mop fell from its upright position behind the now open door, startling Fitz. He quickly checked the rest of the tiny room, seeing only more mops and a couple of brooms on one side. On the other wall, there were empty buckets lined up next to a pile of long since soiled rags.

A janitor's closet.

He leaned out of the room and saw a shape emerge from around the corner, but slow enough that Fitz had enough time to dart out of the small nook. Apparently, they had heard the slap of the mop's wooden handle on the floor, giving away what direction he had fled. Fitz continued down the main hall coming across a set of stairs that led down, deeper into this literal hellhole.

"Forward or down, mate," he said to himself. The skittering grew louder, followed by another sound.

The hell?

The low moan of one of the pursuing cat's softly echoed down the utilitarian corridor. It was answered by another shortly after. At the very edge of his night vision, he saw a figure emerge...and then another.

"Fuck it. Down it is." He took off down the stairs,

taking them two at a time. The hand rail rattled as he hit the landing inbetween the first floor and basement level. The stairs then wrapped around to the left and went in the opposite direction, like the staircase in a parking complex. *Shit.* He knew the clang of the metal bar just gave away his location and he needed to abandon his half-stealth.

Hopefully they'll inspect the open doors first and give me a better head start, he thought, leaping the last three steps to the next floor, twisting his ankle slightly.

Damnit! he thought, gritting his teeth, quickly looking left and then right, hobbling forward. He had hoped to run into the rest of his team by now, but no such luck.

"Come on, guys. Where are you?"

Not having the time or luxury to lollygag, he decided to trust his gut again and go right.

"I gotta' run into them eventually," he said to himself, huffing a breath as he limp-ran, "right?"

Just as he asked himself the question, the first of the lions hit the loose railing with a bang. Fitz looked back, stumbling a little, and saw the steel bar go flying, obviously flung away by either Simba or Nala.

Damn they're quick. He thought he'd have more time to at least get around the next corner. As it stood, he was quickly running out of time.

Through his night vision, Fitz could see a door coming up on his left. He skidded to a stop, just as one of the lions appeared at the edge, materializing like a demon-ghost. What was worse was its eyes. They just stared at him. They weren't like the *undeadheads* you read about in books or like the ones you see on TV. These had life in them, thinking for themselves, planning out their decisions. They weren't just mindless, lifeless killing machines. They were the ultimate predator.

Hard as shit to kill, and *really* hungry.

Strange, he thought. Logan had said that Saami and Pandu acted the complete opposite. They were pure instinct, doing anything for the kill. But he didn't have time to contemplate it any further.

Shaking himself out of his stupor, Fitz looked at the door he stood in front of and instinctively tried to read the label. "Oh," he said, surprised at seeing a word he actually knew. He didn't know a lick of German, but the word was very similar to one in English.

Labors.

Labs, he thought as he grabbed the door's knob. He turned it and pushed open, quickly slipping into the room beyond. The pounding of the lion's paws could be heard as he spun and slammed the door shut, locking it with a simple pushbutton lock. These doors were barely adequate to keep *humans* out let alone the two beasts that chased him now. As soon as he let go of the doorknob, it shook from an impact, making him flinch and jump back, aggravating his already sore ankle.

"Speaking of getting aggravated..." Fitz was getting pissed.

Whump.

Quietly stepping back from the door, shotgun up, Fitz breathed in deep and let it out. He repeated the process twice more as the thin metal door was hit again and again. *If they keep this up...* He let the concern hang in the air—but before he could finish the assumption, he caught movement to his left and wheeled around, finger grazing the trigger. He didn't fire, though. It wouldn't have mattered. What he saw didn't scare him as much as it startled him. The room's low light combined with the shadows his night vision gave him made the reflection of himself in the mirror take on an otherworldly form.

He quickly recognized what the ladies called a 'heavily bearded Jude Law' in the smeared glass. He was almost two years older than Logan, quickly approaching his fortieth birthday—next week in fact. *Just another number, mate.* He always said that a birthday was just the annual anniversary of another day of getting older. It was truly just a number.

Whump.

The door bucked again, bringing Fitz and his Mossberg back around. The hinge creaked and buckled a little as it was hit with an even larger impact.

Fitz knew he could pump every single one of his steel slugs into and through the door, but he couldn't guarantee a kill. These things needed a headshot to go down for the count. He could take out all four of its legs and the thing would still try to carve him a new one. *Literally.* He'd seen the teeth.

Whump.

Damnit, he thought as the door was hit again, bending the hinges further, almost to the point of breaking. *Come on baby, hold on a little longer.* But he knew it was too good to be true. If these things were like any of the other creatures he'd read about, particular the Draugr in that Raven book he read a couple years back, they wouldn't tire or give up so easily. These were the fictional things of nightmares come to life. They'd beat down the door and get in eventually.

Into here.

Chancing a glance behind him for the first time since entering the room, Fitz looked, hopeful at finding a backdoor out of the labs. But what he saw was worse than anything he'd seen so far. There had to be a hundred of them in there with him.

Shreee.

Cringing at the sound of tearing metal, Fitz turned back towards the door and watched it fold in on itself as two of the world's best and most dangerous hunters leapt through.

"Shit." He had just enough to time to audibly curse before he pulled the trigger.

20

CJ yelped in surprise at the bang she heard reverberating around her. It sounded like someone violently kicked a car door shut.

Logan and Jan took up positions to either side of her, pointing their larger, more imposing weapons down each direction of the basement hallway. The boom startled them into action as quickly as it scared CJ. They were soldiers after all.

Logan didn't like the sound of whatever that was. As far as he knew they were alone. No one other than Mo and Fitz knew they were down here, or at least where to look for them.

"Something's wrong," Logan said softly. "We should head back and—"

Whump.

The sound resonated through the corridor again, coming from *both* paths. The square pattern of the hall was throwing off the directional origin of the noise.

Forward? Logan thought. *Or back the way we came?*

Whump.

"Screw it," Logan said, running forward. "Let's move."

Jan and CJ fell in behind him at a dead sprint, nearing the corner. Slowing for just a second, Logan stepped around the left turn, SCAR pointed down the hall. Seeing nothing, he broke into another sprint, this one faster than the last, his adrenaline taking over.

As the lactic acid started to consume his legs, he willed himself to keep going. The square layout of the facility made pursuit of the unknown noise easy. Straight, left, straight, left.

It's like the American's bloody NASCAR races.

The *whump* got louder and louder as they neared the next and presumably last left-hand turn. Logan again slowed as he neared, peeking around the two walls junction.

Whump!

The sound was louder, echoing past him and around the corner to CJ and Jan. It was definitely down here.

"Can't see anything yet," Logan said softly. "We need to keep moving."

He and Jan took point, CJ following closely behind. They slowed to a brisk walk, all the while aiming their weapons in front of them.

CJ plowed into both men as they suddenly stopped.

She peeked between them, her mouthing hanging open like a codfish.

What she saw both shocked and confused her.

Two lions, both males, but too young to have fully grown manes, leapt and slammed headlong into what looked like a random metal door.

Not so random, I guess.

As the two big cats collided with the door, their combined weight, along with the weakened integrity of the metal folded in on itself. As soon as their front halves made it through the entry, the booming of a weapon discharging echoed past them, originating from inside the now doorless room.

Logan and Jan continued forward, bringing up their weapons. They each popped a few rounds, most striking the closest lion in its side, penetrating flesh. To any *normal* adversary, the hollow points and steel slugs would have been enough to shred their organs, killing them where they stood. But alas... No such luck.

If this beast felt pain, it didn't show it. The only recognition Logan got for his efforts, was a look that could have curdled a glass of milk, and a roar that was both feral and accusatory. The Nach was actually pissed that he and Jan had shot it.

Logan watched as the unseen shooter let loose another volley of blasts from inside the room, dropping one of the creatures at the halfway point of the ransacked doorway. The second *living* lion, stepped back and turned fully towards them, screaming one last time before charging down the hall with impossibly quick strides.

Everyone knew a lion had a quick first step, but they weren't marathon runners like some of the other predators the Serengeti had to offer. If you stayed far enough ahead of them, the lion hunting you would eventually give up. Their strength was surprise and sheer strength.

At first they balked at the advancing beast, confused that the injured animal would actually go on the offensive with an obvious retreat just a little further back down the hall. But the shock only lasted a second as Logan, Jan, and CJ all gathered together and tore into the lion all at once.

Just as he pulled the trigger to his weapon, Logan thought he saw someone poke his head out of the destroyed doorway. *Fitz?* The beard was a dead give-a-way. *Why is Fitz here?*

Thankfully, Fitz was smart and dove back into the *safety* of the room, just as the corridor was filled with the deafening roar of the three of their weapons.

It took more rounds than it should have, but finally one of Jan's slugs found the thing's forehead, turning what was left of the creature's brain to mush. It fell, sliding to a stop halfway between them and the door it just beat down. The slick of blood could be seen glowing in their night vision.

"*Fick dich ins Knie!*" Jan cursed, showing true anger, which was a little out of character for the bigger man. His nature was always peaceful, but Logan knew that was just because he'd never seen anything make him go overboard.

"What?" CJ asked, wincing at what Logan knew

would be an awful ringing in her ears. He felt it too, *again*, but had become accustomed to it on the battlefield, having been in his share of close-quarter firefights.

Jan didn't answer her, his rage had consumed him for a moment, lost in it. Logan knew how the man felt. He had experienced the same thing many times when under heavy duress. He knew the tunnel vision would subside and Jan would be back to his usual cool, calm, and collected state in no time.

"Damnit, Logan."

Logan looked up from the dead lion, which he noticed was black as night. But the investigation into the creature could wait. He was just happy to see that his friend and longtime partner was okay.

"Gray," Logan said, walking forward, "you good, mate?"

Fitz patted his chest and legs, mockingly checking for injuries. He then grabbed his crotch and smiled. "You know I am." Limping forward, he met the others next to the prone body of the...

"What the hell?"

Logan looked down and saw CJ inspecting the... Lion? It was then Logan saw that this *definitely* wasn't a normal lion.

"Lights," Logan ordered. He wanted to see this thing with his own eyes, without the green tint of his night vision.

As everyone lifted their various devices away from their eyes, Logan clicked on a L.E.D. flashlight. The others followed suit, illuminating the dead monster, revealing it in its entirety.

"It's a saber?" CJ said, questioning her own assessment of the beast.

"A saber?" Fitz asked. "As in a saber-toothed tiger?"

"Saber-toothed cat—not tiger—there's no such thing," she corrected. "But yes... Well, more or less, yes." Her eyes never left the...*animal*. "It definitely has some of the more recognizable characteristics that a saber would have had."

"Like big fucking teeth," Fitz added. "Bastards were chasing me throughout this whole damn place. Thankfully, they can't see for shit in the dark."

"Why is it black?" Jan asked, standing over its head, Mossberg pointed at its blown out skull. He apparently wasn't taking any chances at a potential resurrection.

"Camouflage maybe," CJ replied, "or, it could be another form of *melanism*—a mutation in an animal's skin causing the coat's color to darken. It's actually quite common in the animal kingdom. Whatever it is, virus or not, it caused these things to change, giving these cats better stealth at night by altering their fur's pigment."

"And the teeth?" Logan asked.

"Better weapons," CJ said, looking up to her brother. "It's like a form of expedited evolution. It's a *Smilodon*, or as they are more popularly known as, saber-toothed cats. Smilodon means 'tooth shaped like double-edged knife' in Greek for those who care. Anyways, they were expert hunters and had canines that could reach in excess of ten inches."

"And *populator*?" Fitz asked. "What does it mean?"

"It means 'he who brings devastation.'"

The group was silent for a beat, but CJ perked up, a thought popping into her head. "It devolved the lion."

"Devolve?" Logan asked. "Isn't that a bad thing?"

"Normally, yes," CJ replied, "but if you could isolate the specific link—or gene—that caused it and eliminated the negative effects, you could, in essence, achieve it."

"So the lion was genetically instructed to revert back to its ancestral form—its stronger form most likely." Jan said skeptically.

"Along with a little laboratory created cocktail too," Fitz added, looking back to the room he found, his own comment making him shudder at what he saw in there.

"That's all fine," Logan said, trying to put a bow on what happened. "But why does this lion look like an extinct saber?"

CJ shrugged. "No idea, but whatever is in the God Blood that Mengele mentioned, seems to bring the *best* out the Nach in their own way."

"You mean, whatever brings out the *worst*," Jan added, shotgun still pointed down at the thing's head.

CJ just shrugged again, conceding the point. Jan was right after all. To the lion it was a best case scenario, but to its prey, it was most definitely the worst.

"What of Saami and Pandu?" Logan asked. "They didn't seem evolved or devolved. They just seemed crazed."

CJ shrugged again. "I can't tell you that. I'm not a

biologist, but maybe the God Blood reacts with different species inversely, creating different mutations. That would be my guess. Mengele's research is over seventy-years-old remember. His equipment was just as old. So was his understanding of DNA. We've come a long way since then."

"Mengele? God Blood? Nach?"

Logan, CJ, and Jan all looked to Fitz. His eyebrows raised to the ceiling, a questioning look on his face.

"What the hell are you guys talking about?"

21

"It's in here," Fitz said, leading the others around the second dead saber-toothed lion. They had to shimmy around its girth clogging the doorway in order to access the room marked *Labors.* His team had filled him in with what they had discovered too. He still couldn't believe most of it.

Fitz also filled in the others with the events that happened after he and Mo had left in the Blackhawk, to find the missing poacher. He described in detail what he saw when the largest of the males changed into a Nach-lion.

"Labs." Jan read the nameplate, rubbing his eyes, confirming what Fitz said as he stepped into the room. They opted to conserve the batteries in their night vision devices, using only their L.E.D. flashlights for now. If things went badly, they'd still have enough juice to get out of Dodge and make it safely back to the vertical shaft entrance.

Logan was last to enter, unable to avoid the congealing goop on the tile floor. It spread like black molasses and he had to be careful not to slip. As he passed by the lion's head, he saw that Fitz had blown out most of its skull, like Jan, with a well-placed shotgun blast, after taking off one of the creature's front legs.

He got lucky, Logan thought. *He incapacitated the thing before it could attack, blocking the second one from fully entering.* Logan then looked over to his friend. *Or he's just that good and stayed cool under pressure.* Knowing their backgrounds in the army, he knew it was probably Fitz's cunningness under pressure that did it, he was definitely talented with a variety of different weapons. *That* was for sure. If Logan was the best—which he believed himself to be— then Fitz was a very close second. Australia had lost two of the best within a couple years' time.

"This place is freaky," Fitz said, splaying his L.E.D. over the room, looking like he was about to retch. "I thought the Nach were bad... But the people running this place were even worse."

Logan immediately agreed with Fitz's criticism of the Wohn Tod as soon as his light found one of maybe a hundred or so *large* specimen jars. He inspected one in particular. Inside this *container* was what looked like a type of mongoose, except it was as big as a Komodo dragon. With fangs to boot.

"I almost crapped myself when I saw what was locked in here with me," Fitz said, laughing a little.

"Lucky for me they're already dead."

"Ugh," CJ said, her face pale-white in the bright beam of their flashlights. "I don't even know where to begin."

Logan didn't either. Every major species that inhabited the Serengeti was on display like some formaldehyde freak show from hell. The room must have taken up seventy-five percent of the basement level, with the middle being dedicated to performing these horrific acts against nature...and man.

He looked up and saw that the ceilings were vaulted. They must go straight up into the floor above, giving the room a cavernous feel.

Now that he thought about it, Logan realized that all of the rooms on the first floor were to the outside of the hall, away from its center. This room was the central hub of this entire facility.

Mengele's pride and joy.

"Are those people?" Jan asked in a low, growling tone. His light showed a half-dozen vertical coffin-sized containers. The bodies were naked, floating in the viscus green fluid. Three were male and the other three were—

"Oh my God!"

Logan shared CJ's horrified sentiment. The men, while stripped nude, looked semi-normal, only having minor signs of physical abuse and scarring from what was most likely some kind of brutal experimentation performed on their bodies. But the women...they were different. They, like the men, were nude and floated lifelessly in the chemical soup, but they also had one feature that was *obviously* dissimilar.

"They're pregnant," CJ said, gagging.

Logan watched as she stumbled away, vomiting beside another of the tanks. This one contained a chimera of sorts. It looked like half a baby giraffe had been combined with half a zebra. It was a strange and disturbing combination, one that he wouldn't even know where to begin to describe it if someone were to ask. He hoped no one would.

"CJ..." Logan said simply.

She shooed him away. "I'm fine—well not fine, but..."

He knew what she meant. No one was fine with this, but the three men accompanying her had been hardened by war. But this wasn't war. This was a crime against nature and humanity. This was evil.

"Logan," a voice said, tinged in German, "you need to see this."

Logan turned away from his sister, who was slowly composing herself. He saw the former demolitions expert halfway across the room, staring into a tank that was easily floor-to-ceiling in height and another ten wide.

He slowly made his way through the operating tables, which were stained with a dark brown coloration. *Blood,* he thought as he swept his flashlight back and forth, splaying the high-powered beam across the space. There were six tables in all, including a sizeable platform that was recessed into the floor, most likely used for *larger* specimens. He walked across it, noticing a hole at the center of the gigantic operating table. It unnerved him. He knew what it was for.

A drain.

Looking up to the darkened glass, Logan could see an enormous shape inside. It was easily twice his height. Jan was only a couple of feet from it, staring into the void, unmoving. As Logan stepped up next to him, he could see the older man had a single tear dripping down his cheek. Whatever was in here had unhinged the otherwise stoic man to tears. And Logan saw why.

"Is that a hippo?" Logan asked, shocked.

"Yes," Jan replied, "and something else too..."

Logan looked closer and saw it. The hippopotamus was standing erect...like a human. He saw various chains keeping it upright and against the rear wall of the room. But the body was all wrong. It had the same thick build as a hippo, but had the proportions of a human being.

"Look at the face."

Fitz had quietly stepped up next to Logan and Jan, a look of revolt on his face as well. They had both seen some awful things in their lifetimes, but this was insane. It was even worse than watching their bullets kill those kids. *That,* again, was war.

Logan looked up from its bare chest and midsection, which at one time or another, belonged to a woman, and saw what Fitz had. The face was all hippo, but the open, lifeless eyes, along with the brow and skull, were human. It even had hair, floating around in the green liquid. *Probably would have been shoulder length if it wasn't floating.*

"I think I know where it came from."

The three men turned, finding CJ, hand pressed up against one of the pregnant woman's tanks. Not one to hide her true emotions, she let the tears stream down her face. She looked back over to them, blinking heavy, containing herself just long enough to finish her hypothesis.

"They weren't just experimenting on them..." She looked back up into the dead woman's face. "They were growing them."

22

"Wait, I thought you said they were trying to develop some sort of super-serum?" Fitz asked, confused.

They had backtracked back upstairs and were now searching a few of the rooms on the first floor they had skipped. They still took every turn cautiously—even though Fitz had confirmed that there were only the two saber-lions in the bunker with them.

"Apparently, it wasn't the only thing they were working on down here," Jan replied. "Mengele and his men were obviously tinkering with the genetic code outside of their primary goal."

Fitz shook his head. "I still can't believe it was Mengele."

Jan thumbed over his shoulder back towards the entrance. "Would you like to meet him?"

Fitz looked at the German, but didn't answer. He just shook his head *no* and continued forward, following Logan and CJ back towards the hallway *not* containing the bodies of Saami and Pandu's. They didn't need to relive that moment, and honestly, Fitz didn't want to see it for a first time.

Rest now, my friends, Logan thought as they passed.

"The Wohn Tod were evidently looking into cross species experimentation as well as their fabled God Blood," Jan said.

Logan knew it honestly didn't matter why they did what they did. It was done and over with and now they were tasked with cleaning up the mess. Either way, they needed to contact the Bullpen and figure out their next step in this fight against this plague.

"But why the animals and the cross-breeding?" CJ asked, unnerved.

"Could it be that they were just fucking nut jobs?" Fitz asked, getting some of his wit back.

"Clearly," CJ added, "but there has to be a reason why. Like you said, the serum makes sense. They wanted to create stronger, better soldiers. Maybe even turn the tide in the war."

"I don't think so," Jan countered. "Remember the note the doctor left? It said something about leaving Hitler behind and moving on."

"Desertion?" Fitz asked. "They were going AWOL?"

"Sure sounded like it," Logan said from the front of the pack. "We're pretty sure this entire complex was off the Fuhrer's radar completely. The Wohn Tod didn't believe in what the Reich stood for. They wanted more."

"A secret organization operating under their noses," Fitz said. "Most likely using Nazi funds as well." Then he thought of something that didn't fit, motioning up. "What of the SS logo on the hatch above? You think they had some help from within the Schutzstaffel?"

"I think it's pretty safe to say they had agents within the SS. Stealing the building materials from a Nazi warehouse and sneaking them out of Germany overnight would have been easy too."

Fitz nodded his agreement. If anyone knew their German history, it would be Jan. He knew the man had no ties to the radical group, and it was honestly a blessing to have someone with this kind of knowledge right now. They needed any advantage they could get.

"How did this all start?" CJ asked, making the three men pause mid-stride and face her. They had just made it around the corner, back into the entrance tunnel back to the stairs.

"What do you mean?" Jan asked.

"What I mean is... How did this all start in the first place—how was this virus unleashed?"

"From the poachers in the pit topside," Logan said, remembering their first encounter with what they would later dub, the *Nach*.

The screams.

The glowing red eyes.

The bloodied chaos.

"Correct," CJ agreed. "We need to somehow investigate the burial for clues to how they were infected." Her face fell. "But... It may not be safe. If it's contagious then someone like the CDC should take care of it."

"I'm not going in there," Fitz said. "I say let the experts handle it. I'm just here to kill the sons-of-bitches."

"So," CJ asked again, "what was it?"

"It, uh... It wasn't blood obviously," Logan said, his mind in three different places. "That would have dried up long ago."

"Anyone know of some other protein that could have lasted seventy-plus years buried in the ground and then transmitted to a human?" Logan, Fitz, and Jan shook their heads, their night vision devices swaying back and forth. They opted to use them again, keeping their hands clear for their weapons. Just in case.

"Anatomy and biology weren't exactly my strong suits in school, CJ," Fitz said laughing. "I was a natural with a rifle and had shit for grades. The army was an easy choice."

"Same here, mate," Logan said.

"It's possible," Jan said, continuing the conversation. "We don't really know what is in the *Gott Blut*—the God Blood. If it's something synthetic, then, who knows? It could last forever in an ice box even."

"But, yes," he went on as they reached the bottom of the metal stairs leading back up to the surface, "I'm no expert either. I made things explode for a living. If it were an explosive I could dissect it and tell you everything. But this..."

Logan perked up at a memory. "Wait, remember the note?" Jan and CJ nodded, Fitz just shrugged.

"Only what you've told me," Fitz said.

"Right," Logan said. "Anyway... It stated that the *earlier* versions of the elixir caused the subjects to turn violent, craving flesh and blood." He pointed up. "I'm willing to bet the farm that's what we've got here."

"You think we are dealing with the more...*unstable*...version?" CJ asked.

"Yes," Logan replied, a-matter-of-fact, "I do. It all fits the behavior."

They stood there motionless, everyone waiting for the other to say something, but no one chimed in. What else could be said?

"Alright," Logan said, doing his leader thing, "let's get topside and call in Mo. We need to get the hell out of here and regroup."

"They're on their way, mate," Fitz said, grabbing the ladder. "I sent Mo back for the others...just in case. Adnan is going to stay behind and hold down the fort."

"ETA?" Logan asked.

Fitz looked down at his watch, calculating the time the chopper would arrive. "If Mo is flying like a banshee with her dress on fire, they should be here shortly."

Logan nodded and motioned for Fitz to climb. They needed to get back to base in one piece and retool for a heavier enemy. Their current weapons weren't going to cut it if these things got bigger.

Like the freak in the jail cell downstairs. He looked at the floor, visualizing the large skeleton with ragged flesh strapped to the chair on the floor below. He didn't want to admit it to anyone, but he had become intrigued with everything happening. Call it the result of a boy's natural interest with dinosaurs or with Kaiju like Godzilla and Nemesis. His mind shouted at him to flee or fight, but his inner voice told him to investigate it too. Find answers.

What made matters worse is, he knew of some pretty horrible possibilities out in the plains that, if infected, could wreak havoc on them. *Shit,* he thought. *Some of them aren't even carnivores.* But he knew better. The God Blood would see to that nicely and turn the most docile giant into the worst monster imaginable.

OUTBREAK

"Let both sides seek to invoke the wonders of science instead of its terrors. Together let us explore the stars, conquer the deserts, eradicate disease, tap the ocean depths, and encourage the arts and commerce."

~John F. Kennedy

23

Tanzania, 1946

One year, he thought to himself. It had been a year to the date since he had taken a permanent leave of absence from his post at Auschwitz to set up his little *side project* in the south of Africa.

He leaned back, rubbing his temples, recalling some of the information he had just read. The reports were promising, but the results were lacking. He needed more men that thought like him, but he recognized that wasn't possible.

He knew it was senseless to think that way, though. There was only one of him. There was only one Mengele. He was unique. He believed himself to be...special. It was the reason—the purpose—of starting the Wohn Tod. The Fuhrer had no idea what the Gott Blut could really be used for. Yes, it could turn the subject into a near immortal—a god—but it could also do so much more.

It will do more.

Staring at his notes, Mengele sighed, beyond exhausted. The initial tests of the current serum were encouraging, but it still wasn't right. The desired physical changes had occurred, but the changes to the mind was still an enigma as to what was causing them.

What would turning into a god solve, if you are to only act as a brute?

He rubbed the weariness from his heavy eyelids and sat straight. He knew it would take every single spare second he had here at the *Wohn Tod's* secret location to get it right. Someone would eventually come for them. It would only be a matter of time until someone survived an encounter with his men roaming the plains and report them.

By now the Allied forces were busy chasing a figment in South America, following a false trail he had set up to keep them occupied while he moved full-time to this outpost. If all went accordingly, they would believe him hidden away, living his life in peace in the jungles of the Amazon.

Mengele thought the Allies were fools. If they were as learned as he, they could have easily followed the trail south of Rommel's camp and found them here. Then again, there had been no reports of the Nazis continuing any farther. So why would they think such?

His initial estimate of the place was correct. It was plentiful with life, specifically the mammalian DNA the

Gott Blut required to work. For a reason that still escaped him, he still couldn't figure out why the elixir had no effect outside of mammals. He had always wondered what the serpents of this land would become if given the Gott Blut. He couldn't complain though, he still had an abundant amount of viable species at his disposal whenever he called for a new...specimen. It's all they were to him.

Mengele believed them *all* to be expendable—even his own men. His own life was truly the only one he believed mattered.

He had used some of the lesser soldiers stationed here—the ones that had started to second guess the cause as the months went by. It was an understandable situation, but it was also a feeling that needed to be squelched immediately. The last thing he needed was a mutiny. He knew it was rational for some of the men to feel that way. They were, in fact, originally told that they would be relieved after a few months. But no one would be coming. The only time frame they truly had was when they ran out of food and water... Which would be never. They would hunt food and collect water if needed.

"Doktor?" A shaky voice asked from the doorway of his private quarters.

He turned to find the younger man standing at attention, waiting for him to reply. The man, whose name he had yet to learn, was visibly uncomfortable, sweating profusely, his forehead beading with the salty liquid.

"*Ja?*" Mengele answered, seeing the soldier flinch

when he spoke. The people here were still terrified of him after all this time...and it served him well. They obeyed him to no fault, and they never second guessed one of his decisions. Particularly ones like this. If it were a more seasoned soldier... He didn't have to worry about that, however. *They* had all been slowly taken care of. The only soldiers left were ones he could control.

Smiling at the private, he knew why he was summoned. The men here had strict orders to retrieve him once the newest test subject was prepped. It was to be the first experiment with the latest of the serum. A new strand made from the oldest lot.

His heart pumped with excitement at the possibilities the most recent combination would provide. A truly *unique* outcome. And based on this result, they would proceed with the next phase of the project.

"Er ist bereit?" Mengele asked. The soldier nodded, confirming the subject was, indeed, ready.

He stood and approached the man. The younger *soldat* was maybe in his early twenties and easily could have physically overpowered Mengele. But the *Angel of Death* didn't need to use muscle to intimidate. He used something better. Fear... Reputation.

If anyone here crossed him and didn't kill him, they knew they would become the next in a long line of experiments. And that...was something even worse than death.

"Nimm mich," Mengele said, shooing the man forward. The soldier was nothing more than a lackey for the *Wohn Tod's* scientists now—an errand boy. With most of the commanding officers dead from *predator* attacks while out on *hunting expeditions*, Mengele was truly in control.

They quickly marched through halls with practiced strides. Both men could have done this in the dark, having moved through the corridors hundreds of times.

After a hard turn right, they found stairs not too much further, descending them swiftly. Mengele's hand touched a railing on the landing between levels, rattling slightly, coming loose a bit from the wall. He was about to question it, but the soldier quickly informed him it was to be taken care of in the morning.

The lower level's destination sign came into view moments later, and they immediately went right, towards the prisoner quarters. In some cases, like this one, it was set up as an experimentation suite.

The detainee was far too valuable—and dangerous for that matter—to be taken to the designated laboratories section of the underground facility. *He* needed to be under heavy watch twenty-four-seven. Mengele had even added an additional guard, just in case.

They rounded the final turn and came upon the barred door of the cell. Inside were two other scientists, loyal only to Mengele. They were his favorites from Auschwitz and would follow his orders without a second thought.

The imprisoned man screamed, not in pain, but in fury. He did his best to verbally berate the men who stripped him down nude, strapping him to a slightly reclined examination chair.

"Guten abend," Mengele said, stepping into the cell, formally greeting the prisoner.

The man looked up, fire in his eyes.

"Mengele," he said with a growl, speaking the doctor's name with disgust.

Mengele just smiled, like a wolf. *"Hallo, Generalfeldmarschall."*

The captured and transported test subject, Commander of the Afrika Korps, Erwin Rommel, sat in what would become his place of death. The normally clean cut soldier had at least a year's worth of growth on his face, showing how long he had been kept prisoner before being brought here. Mengele had two of his field agents back in Germany *apprehend* the general late one night.

Finally resided to his fate, Rommel stopped fighting—he stopped struggling altogether. He knew better than anyone what a losing battle was. He would let death come, they had already *killed* him back home, faking his reported suicide.

He had scoffed at the idea of telling the people of Germany that he killed himself. They really had no idea what kind of man he was. Rommel was a true soldier and a man of integrity. Even the notion that he would end his own life for someone like *the Fuhrer*, was laughable.

The one thing Rommel regretted more than anything else, was not seeing the treachery quicker. He had unknowingly cleared the path Mengele used to come to Africa. He was a stooge at the end of the day. A common lackey.

He remembered the orders from Himmler and now questioned the man's involvement in this. Was he a part of the grander scheme? Were he and Mengele in cahoots with each other? It was unfortunately an answer he would never get.

Mengele stepped forward and immediately injected a thick syringe into Rommel's neck, pumping the newest blend of the Gott Blut into the man's carotid artery.

This would be the most interesting test yet. The *general* would be given a special mixture containing some of the DNA *acquired* from the Gott Blut's *original* host. Ever since the first subject, Mengele had only used synthesized versions of the genetic matter, stating the extreme danger of administering the potent cocktail containing some of the tribesman's undiluted blood.

He was a tricky one to bring down. Mengele fully remembered the night when eight men died trying to apprehend the...*man*. What was even more spectacular, is that those soldiers then perished at the hands of an eighty-year-old local who was *armed* with nothing but his fingernails and a set of amazing sharp teeth.

The memory of watching the small *man* move like a ghost in the dark. Both silent and deadly. Both crafty and brutal... It still haunted Mengele's dreams to this day.

Man...

He used that term loosely. The tribesman was most certainly *not* a man in the obvious sense of the word, but Mengele didn't really know what else to call him. It's when he started to eat the dead... That's when he knew the creature was *NO* man.

The agonizing howl broke him from his thoughts. It also shook the room with a rumble of stone and earth that would have brought a lesser built facility down. The overhead light shattered, cascading the concrete cell into darkness.

In the pitch of the cell, Mengele heard his colleagues scream in agony. Had the prisoner escaped? *No,* he thought, *that isn't possible.*

In a moment of what he would later describe as *stupidity,* he rushed forward to help, but he didn't make it a step. Something quickly clamped down on the webbing of his hand and slashed, tearing the smallest amount of flesh.

He fell back in shock—not from the pain. But from the giver of the wound. The monster that the general was becoming, had bitten him.

Dr. Mengele stared in disbelief.

He was a dead man.

24

Whup. Whup. Whup.

The Blackhawk came in low and fast, ready to pluck the four SDF troops from the peak of the koppie. CJ stood towards the center waving her hands, signaling Mo. The three men, weapons raised, took up positions around her, and waited for anything that got close.

"Logan. This is Mo. Over."

"I read you!" Logan said, having to shout over the incoming noise of the low flying aircraft. "EVAC ASAP. Get us the hell out of here!" He then lifted his night vision, having to compensate for the brightness of the chopper's lights. Fitz had insisted that Mo come in with them ignited like the sun itself.

The front spotlight on Kipanga blinked twice, signaling the message was received loud and clear. It then slowed, kicking up a plume of dirt and grime as it pulled into a hovering position directly overhead of

Logan and the others.

Once we get in the air we'll call for backup. Then, we'll get the hell out of here and regroup, Logan thought, watching cables descend from either side of the Blackhawk. But Logan knew it wouldn't matter for the time being. Help was still hours away from arriving even if they called now—which they couldn't. Their personal comms weren't strong enough to reach Kenya. They would have to call from HQ and burdening Adnan wasn't an option. The younger man wilted under that kind of pressure. Logan would do it himself.

Calling for assistance wasn't something Logan liked to do either. It didn't always work out. He and his team were quick to act and didn't need a bureaucratic okay to get moving, the rest of the world did. He knew the approval to assist them could take hours to come in and then another few to get to the base. It was always a last resort to call for help.

This was definitely one of those times.

Normally, they were in, every sense of the term, 'self-sufficient,' minus the monthly air drop of supplies that is. They would receive their food supply, including water and other nonperishables, specially ordered weapons and ammo, and whatever other personal things each of them needed/wanted. The Bullpen even had its own power source. On one side of the roof was the helicopter pad and on the other was the latest and greatest in solar panel technology. It was the same ones used in some of the most remote parts of the world.

Kind of like here. It's what CJ had said when she pitched the idea.

As long as they didn't abuse it, no one seemed to care that they could basically ask for whatever they wanted. They were never questioned. They paid for everything they ordered mind you, but the service was still pretty over-the-top if you asked any of them, and they were thankful for that. Hence, they didn't exploit the charity.

Like what I have back at base waiting for me in the garage, Logan thought, thanking God that he, Mo, and Dada had the sense to finish putting it together a few days ago. It would definitely come in handy if things got any worse. *Which they will.* The feeling was all but assured when Mo cried out from Kipanga.

"Incoming from the north! Multiple targets, coming in hot!"

Logan, Fitz, Jan, and CJ all looked north, their heads shifting in unison like a group of prairie dogs on a hill. Each one of them gasped in harmony too. Neither of them could believe what they saw. Just on the fringe of the dark, aided by the various spotlights attached to the aircraft, was a herd of Grant's gazelle and wildebeest, maybe a hundred in all.

"Aw, damn," Fitz said. He looked down at his Mossberg, the shotgun feeling completely inadequate at the moment. "Logan, we can't fight this."

Logan agreed and passed on the sentiment to Mo. "We need EVAC right now, Mo!" The widespread herd, quickly narrowed and became a living column of death. He watched as hooves and horns, barreled straight for them. "Right now, damnit!"

Mo gently nudged Kipanga left, closer to the four stranded teammates. The flat black phantom glided to them, just as the first wave of wildebeest hit.

Two-dozen of the largest—some six hundred pounds in weight—slammed into the footing of the tall rock formation, trying to desperately climb its smooth, weather worn surface. The larger, clumsier species failed and slipped back down the koppie. Another smaller group, consisting mostly of the more agile gazelle, leapt up onto the wildebeest's backs, successfully bounding up onto the rocks like a mountain goat in the American Rockies.

Firing a volley, Logan could clearly see the swarm of red eyes in the bloodthirsty mob. The first set of bullets tore into the closest gazelle, sending it spinning away into the ever-growing throng of *Nachivores*. Then, as quickly as the foremost creature arrived, a second took its place, hopping up the steep climb. Logan caught a glimpse of the creature in the chopper's overhead light.

The ever common Grant's gazelle was around three feet in height to the shoulder and had a set of lyre-shaped horns roughly the same tallness. Their best evolutionary gift was their speed and agility in the open, reaching speeds of 50-mph. These gazelle, however, were not the typical ones found numbering in the hundreds-of-thousands all over Tanzania.

Logan flinched when he saw the horns. Usually, they would be turned back a little, acting more like a club during territorial disputes, or when fighting over mates. These were turned sharply forward, acting as perfect weapons for close combat. If they got close, all they'd have to do was use their exceptional speed, get close, and strike, spearing anything that got close. It would be just like a bull goring the bullfighter.

Or us, Logan thought. *Plus, there is usually only one bull.*

A shotgun blast took the animal's head off, sending a shower of blood and bone to the grass below. Another boom shook him from his daze, as Fitz fired again, killing another of the crimson-eyed beasts that tried—and failed—to get to close.

Rapid-fire machine gun discharge sounded from above as Dada and Kel fired, leaning out from inside the Blackhawk via the side doors. Each man was secured by way of tether, just in case the ride got bumpy and one of them lost their footing and fell.

A screech from somewhere behind the horde echoed around them as they continued their defense against the rampaging grasslanders. Logan recognized it for a second, but dismissed it immediately. It couldn't be what he thought. It sounded and looked too big.

The scream erupted again, almost jittering as it called. It was then that Logan's initial judgment of the noise's origin was confirmed. Only...this wasn't your average spotted hyena.

First off, it was covered in blood and looked like it went toe-to-toe with Wolverine and survived. It had flesh hanging from its face and half its lower jaw bone was exposed. Secondly, it was huge, easily a hundred-plus pounds heavier than the average one that inhabited the plains.

"It's a *Pachycrocuta*," CJ said, seeing it for what it was. "It was the largest of all the hyena, dating back some three million years. They were said to be the size of lions—maybe bigger."

Logan knew plenty about these things, and with this one's misshaped and extended jaw, it could probably cleave a limb off with just one bite. It had a wicked under bite, causing its abnormally large lower incisors to stick up in the air like a row of office buildings. He quickly went through his studies in his head, but *none* of what he read was worth exactly two shits at that moment. No amount of research could have prepared him for this.

How the hell did it get so big so quick? Logan thought. The only thing he could figure is that it was a side effect of the virus, accelerating the changes in some, but not the others. *Probably a random result depending on the species.*

"Logan!" Mo shouted through the swirling wind. "Clip on and we'll pull you up!"

With the cover fire from Dada and Kel, Logan, CJ, Fitz, and Jan, fastened themselves to the carabiner clips already attached to the ropes dangling just inches away. Then, as one, they were yanked off the top of the thirty-foot rock—just as it was overtaken by the masses. They were quickly lifted into the air, shooting the entire way up. It's only until they reached a *safe* height of a hundred feet did they stop firing and take in the full scene around them.

It was bedlam, and all of it was looking their way as they clambered into the rear hold and sped off. Mo angled them away and accelerated to Kipanga's top speed, back towards the Bullpen and what Logan hoped was safety.

25

If the helicopter hadn't drowned out the sounds of the surrounding terrain, its occupants would have heard a thunderous roar emanate from the fringes of the burial pit. The massive form of Shetani was easily seen and was now nine feet tall and weighed close to five hundred pounds. He pounded through the long since dead corpses of the men and animals buried long ago, having just arrived. Something in his mind recognized the site, but he paid it no attention. He had other things to deal with.

He emerged seconds later climbing the koppie with ease and watched the black silhouette speed off into the pitch-black sky.

Sneering in hatred at the prey he had detected earlier, he sniffed the air around him and bellowed again. To his surprise, the undead wildebeest and gazelles calmed some. He was originally expecting a fight. Now, he wasn't so sure.

The animals still reared in anticipation, stamping their hooves, crying out in frustration, but they...listened. Is that what this was? None of them spoke *per se*, but they instinctually knew to fear the monster perched above them. It could easily tear them to shreds without so much as breaking a sweat.

Shetani sniffed the air again and looked to his feet. His *six* red eyes locked in on the opening, peering into the darkness of the vertical entrance. He didn't know what this place was, but he instantly felt at home here, feeling some sort of natural bond to something inside and below.

He leapt into the air, raised his arms, and closed his legs, narrowing his body as much as he could. It was a tight fit, but he cleared the edges by mere inches. He fell like a missile, feet first, as if he were a diver entering a pool.

Sensing that the floor was rising up to meet him, he braced himself and landed with a crunch of concrete and tile. The room shook following his arrival, making him grin at the sight and sound of the cracked earth beneath his girth.

He sniffed the air again, detecting what he smelled from up above. He looked, seeing the stars overhead through the square opening above. He could even hear the huffing of the mindless drone army—his army—outside, waiting for him to return. For some reason those beasts thought of him as their leader. Maybe it was an animalistic intimidation—or possibly it was something else. Something deeper—a connection.

But, before he returned to them. He needed to explore this place. He needed to discover what drew him here.

He continued down the tight hallway, squeezing his wide shoulders and barrel chest through until he emerged at a two-way T-junction. He could go right—he looked that direction seeing only emptiness—or he could venture left. He turned his massive head left, noticing the veins of glowing blood that lit his way. They pulsated just enough to light up the walls and ceilings like a bioluminescent fish would the open water. It would aid him in the depths of this place and possibly even outside, but it would also give away his position to those who would be looking for it.

Like the ones that just got away.

It's then he saw the bodies. And it's then he smelled them. They smelled familiar, but not. It was hard to tell with the overwhelming fragrance of metal and... *Gunpowder?* The offensive odor clogged his nostrils, making it hard to correctly identify the dead.

His hulking form glided forward, each massive foot landing with a boom. There was no need for stealth down here. He stopped and kneeled, inspecting the dead, inhaling the different scents that were glued to every surface.

These are fresh, he thought.

He stepped over the first figure. It was torn to shreds by what looked like gunfire. He didn't remember ever firing a weapon, but he understood what the outcome looked like. Bloody and violent.

They were here.

The thought of the prey that had just gotten away

burned in his memory, but he knew it would have to wait. He *needed* to continue his search. He *would* find them eventually.

The next body was in much better condition, having only been stabbed with a blade. The wound through the dead man's chin was a given. He leaned forward and again inhaled. The man buried deep inside his mind glowered at the scent, but the creature within—the dominate personality—smiled. He recognized it, but it didn't come from the newly dead. It came from something older.

Still on hands and knees, Shetani craned his head to the left and looked into an open doorway, seeing what looked like living quarters. He sniffed the air, tasting it, and stood.

He ducked and entered, barely fitting into the tight confines. Pieces of the wall encasing the door's frame cracked and broke as he forced himself through. He then saw what he had smelled, a long rotted corpse sitting at the rear of the room. It may have once been a decent sized space for its inhabitant, but it felt like a cramped hollow to Shetani. He felted caged.

He kneeled again, coming face-to-face with the seated dead man. Maybe it was the sickly grin that all corpses had, but it kind of looked like it was smiling.

He sniffed again, and gagged, swiping at the body with one of his massive clawed hands. The wild swing missed, decimating the bookcase to his left. Books and rotted wood went flying in every direction, sending up a plume of dust in the process.

Shetani stumbled out of the room and collapsed on

the floor just outside the quarters, crushing the fresher dead man under his weight. Breathing heavily, he sat up and peered again inside the space, through the miasma clogging the air.

He knew the smell. It was easily identifiable in the unspoiled room, unlike the hallway. The seated figure's scent hadn't been masked by the noxious stench filling the corridor now.

He lifted his arm and sniffed his own flesh, focusing on the specific scent.

The same, he thought. *We are the same.*

He recognized the scent of his current form, but he also recognized the smell of something else. The army outside smelled only of the *devil* in him. The scent that attracted him to this place was unique, like him. There was another that the scent had in common with... The ones that fled from here. Shetani knew that deep down he was similar to them.

Was... But not anymore.

Confused at the notion of what he was, Shetani leapt to his feet and pounded down the corridor, smashing what was left of the body's head under his foot. He took the first right at a sprint, pushing off the wall as he made the turn. The plaster crumbled beneath his strength.

He understood what the seated dead man was to him—he just didn't comprehend how it was possible. He could also tell this place was old—too old for him to have anything in common with anyone here.

The human aspect of his mind was still functioning well enough for him to know and understand things he took for granted. He knew this was a man-made structure and that it was old. But he didn't understand the finer details, like the Nazi paraphernalia or the subject matter of the books in the office... He even knew it was an office and not some primitive cave, the knowledge popping into his head just now.

But instinct was overthrowing knowledge and primitive aggression was subduing caution. He felt no fear...until now.

Is something changing in my head?

In something of a panic—another new feeling—he skidded to a halt at the sight of a staircase leading down, his oversized heart pounding like a drum. Again he could go in two different directions. Straight or—

The other scent hit him like a slap in the face and without another thought, he dove down the stairs. He jumped from level to level, landing hard on the basement's tiled floor in one large leap, crushing another section of flooring. Upon arriving he squatted, claws outstretched, ready for anything.

The smell of what drew him radiated through the tight confines of the underground facility. It was faint though, having been here for a while, dissipating over time.

Like the seated man.

Just in front of the stairs was another T-junction. He gave pause and sniffed the air. The overpowering scent, matching the one from the hallway above his head, struck him hard. He would not go left. But the smell coming from the right was different.

This time he breathed in deeply, letting it absorb into every square inch of his nasal cavity. The aroma caused an almost euphoric bodily response. His muscles relaxed, squelching the abnormal nervous twitching impulses throughout his body. His nerves calmed and his self-control returned. It was similar to the seated man, but not, like only a fraction of it had been instilled into the other.

The thought of the pure scent was too much. He leapt down the hallway. He was this close to identifying what called him here.

26

On all fours, like one of the other killers outside, Shetani continued forward, exiting the small hall between the stairs and the next T junction. His other two, newer, appendages were still folded atop his thick back. He tried to move them and found the effort less painful than before, but they still weren't ready to use. He could also feel a slight itching sensation emanating from them—annoying more than anything else. He breathed in again, focusing his senses on what was around the corner rather than on something as insignificant as an itch.

He went right, towards his unknown destination. Following the same layout as the floor above, he made the sharp turn—immediately passing through what could only be described as an invisible odor barrier. He shook his head, slamming it into the right hand wall of the dark corridor, but he didn't stop. It was the scent he had picked up earlier, and it became more and more overwhelming the closer he neared its source. The smell-wall he had just passed through, overstimulated his senses, causing his mind to momentarily buck, reverting back into the primal beast he continued to evolve into.

Physically, he thought, *but not mentally.* Something continued to change in his mind. His body grew stronger and more overpowering. His mind was growing stronger too, but in a much different way.

Slowing, he stalked forward like a cat, claws ready to slash and gore anything that appeared in front of him. But nothing did. It was as still as death down here and had been for some time.

He stopped when he saw the barred door, staring at it with mixed emotions. Whatever he was drawn to, it was in that room, behind the cage-like barrier.

He again moved closer, breathing heavy with anticipation. He *needed* to see what was in there. It beckoned him forward.

Inhaling, Shetani tasted the air. The human scent was thick here too, covering the bars themselves.

Human?

The revelation caught him off guard. Something was definitely happening to his memory. Images from a past he still couldn't fully recall flashed through his mind. Just a few moments ago he had no idea what the scent was that drew him, but now he could confidently say it was human. The *people* that fled in the flying machine had also left a trail here.

Flying machine. Information, like ants marching

one-by-one back to their homes, came. One at a time, small bits of his memory returned, feeding his subconscious.

He stretched forward smelling the metal, catching a whiff of one the humans. Its fragrance was sweeter, softer, more...feminine. He glanced up from the bars and froze when he saw what was on the other side of the cell's door.

Slowly standing tall, he never took his arachnid-like gaze off of the creature that sat inside the prison, strapped to a chair. He gripped the heavy door and with one raged-filled roar, yanked it from its hinges, flinging it down the hall. He stepped inside, peering closely into the dead eyes of...

We are the same. It's the second time he had the thought.

He leaned in closer and sniffed, rearing back at the scent. It was like before, but ten-times stronger. It would have again sent him sprawling to the hard floor, but he anticipated the reaction and reached for the wall outside the room.

It's the second time that has happened as well. Something as simple as a smell had caused him to react like that. *Fool.* He hadn't felt the least bit clumsy or frightened before this. Whatever the two monsters were, they were something even he needed to have caution with.

Monsters.

The one upstairs wasn't a monster in the literal sense, but he had obviously been one. It wasn't as overpowering either. *Maybe because it still looked human?* He wasn't sure exactly how much monster the person had in them before they died. Regardless, the two definitely had the same human scent.

Like me.

He again smelled his own flesh, comparing it to the dead here. Smiling for a second, Shetani lifted his other arm and found it covered in the fluids of the dead. It belonged to the one he fell on outside the office upstairs. It too held an identical odor, along with the putrid smell of their weapon's discharge.

Weapons. He looked to his hands, grinning. He didn't need weapons.

He reentered the cell and reached out, cutting away the thick leather straps keeping the arms tied down. *Four arms*, he thought. Next, he lifted one of the primary arms, surprised to find it much more flexible than he would have thought. He knew the older of the dead were supposed to be stiff and brittle. This was most definitely *not* that. This was like a taut kind of rubber or something close to it.

Slowly, Shetani placed a heavy palm on the dead creature's chest—flinching away after feeling something that didn't belong. A faint, barely noticeable thump twitched under his prodigious hand.

Alive?

The severely dehydrated beast was...alive.

How? Even he knew that most living thing's needed sustenance to survive.

Living... He felt his own chest, finding nothing.

NOT alive. The realization struck him hard. He was dead... He flexed his arms.

NOT dead, but not alive.

He shook off the discovery. He was *Hai Wafu—Living Dead—*and it made him smile. He was the best of both.

Shetani looked back over his shoulder, sensing the pounding of the hooved throng above him. The reverberation could be felt under his feet and in his ears, thanks in part to his heightened senses.

Looking back down to his *relative*, he had an idea, grinning as he turned. He quickly headed back the way he came. He knew exactly what to do. It would take time, but in the end it would be worth every second.

The best part was that there was a stable and almost willing source of fuel just outside. *He* wouldn't feed on the others here, though. They didn't possess the new meat and fresh blood he now desired. *But what of the other?* Shetani didn't think the mostly dead would mind how new or old the meal was. He was sure it would just be happy to be *alive* again.

27

"Right…" Logan said, leaning forward on his knees. "What do we know?"

Along with CJ, Fitz, Jan, and Adnan, Logan, seated at his desk, had gathered his team inside the inner ring of racks and shelves. In front of each shelf was a metal table, each one being filled with recently outfitted and customized weapons. The ones that were empty held a couple of his friend's butts.

Dada and Kel were elsewhere, checking that the compound was locked down and sealed tight. The only entrance would be from the garage at the rear of the complex. Its door was thick and heavy, and impossible to open from the outside without a remote.

"Infrared, huh?" Fitz asked Mo, who was standing, leaning against one of the racks that encircled Logan's workstation.

Mo nodded. "I was curious and flipped on the unit

equipped to Kipanga's belly—the one we installed last year, but haven't really used. Normally, it would show anything alive within a few degrees of our blood's temperature as an off-white blob." He took a breath. "But the Nach..."

"What of them?" Jan asked.

"They read as white-hot—" Mo replied, "off the charts white-hot—like they had a spike of internal temperature—"

"Like a fever?" Logan asked.

"Could be," Mo said, "but it's not like I had a thermometer handy."

"You can borrow my rectal thermometer if you want." Fitz said with a smirk on his face.

"What do you think it is—the God Blood, I mean?" CJ asked the group, rolling her eyes at Fitz. She threw out the question for everyone and anyone to answer curious at any and all opinions.

"I thought we nailed that one already?" Fitz replied. "It's some sort of World War Two-era super elixir, administered to human and animal subjects, giving them a steroid-user's wet dream of results and a cannibal's wet dream of an appetite."

CJ's nose flared in disgust.

"Some of them were Nazi soldiers too," Jan added, shaking his head. "They really didn't care who they tested it on. Just as long as they got their damned results."

"Probably some blokes that didn't exactly agree on what they were doing there," Fitz said. "The *real* SS soldiers stationed there, I mean—not the Wohn Tod traitors."

Everyone nodded. It was clear that they staged some sort of coup and took over the facility from the inside out. Whoever was actually a part of the Reich was eventually captured and experimented on like any other POW. Once the bunker was in the hands of Mengele and his men, they must have gone into full-blown psycho mode.

"That's not what I meant though," CJ said. "What I meant was, *what* is the virus—the God Blood itself? What is it doing to the things that call this place home?"

"Turning everything infected into fucking monsters, that's what!" Fitz said, getting up and pacing the room.

As ridiculous as it sounded, Fitz was right, and Logan had no idea where to go from here. How do you fight something like this on a wide scale? You can't kill everything in the Serengeti to prevent the spread, and you can't hunt down everything that has already been infected. The square footage was just too great. Even if he had a hundred men it wouldn't be possible.

"It's also altering their DNA at its finest levels," Jan said. "It's changing them—"

"The saber-lions," Logan said.

"Exactly," Jan agreed. "Whatever the *Gott Blut* truly is, it's giving the animals and people infected added aggression and the means to become true super-predators. It's tapping into their ancestral traits and bringing them out after the virus invaded their systems."

"Like foot long teeth and camouflaged fur?" Fitz asked.

Jan just shrugged.

Logan looked up to Adnan. "Any word back from the military?" He had asked the I.T. guru to call it in, even though he had planned on doing it. If contact was made, Logan would take over. He asked Adnan to do his best to explain what was happening without bringing up the undead packs of animals now roaming the plains.

Adnan shook his head no. "Not yet, but I left a message with them and implored them to ring us back as soon as they got my call." His face fell a little.

"What?" Logan asked, noticing the change in body language.

"I'm just not sure how seriously they are going to take it. It may be hours before we hear something back from civilization."

Logan nodded.

"Okay," he said, standing and walking to the nearest table. He lifted his slightly modified SCAR, checking the scope that now sported an infrared feature. "We stay in the Pen until we hear back from the outside and hunker down. We can patrol the grounds outside in the Rhino. Two man teams. No one goes outside alone."

The *Rhino* was Logan's brand new technical. It was a military grade Hummer outfitted with a .50 caliber M2A1 heavy machine gun and bullet proof glass. The steel siding would protect anyone on the inside from the standard ammo used by poachers. The Hummer also had steel plating covering each of the tires, making them invulnerable to attack from the sides as well. It had yet to see action since the SDF recently acquired it.

"Mo," Logan said, looking to the pilot, "how's fuel?"

The man shrugged. "Fine, but no long trips unless absolutely necessary."

"We need to go back to the site," Fitz said, getting everyone's attention.

"What—why?" CJ asked, her eyes wide in fright and shock at such a request.

Fitz held up both his hands, pleading for her to calm down. "Easy, mum... I just want to get the Rover back that Jan and I left there. It is fully stocked and we may need the extra wheels if we have to bail and head for the hills."

No one spoke, unsure of what to say. But Logan, being the leader of the group, did what all men in charge would do.

"He's right and I'll go."

Several voices argued about it, but he squelched it down with a loud bang, his fist punching the metal table. The equipment atop it rattled, causing everyone to quiet immediately. They knew how serious he was if he lost his cool or raised his voice a decibel higher than usual. If Jan was as calm as he was, Logan was the Buddha himself. Logan's demons caused him anguish on the inside, but on the outside he was as passive as a statue.

"Mo will fly me out and drop me right on top of it," he said. "Then I'll high-tail it out of there and head back here ASAP."

"Like hell you are," Fitz said, standing in defiance. If there was one person in the room Logan would listen too, it was Gray Fitzpatrick. Logan respected his words above all others when it came to things of this nature— even more than his sister's.

Logan was about to argue, but Fitz just calmly held up his hand and added, "At least," he smiled, "not without me you're not."

"Gray—" Logan said, but was cut off.

"Don't even try, mate," Fitz said. "You and I both know that going out there alone right now is the wrong thing to do, and there is no one better by your side than yours truly." He emphasized the last point my sticking his thumb out at himself.

Logan conceded, rubbing his forehead, trying desperately to ward off the incoming headache. It didn't work though. The slight pressure behind his eyebrows increased with every second that passed.

"Plus," Fitz said, with a smirk, "I have a new toy to try out."

28

They were in the air fifteen minutes later, heading back towards ground-zero. Knowing the flight would take roughly thirty minutes, Logan and Fitz went over the plan again, Mo listening the best he could while still flying straight and true.

"What the hell is that?" Mo asked, interrupting the huddle when seeing Fitz's new *toy*. It was unlike anything he'd seen since joining up with the SDF.

The Aussie grinned patting his recently acquired XM-25 grenade launcher. It was black in color, like their new BDU's. They opted for the new clothes for nighttime concealment with the hopes of leaving as small a footprint as possible until they reached the Land Rover.

That's the plan, anyways, Logan thought, listening to Fitz.

"The XM25 Counter Defilade Target Engagement

System features a state-of-the-art targeting software that calculates the mark's range with a push of a button." Fitz flipped over the weapon, showing Logan the red button. "It then transfers the data to an electronic fuse built into the 25mm round." He held up one of the large shells and continued. "These projectiles are capable of exploding directly above the target in question when programmed, peppering the enemy—in this case the Nach—with shrapnel."

"Does it have to be programmed?" Logan asked.

"No," Fitz replied. "You can just point and shoot like any other weapon. The targeting system is just an option."

Logan took the weapon, hefting the fourteen-pound beast, inspecting the futuristic looking grenade launcher. "A little heavy, don't you think?"

Fitz only shrugged. "Normally, I wouldn't recommend carrying such a bundle, but considering what we are going up against..."

He didn't need to finish, Logan understood. This wasn't your normal everyday situation. They need to bring out the heaviest of the heavy and get this thing under control. The only problem was that he still had no idea how to do that. He feared it would be a large scale invasion on every living thing in the Serengeti. Animals *and* people would become the hunted, and in other cases...the hunters. Some would be killed—maybe all of them if this pandemic kept consuming everything it touched.

"Ten minutes out!" Mo shouted from the front.

"Right," Logan said, "let's do this."

Both he and Fitz stood and prepped the twin lines, one on each side of the Blackhawk. They would then quickly throw open the bird's doors and leap out into the night sky. If Mo did his job like he always did, the two men would practically land atop the vehicle they sought.

Better be worth it, Logan thought, starting to second guess the idea of returning to the pit again. *Was a truck really this important?*

He knew it was, though. If, and possibly when, they need to evacuate the Bullpen, he wanted enough wheels for everyone who was left to get out quickly and safely. That meant the Land Rover they now pursued. If they lost any of the vehicles back at HQ and this particular vehicle was still sitting here, he'd hate himself for not getting it.

"Get ready to drop in thirty seconds!" Mo yelled as Logan felt Kipanga level out and slow to a hover. He was so lost in thought that he hadn't even realized they had arrived.

Okay you bastards... Let's do this.

He gripped the door, ready to throw it open, but was stopped by the quiet and shaky voice of Mo in his earbud.

"Um... Captain?"

Logan glanced up front to the pilot, seeing only the back of his head. He then noticed that the Kenyan was looking out his side window and down. Logan tried to do the same, but the angle wasn't right. The only way he was going to see what Mo did was if he opened the cargo hold's sliding door.

He pulled and froze.

"The hell?" he asked himself.

The ground below was moving. It was like a sea of bodies, roiling like an incoming wave. Every species of inhabitant was accounted for. He saw lion, leopard, hyena, gazelle, wildebeest, smaller creatures that looked like a mongoose, and something else. Something that he didn't recognize.

"Holy shit—pull up!"

The helo accelerated straight up, throwing Logan to the floor of the rear hold. Fitz's warning had come so quick that he wasn't able to properly brace himself for the violent upheaval underneath him.

The motion caught Fitz off guard as well, but he was able to stay on his feet. The jarring motion did, however, cause him to flinch, flexing his finger down on the trigger of his XM25.

A round sailed out into the horde below, exploding on impact, turning six of the things to pulp and maiming another handful. But as quickly as they died, another group took their place in the ever growing mass.

Laying on his back, Logan turned and looked out over the edge, seeing what looked like a gorilla in midair, heading back towards the ground.

No, not a gorilla, Logan thought, not believing what he saw.

The monstrous beast, descended the next forty feet, having leapt from the top of the koppie, and landed directly on top of the Land Rover they sought, crushing it like a tin can. The creature was covered in hairless black, leathery skin and had what looked like pulsating red veins crisscrossing over its body. It sort of resembled what a dehydrated power lifter's veins looked like, protruding from its skin. He noticed that they rippled too, pulsating with glowing blood.

Except, that's not a powerlifter or any other kind of man, he thought. *Not anymore at least.*

The only thing that made it look human was its *humanoid* shaped body and the intelligence it moved with, but besides that... Nothing. It looked like it had just awoken from a deep sleep in Hell...

And boy does it look pissed, Logan thought.

The six eyed behemoth looked up to them and roared. The sound was low like a lion's—and at the same time high, like a chimp's. They could even hear it over the wash of the Blackhawk's rotor blades. It stared back up at them with a venomous glare. Never blinking. Never backing down.

"Fitz, hit the truck!" Logan shouted, coming out of his stupor.

Fitz immediately aimed at the crushed form of what was once *his* Land Rover and fired. The 25mm explosive round quickly navigated itself towards the ruined vehicle. It would make a perfect addition to the explosion, adding even more punch.

"So long," Fitz said to the Land Rover as he watched.

A split second before the projectile hit, the creature leapt into the air again, landing atop the koppie. In another fluid motion, it jumped again, disappearing from view into the mass grave site on the other side.

"Eyes!" Logan yelled, as he, Fitz, and Mo, who were

all wearing night vision devices, quickly shut their eyes. The detonation, aided by the SUV's gas tank, ripped through the throng of Nach like a knife through butter, cutting down a large group of them.

Maybe it was the concussive force from the Land Rover, or maybe it was the fact that the creature had fled, but without their 'leader' the other monstrosities scattered in all directions. It's like the hive just lost their queen and had zero direction of their own. Having no reason to stand there and wait to be next on Fitz's widening shit-list, they bolted.

A roar, throatier and raspier than the man-thing's, echoed through the area surrounding the koppie. It had an instant effect on the other creatures, calming the thrashing mob of hooves, horns, and claws. As the feral cry faded, so too did the stampeding of the other infected beasts. Hundreds of sets of eyes simultaneously turned up to the hovering aircraft, all having the same hate filled, hungry look.

"Ah, shit..." Fitz said, looking out his own open door. "That can't be good."

The obvious differences in the two roars was disconcerting, but what was even more disturbing to Logan was that it came from *inside* the underground complex.

No...

He hoped he was wrong. The memory of the creature he'd seen in the barred jail cell on the basement level had unnerved him, but the thought of it being alive was even worse. He didn't know how it could have lived after seventy years of rot and decomposition, but somehow, it had.

He glanced back down, seeing the large beast moving within the pit. The first monster was still above ground, confirming his suspicions that something was definitely alive in the bunker. The thing in the basement was one of these, but older—more ancient.

"Mo," Logan said, quietly, "take us home." He then noticed the blood running down the koppie's exterior. There had to be gallons of it flowing from its top, like a demonic waterfall.

He then climbed into the front passenger seat, seeing the terrified look in Mo's eyes. "Quickly, my friend."

29

Shetani watched from inside the pit as the men escaped...alive. He seethed at the thought of them fleeing again. He wanted them dead. All of them.

The hatred for them came naturally and he wasn't exactly sure why. It just felt right to want them gone. At first, he was curious, but now, he was furious. It must have come from the changes happening both physically and mentally, becoming a part of his new identity... Shetani... *Devil*. The name he now realized was new too, even though it was the only one he could truly remember. He was most definitely something else—*someone* else—before he awoke in the burial pit. But not anymore. He was only *Shetani* now.

He reached up and began to climb the backside of the koppie, barking out orders for the cats to follow as he moved. He didn't know how fast they were now, but he was sure that in their current state they'd be able to keep up easily. It came out as garbled, saliva filled snarls, but they abided his wishes, turning and sprinting away.

Speech was new, too. He hadn't tried to speak other than a sustained roar, but that was more involuntary, being brought by emotion, not thought. The notion of verbal communication with his brethren had just come to him...and it obviously worked.

Halfway up the boulders, a large talon tipped hand emerged from the opening leading underground. Shetani silently paused his ascent, watching the three fingered hand grasp at the smooth stone surrounding the open hatch. It was bigger than his by quite a bit too, and was built differently.

His hands were strong and powerful, like the rest of his body, but these were long and spindly by comparison. He wouldn't have called them weak by any means, either. They were plenty strong, having seen the way his...ancestor...tore into his meals. The precision of the strikes was incredible.

The fact that it was down in the underground facility also stated that it was old—older than him and so *ancestor* felt like the appropriate term.

Dragging the live meals down the halls wasn't easy. If they had fresh prey, Shetani would have probably fed on them himself. These weren't fresh, though. These were the newly made. They still had enough blood and other viable substance to help his ancestor's rebirth.

Shetani wanted nothing better than to take off after the enemy, and hunt them down, but he needed to help awaken his... *What was he to me? Grandfather?* Regardless of who, or what, he was to Shetani, he needed to reawaken him first. It was another of the many things nagging at the back of his head.

He didn't know if the thing he now called his ancestor was actually related to him in some way or not, only that they were similar in... He didn't even know that. It was the scent that spurred him into action. He knew they were of similar species, but beyond that...

As the changes in his mind continued, some of his intellect returned, backseating the barbarity from before. He tried to focus on the things before he *awoke* in the pit surrounded by death, but he couldn't. Every time he got close to seeing a memory it disappeared, causing his anger—his savagery—to rise anew.

A scratching sound returned his attention back to the top of the koppie, and he watched as a second identical hand emerged from down below. It was then followed by a third...and a forth. But before the creature could pull itself up, its grip faltered and it fell, landing hard on the floor below.

Shetani would need to help him back to the chamber below so he could continue to feed. It was obvious that his ancestor wasn't strong enough to leave the confines of the underground structure yet. He would need a little more time.

Before he dropped back down through the opening, Shetani looked back off in the distance. He visualized the direction his prey had gone, burning it into his memory for a later time. He *would* find them.

He breathed in deep and blocked out the stench of those around him, singling out the noxious fumes that emanated from the aircraft. He grinned and leapt into the air, dropping into the darkness below. The scent of the machine was easy to pick out... It wouldn't be hard to track.

* * * * *

The only problem with quickly evacuating the area, is that the Blackhawk made a lot of noise and kicked up a ton of dirt, spooking the already on edge animals. Some fled away from the aircraft, some didn't. About half of the Nach pursued the aircraft, following them back towards their base of operations.

Mo throttled up as fast as he could, but couldn't shake the quickest of the animals. There were about eight or so, that kept up with them, traveling over 150-mph.

"That's not possible," Fitz said, watching the spotted cats as they sprinted after the chopper like a group of fang filled sports cars. They were clearly some kind of cheetah, but the virus had definitely given them some *upgrades*.

"No ground animal on earth can keep up with anything at this speed," Fitz said, turning to Logan. "Thank God we didn't actually make the Rover." He shook his head. "We'd be done for."

Logan silently agreed, keeping vigil, watching the extra-large cats as they ran. It was like nothing he'd ever seen before. The altered cheetahs bounded like any normal one would, except that it would stay airborne for what seemed like seconds before its thickened forelimbs and hindquarters met the ground, pumping hard again. What was worse, is that they didn't even appear to be overly exerting themselves. It seemed like just another midnight stroll through the Netherworld for them.

Their physical appearance didn't look much different—minus the obviously larger bone and muscle structures. A normal cheetah would get around to the size of a large dog, maybe a hundred and sixty pounds. But these things... They had to be twice that.

Black fur too, Logan thought. *Perfect for concealment out in the open.* He could just make out the off-black spots covering its body, giving it a two-tone, black-on-black appearance.

"Mo," Logan said, formulating an idea. "Slow us down and bring Kipanga lower. I want to see if these bastards can dodge one of Gray's 25's at this speed."

Without acknowledging Logan, Mo slowed Kipanga to 70-mph and lowered them to just fifty feet off the turf.

Logan then turned to Fitz. "Clip on just in case you get thrown and light these assholes up."

Grinning like a kid about to do something he knew he shouldn't be, Fitz stepped out onto the left landing skid, letting the military grade tether hold him in place as his upper body leaned out into open space. He pivoted, turning his hips and shoulders just enough to aim his weapon down and to his left. The XM25 was leashed to his belt, and so was the tether that held him to the chopper. He then picked out the front most cat, leading it a few feet in his sights, and pulled the trigger.

The back half of the Nach-cheetah exploded in a cloud of gore as its front claws dug for purchase, about to make its next stride. The remnants were then shot away as a resounding thunderclap resonated through the air, sending the remaining creatures into a frenzied zigzagging pattern.

"Keep at it!" Logan yelled over the swirling wind. "We need to cut down as many of these things as we can before we get back to HQ."

Whether or not Fitz heard him was a mute question. He let loose another projectile, continuing his own war with the Nach. Logan peeked out behind his friend and watched as another cheetah burst, turning to cat-slush. *He heard me,* Logan thought, grabbing a satchel from behind his co-pilots chair.

Reaching into the dark olive canvas bag, Logan pulled out two of a dozen flashbang grenades. He then quickly scurried back to his position next to Fitz. Clipping on like his friend did, but staying seated, Logan swung his legs over the side, dangling them over the open air below.

He pulled the pin belonging to one of the flashbangs and yelled, "Flash out!" directing Fitz and Mo to shut their eyes. The last thing they needed was a blind pilot.

Through his shut eye lids, Logan saw a slight flash

and then opened them, watching two of the large cheetah stumble and slow. Mo followed the movement, slowing the helo so Fitz could take the shot.

It's what he needed.

The other Aussie, let fly two more 25mm rounds, obliterating the stunned cats. *Four down,* Logan thought, counting the remaining creatures. *Four to go.* He then lobbed another flashbang out into the void of the darkened African sky.

I hope Fitz brought enough ammo.

30

"Well, that didn't go as planned," Fitz said, falling into one of the lounge chairs on the second floor living area. He then leaned back and kicked out the foot rest, closing his eyes while rubbing his temples.

The second floor was sectioned off into three parts. A third of it was where half of the remaining SDF team now found themselves, including Logan and Fitz. The latter adding an ice bag, laying it across his forehead.

"Ya' think?" Logan replied, equally exhausted, and sprawled out across the sofa on the other side of the living room. Both men were still dressed in their black BDU's, but had cleaned up and showered, changing into new clothes. They didn't want to take any chances and not be ready if things went south... Which it undoubtedly would.

Logan recalled the hot, scorching shower and thought about taking another one. The first was to clean up his body. The second would be to clean up his mind. Maybe try to forget some of the horrors he'd seen...

He got up as the flat screen mounted above the faux electric fire place blinked to life, quickly resolving into the form of Adnan. He was still manning the third level's communications and had continued trying to call for help.

Logan turned. "Anything yet?"

Adnan just quietly shook his head. He had tried several times, in fact, to reach someone from the local American command. It was number one on their "Holy Shit We Need Help List," knowing they would have been fully resourced and have the capabilities to send the assistance needed. It was either the late hour or the moronic sounding cry for help stating that, "the animals have gone berserk and are killing everything in sight."

It's no wonder they hadn't gotten back to them, Logan thought. If he had been one of the Americans, he would have agreed. It sounded completely absurd.

Looks like we're on our own for now.

He turned away from the screen as it blinked out, heading around the catwalk that also housed a set of stairs that looped around the inner wall of the large building. It also held an open air freight elevator, like the ones you see in some old style buildings, or in the movies. It even came with its own roll down wood barrier to keep the riders from falling out. The biggest difference was, that this one could fit a Hummer on it.

"Captain?" Fitz said, lifting the ice bag off his head,

opening his eyes. "You alright, mate?"

Logan nodded. "As good as it gets, Gray." He pointed to his temple, tapping it. "Just need to clear the ole' noggin."

He continued right, his boots pounding over the metal utilitarian catwalk. The Bullpen was in fact just a large, vertically built cylinder divided into three floors—four if you counted the small fallout shelter in the basement beneath the garage. It was another of Logan's paranoia induced precautions.

Garage Level was technically two stories tall and encompassed ninety percent of the lower floor. The other ten percent made up a small gym, with a boxing ring. The garage mostly housed all of the vehicles the SDF had at their disposal, which was now one SUV short. They had one more, though, along with the Rhino, a pair of dirt bikes, and a specially made four-wheeler. They had always lived by the motto, "The more the merrier," hence the decision to go back for the other 4x4.

The other two sections of the second floor *Living Level* housed the showers and bedrooms. The former was equipped with a small, but very effective swimming pool. It was ten-feet-long and another four-feet-wide and four-feet-deep. It was specifically to use for swimming against an artificial current, helping with overall stamina and low impact exercises. Perfect for rehabbing minor injuries like muscle pulls or ankle sprains.

Logan turned right, entering the bathrooms once again. Through the open walkway, were the stalls holding half a dozen toilets and sinks. Each one was outfitted to look like a normal private restroom back home. They came complete with locking doors for some much needed privacy too. It reminded Logan of the trailered-in bathrooms some state fairs had. *Shitter on wheels.*

He turned left, following the left side wall past a row of mirrors and entered the shower room. He undressed, hanging his BDU's and underclothes in his specially marked spot. Each one of them had their own locker-type area at the entrance to the shower room. They had trained to dress fast, in case of emergency, and needed everything to be quickly accounted for if and when that time came.

Now naked—they didn't bother with men's *and* lady's showers, CJ made due with a bikini stating, "Once you've seen one, you've seen them all." Logan smiled at the thought. It had helped break the ice when she had first walked in on four of the men. They scattered like field mice, causing her to laugh hysterically. Logan had been the only one not to flinch and run. CJ knew what she was getting herself into when she signed up for this gig.

He turned from the happier of his memories and looked at himself in the full length mirror just outside the showers. His body was still chiseled from head to toe, barely sporting any body fat to speak of. He had been a little thicker in the service, maybe another fifteen-to-twenty pounds, but decided to clean up his diet when he moved here. He felt thirty-eight, but could physically pass for ten years younger if he ever bothered to shave regularly. Which he didn't.

The last real *relationship* he had ended when the girl said he reminded her of a grittier Hugh Jackman. While normally a guy would be pleased with hearing something like that, Logan, being an Aussie himself like Hugh, took offense to it. Especially, since she was a ditzy, Kardashian loving American. Plus, one night she screamed the actor's name while they were *between the sheets.* That was the final straw.

He shook his head at the now funny memory, rubbing the scruff forming on his face. He had been lonely and she was there waiting for him. It was a win-win for them both.

He moved on, past the showers, and straight into one of two heated hot tubs, bypassing the showers altogether. He slapped a button as he climbed in, starting up the jets. The churning water beckoned his beaten body and psyche forward.

As soon as he settled in and closed his eyes, he heard footsteps clunking their way towards his short-lived respite.

Ugh...

"Logan?"

He didn't open his eyes to his sister's question. He knew it was her and he wanted her to go away.

"Can it wait?" he replied, his eyes still closed, head tilted back on a makeshift pillow made from a rolled towel.

"Sorry, brother, but I don't think it can."

He grunted, opening his eyes, wiping away his matted down mop top, clearly seeing the horrified look on her face.

"What is it?" he asked, unsettled.

"They're here," CJ replied, swallowing hard, instinctively glancing behind her.

"Who's here?" Logan asked, standing.

"The Nach... Some of the animals just passed our 500-yard barrier and are making their way here. Our northern sensors are going berserk."

He waded out of the tub, not concerned about his nakedness in front of his older sister. He rushed to where his clothes were and threw on his boxers and pants while CJ continued.

"There are around 25-to-30 of them—all different species."

She rattled off a few of the breeds, but Logan didn't hear, he was mentally trying to put together a battle plan. They weren't here to negotiate a truce... *That* was for sure.

He headed for the catwalk entry, throwing on his shirt. CJ then handed him his vest, helping him dress as he made his way for the stairs. He rarely used the lift, wanting to get as much exercise as possible. Plus, it was just too damn slow for his liking. Logan had one speed, fast, and he and the elevator butted heads with that.

Taking two at a time, Logan quickly made it to the top landing and entered the Observation Deck, pounding forward to the northern section. He could see from here that everyone left was situated around Mo and his large screen array and it was currently set to using its night vision function. He glanced at one of the monitors and saw a green tinted blur rush by on all fours.

Towards us...

"What do we have?" Logan asked, toweling off his hair, not needing to formally announce his presence.

"Everything, Captain," Fitz replied, speaking up first, leaning over Mo as the other man tapped furiously on his keyboard. "It's a full-scale assault. More are heading in across the Serengeti, as we speak, and will arrive within the next few hours."

Fitz then stepped back, grabbing his reloaded XM25 off a nearby table, a look of determination only a former soldier could have. He regarded Logan. "Africa has waged war on the SDF."

31

"Let's move!"

Everyone, minus CJ and Adnan, who stayed and continued to try and raise the Americans, rushed out of the elevator, equipped for war. The stairs wouldn't get used this time. They needed to conserve what little energy they had left.

Outfitted with what looked like riot gear, but could handle everything except the highest of caliber of rounds, the six men hustled forward, also carrying an assortment of weaponry.

Kel and Dada made for the front door, through the gym, heading outside to the northeastern and northwestern sentry towers. There were actually four towers in all, with the other two being constructed at the southwest and southeast. They were situated thirty feet away from the Bullpen's main structure, acting like concrete and steel guardians.

Each man made their way to their respective positions, sporting the British made, Accuracy International AW SR-98 sniper rifle. It was standard issue for soldiers in the Australian Army. A little gift from Logan.

Fitz wanted them to use Logan's more powerful M82, but neither man had enough practice with the much larger weapon. "Stopping power means nothing when you can't hit the damn target," Logan had replied to Fitz.

Kel and Dada's jobs were to pick off any of the Nach that got past Logan, Jan, and Mo, who would be riding in the Rhino-Humvee variant. The three men would be out in the open, dangerously in the thick of it, but that was the plan. They needed the incoming swarm of creatures to view them as the real threat while the actual danger rained down upon them... Fitz.

Looking skyward, Kel could just make out Fitz leaning out over the concrete ledge of the Bullpen's roof, XM25 around his shoulder. Then the Aussie knelt, dropping the heavy satchel containing his spare ammo beside him and gave a thumbs up.

Kel smiled and returned the gesture as Fitz did the same to Dada, signaling both men that he was ready. He was the key to this crazy plan. Hopefully, the Nach would go after the armor-plated Hummer, giving Kel and Dada an open target. Fitz was the key though, raining down explosives from above, blowing the creatures to kingdom come. The grounds outside the Bullpen were about to get very messy.

Even from this distance Kel could hear the roar of

the Rhino's engine come to life behind him. Tires squealed as it peeled out of the southern-facing garage door, veering hard to the right. It skidded in a tight arc, finally finding purchase on the concrete. Tires grabbing, it made its way around the western side of the Bullpen and headed his way.

Through his night-vision, Kel could see Mo driving, and waved at the man. Mo gave him the customary "Good Luck" thumbs up, and veered left around the sentry tower, heading for the front gate.

As they went by, Kel could see Logan, rifle at the ready, sitting upfront in the passenger seat, no doubt intending to use the FN40 grenade launcher attachment to its fullest. Jan was harnessed into the rear of the truck, holding onto the twin hand grips of the massive .50 caliber machine gun mounted to the technical's bed.

Kel didn't like that Jan was out in the open, but knew it would take an army to get through the side and rear metal armor encasing most of the thing's rear. The only part of him not protected was the top and the front facing opening, but it shouldn't be an issue. That's the direction he'd be firing. Kel doubted anything would be able to get close enough for the weakness in the protection to matter.

The northern *gates* remotely opened as they neared, the motion sensors having automatically granted them egress from the fenced in compound. There were, in fact, *two* protective fences, spaced fifteen feet apart from one another. They encircled the Bullpen, keeping anything unwanted out. Each fence also sported some nasty razor wire atop them, giving an intruder another reason to go away.

The motion censored gates were a handy feature when in a hurry, but wouldn't work from the other side. Reentrance would need to be opened manually, either by remote from inside the Rhino, or from someone on the third floor in the command center. It was a security measure Logan had insisted on and no one had a reason to argue.

Until now, Kel thought, hearing the faint click of the steel gates shutting and locking.

"Get ready," Logan said, through their comms system. "We should be encountering resistance in twenty seconds."

Kel leaned into his rifle, peering through the tactical scope. He followed the Rhino north, then shifted his sights left, gazing further into the distance past his friends. What he saw made his stomach drop.

It was a veritable army of monsters. Some of them were, indeed, predatory by nature, some weren't. *Now ALL of them are,* he thought, yanking on the rifle's loading mechanism. He chambered the first of ten rounds into the bolt-action rifle's breech and waited, picking out his first target, a giraffe.

"Or what used to be a giraffe," Kel said to himself, shuddering at the normally gentle giant's current state.

It was still built like your run-of-the-mill giraffe, but had shorter, more powerful looking legs. He also noticed the way it ran. Instead of its normal awkward gate, it ran like a thoroughbred, pounding over the flat terrain. He scanned further up the thing's neck and flinched. *The hell?*

The Nach-giraffe's head shot down, like a cobra's, and snapped at one of the passing wildebeest that almost meandered into its path. The speed and ferocity of the attack was like nothing he'd ever seen before. *Their necks just don't bend that way,* he thought. He shook it off immediately, refocusing to his task. These weren't the same animals he'd grown up around.

An explosion ripped through the plains, echoing against the Bullpen's solid walls. Kel watched as a group of three lions blew apart, turning to puffs of red gore.

"Still a little pissed at the cats are you?" Dada asked, over the radio.

But Fitz didn't answer, he launched another of his payload into the cooling air, unleashing hell.

Then all at once, Kel, Dada, and the Rhino spurred into action, following Fitz's example. But Kel knew it was going to be close. There were just too many of them and who knew what other kinds of new ways these things could attack. If they were the average beast, they could be taken out easily.

But these aren't those animals, Kel thought, pulling the trigger of the SR-98. He did his best to pound the idea home that these weren't the same animals they were used to. They needed to throw out the boot and start fresh with the Nach versions.

He watched the round strike the giraffe in the chest, halting the creature, stumbling it, but not dropping it. He chambered another round and pulled the trigger again and again, finally dropping the thing after the fifth round found its mark, severing the spinal cord at the base of the neck.

He looked down at his feet and recounted his spare magazines. *Ten more—a hundred more bullets.* He looked up and watched the Rhino skid around in a sharp donut, Jan never releasing the trigger of the machine gun. He unloaded into a large beast that may have been a rhinoceros at one point, taking off its front legs.

Kel laughed at the absurdity of seeing *the* Rhino just take down *a* rhino. He then peered closer through his rifle's scope and saw the glowing veins beneath its skin as the animal tried to right itself.

He aimed and put a clean hole through its skull, silencing it forever. Breathing hard, he looked back down to his extra ammo, recounting it again.

"Let's hope it's enough."

32

BOOM!

Logan flinched, ducking back inside the passenger side window of the Rhino, dirt spraying into his face. He quickly blinked away the grit, leveled his assault rifle at the rapidly approaching creature, and unloaded the rest of his magazine into its muzzle.

The hyena, the biggest he'd ever seen, was down for good, its head in pieces. Its initial appearance, while frightening, also confused him.

It had first charged out from behind the carcass of the dead giraffe—the one that had been taken out by sniper fire—and lunged straight for Logan's open window. Thankfully, Mo had seen it coming and turned *into* the thing, clipping it with the truck's front push bar. It was sent flailing to the side, where Logan caught a look at its flank. A huge bite mark could be seen in the large female's side, causing the hair on his sweaty neck to stand on end. Nothing he knew of had jaws built like that.

Doesn't matter, he thought, turning in his seat to take it out once and for all. *A question for another day.* He then unloaded into it, killing the creature...again.

Thinking of these things as *dead*, was the easiest way for him to pull the trigger. Logan had taken a vow to protect everything that called the Serengeti home when he took this job, even if it was more for CJ's sake then his. She was the animal lover, not him, but he had soon seen that the inhabitants of this place were worth saving. The people that hunted them were killing them for profit, selling their bodies, or at least parts of them, and it pissed him off.

He was never a hunter growing up, quite the opposite actually. Surfing was his love as a kid... At least, until one of his high school classmates was attacked and killed by a Great White. It was a freak accident and most who surfed that particular beach went right back into the water a few days later. But not Logan. He had been scarred for life.

"Captain!"

The voice broke Logan from the memory of the blood-red waves and he looked out his window to see blood-red eyes. Then, they were gone, lost in a cloud of blood and meat.

Above his head, Jan's M2A1 roared to life again, just as Logan heard the echoing report of a sniper rifle. One of the men, Kel or Dada, had just taken down the spear tipped Grant's gazelle about to thrust its horns into his face. As he said a silent thank you, the big

German cut down another zebra, this one attempting to ram the truck with what looked like a boney growth on the top of its skull.

Right then, he thought. *Back to work.*

He loaded another 40mm grenade into his weapon's launcher attachment and sent it flying into the air. The explosive struck the base of a nearby tree, obliterating what was left of its trunk, crashing it to the ground. A group of two gazelles and a wildebeest were crushed beneath the Acacia's girth, hopefully killing a few, if not all of them.

Mo yanked on the wheel hard to the left, nearly clipping one of the dead, sending up a spray of dirt. Logan grabbed the door frame, steadying his bouncing form, and breathed a heavy breath. It would be horribly bad if they were to tip and roll with at least a dozen of these things still kicking. They needed to put an end to this now and regroup back at the base.

He didn't get to issue the next order.

The truck lurched hard on its left wheels, reeling from an unseen impact. Mo kept them under control, driving on only the driver's side wheels for a split second. Eventually, gravity took over and slammed them back down on all fours, rattling its occupants like they were inside of a shaking paint can.

Damn, Logan thought, trying to get his bearings. He could feel liquid flowing from his head and over his right temple. Touching it, his hand came away red, covered in blood. *Must have hit my head...*

Then, he was tossed from the missing passenger door of the Rhino and into the carnage of the current battle. He felt a pinch as something large had dug into his BDU, gripping his Kevlar vest and pulling. Reflexively, he brought up his SCAR which was thankfully secured around his shoulder and blasted the first thing he saw.

The body of the large cat, a breed Logan didn't bother identifying, slumped to the crimson stained grass. Three clean rounds had found its face point blank and another two had pierced its chest.

He dove over the carcass as a blur of motion came barreling towards him from his right, just inside his peripherals. If the zebra had been a few feet to his left, he'd have been blindsided and smeared, not seeing the attack. But he had. And he ran. He needed to get to higher ground.

The only thing he could see through the haze of smoke was a smaller koppie, jutting out of the ground fifty feet to the east. *Good enough*, he thought, sprinting for the protrusion. He dodged smaller creatures, not caring what they were. Turning and fighting on even turf was a serious disadvantage right now even with his current arsenal of weapons.

Twenty feet separated himself from death and maybe surviving being thrown from a speeding vehicle. A bullet zinged by, felling another of the creatures, another charging gazelle, its talon-like horns ready to gore him.

At least I've still got some cover fire.

He jumped, feeling the bottom of his right foot get clipped by something. He spun and fired, knowing that whatever he shot was here to kill him.

Another zebra, probably the same one that had slammed into the Rhino, fell under the barrage of fire. He emptied the clip into the beast, scurrying backwards on his rear, getting further from the edge.

"Captain!" a voice yelled in his ear. "Hold tight, we're on our way!"

Hold tight, he thought. *Right...*

"Step on it, Mo!" He then drew his side-arm, having no time to reload the rifle. His Desert Eagle L5 boomed across the field, killing an incoming wildebeest, its front claw-shaped hooves scraping across the rocky surface of the koppie, just missing his outstretched leg by inches. It had tried desperately to reach him, attempting to climb the smooth, weathered stone.

The flat black .50 caliber handgun was the newest addition to his personal arsenal. He had added it immediately after the initial encounter with the lions in the Nazi bunker. He wouldn't venture out into the night without anything weaker. The weapon's single downfall was it only held seven rounds.

But they're big ass bullets, Logan thought, pulling the trigger twice more. Another wildebeest had attempted to follow its brother up the koppie, but Logan had been ready.

As the limp form of the animal slumped to the ground, a grinding noise filled his ears. The Rhino came into view, half-sliding through the grass as it slowed to a stop. Logan saw Mo yank on the wheel and throw the back end around, slamming the driver's side of the truck into the koppie, pinning the body of the dead wildebeest between them.

"Jump!" Mo yelled from inside the Hummer, begging him to move.

Logan didn't need to be asked a second time.

He leapt.

33

Logan slammed onto the roof of the truck, landing hard on his stomach, feeling every single bump and contusion his body had suffered so far. Hurriedly, he ungracefully rolled across the metal surface and spun his body, laying on what could only be bruised ribs, his feet hanging over open air for a moment. He kicked out and felt the solid door frame under foot, repositioning himself. After doing a quick mental countdown, he half-shambled, half-dove back into the now doorless front passenger seat, crashing into Mo, causing him to jerk the wheel slightly.

"Throw it in reverse!" Logan yelled, sitting up, hurrying to reload his SCAR assault rifle. "Jan! Get ready!"

Mo did as he was told and screeched to a stop, shifting the Humvee into reverse. He slammed his foot on the pedal and shot the truck backwards, quickly accelerating to 40-mph.

Logan looked down at the dash, smiling as he saw the plains behind them in the camera mounted on the underside of the Rhino. From the thing's low perspective, he could unfortunately see the blood stained terrain whiz by, including pieces of some of the creatures.

Another sight I'll never get rid of...

The rumble of the vehicle's unrelenting backwards trek would have been enough to shake his teeth loose on its own, but it paired with the .50 cal's deafening roar was enough to make his vision dance. One after the other, the remaining beasts dropped under the heavy machine gun's unyielding barrage. Then the ground in front of the Humvee exploded into a fireball as Fitz let loose with his XM25, annihilating anything Jan didn't.

The Hummer slowed as Mo lifted his foot off the accelerator, not seeing any movement through the Rhino's windshield. It stopped a few yards later as Logan made a visual inspection of the land.

"We're clear up here," Jan said, giving the all clear.

It was hellish to say the least, looking like a bomb had gone off at a petting zoo. Not seeing anything *alive* either, Logan climbed out of his already open door, regretting it as soon as his boot found a mush of blood and what looked like something's innards.

Feeling the bile rise in his throat, he turned to sit back down, but heard something mewling off in the dark. "Cover me," he said to no one in particular. He didn't have to though. His men would all do their duty and cover his six.

Logan calmly strolled fifty feet forward, his aim never wavering. He stopped, confused, only seeing the body of the rhinoceros they had killed at the onset of the battle. He looked around, seeing the battlefield in a new light now that the initial conflict was over.

Bodies littered the field. Some weren't even whole anymore. The lethal combination of Jan's heavy machine gun and Fitz's explosive XM25 had done the trick...and that's not even accounting for the sniper attacks carried out by Kel and Dada. Each of the four men, including Mo's death-defying driving, had done their jobs admirably.

And then some, he thought, turning back to the truck, shrugging. He couldn't find anything alive that could have made that sound.

Maybe it was just in my head. It wouldn't have surprised him considering what he'd physically and mentally endured so far tonight. Delirium could do that to you, whether caused by being overtired or stress or even—

Merrr.

But then he heard it again, behind the corpse of the endangered animal—the rhinoceros. It pained him to even think about it. They had single-handedly killed it and a few other rare species—some of the scarcest alive today. But what could they do? The irony was like a slap in the face. The very animals they swore to protect had become the very thing they now fought against.

Merr.

The cry sounded again. It almost made him think of a baby cow or some other harmless farm animal. He rounded the body and saw it for what it was. It was another rhinoceros. A baby.

Logan stopped when he saw the mutilated, but very much alive infant Nach. While still much heavier than he was, the young rhinoceros may have only been a few months old. He breathed deep, knowing what he needed to do next. The glowing eyes and fang-filled maw helped him with his decision.

He raised his SCAR to his shoulder and took aim down the sights, aiming it at the zombie brood's head. Even though he knew this thing would tear him apart if it could walk, he pitied it—what it used to be. As he stood there the thing's eyes became even more enraged, like his very presence angered it.

He pulled the trigger, blowing a clean hole into the thing's forehead, ending its escalating fury filled shrieks for good. He blinked back a tear and marched back to the Hummer, climbing in.

"Back to base."

Nodding, Mo threw the truck into gear and hastened back to the northern gate, all under the ever watchful eye of the last remaining creature. It was hidden among the dead, within the felled tree, peering through the foliage, waiting for a perfect time to strike.

The black leopard slowly climbed out of its hiding spot and crouch-ran after the Rhino, its two-tone black fur camouflaging it from its attackers. It kept its distance, just out of range, but easily kept pace. Sneering as its *equally* large prey fled, it gave chase.

34

CJ fell back into her seat and closed her eyes. The initial assault on the Bullpen was over and she was relieved that everyone made it back alive. She didn't need to think about another incident like what happened to Saami and Pandu.

The chair next to her creaked as Adnan leaned forward eyes wide. He had been trying to contact the American's through the entire battle to no avail. He thought something was messing with their signal or something. She just nodded and let the man explain, even though she didn't understand a lick of it.

Quick as a rattler, he grabbed CJ's arm, eliciting a shout from the startled, nerve wracked woman. He then flicked a switch on the console in front of him and a voice boomed over the speakers.

"Come in, SDF. This is United States African Command at Manda Bay. Over."

Manda Bay, CJ thought. *The Americans are responding from their base in Kenya.* She sat forward. *Thank God for Logan and Fitz's connections within the military.* When the local bases had heard that a former soldier was taking over as game warden, they had reached out to them, offering help in an emergency. The SDF had never needed it until now.

"We read you, Manda Bay," Adnan replied. "This is Adnan Drees of the SDF." He sat up straighter, emphasizing his next words. "We are under attack and need assistance immediately. We have men down and the situation is escalating."

Adnan knew as well as everyone in the SDF that Manda Bay had the capabilities to help. They were part of the U.S. military's AFRICOM—African Command—and were originally set up to fight against the various Post 9/11 terrorist cells. They had men there that knew how to get things done quickly—and more importantly with anti-terror units... They got it done quietly.

The soldier on the other side of the radio sounded a little thrown off and expressed as much. "Say again, SDF. Our comms have been down and we are still experiencing some interference."

Frustrated, CJ took the helm. "Manda Bay, this is Cassidy Reed. We have multiple casualties and are under heavy attack by the local populace." The American was about to interrupt, but CJ cut him off. "Look, mate... We don't really know what the hell is going on, but the local inhabitants are going berserk and killing everything—including two of our men. We need help, now!"

There was a rustling sound emanating from the speakers as the man on the other end moved something around, like shuffling paper. Then, in a low and murmured voice, he was speaking to someone else nearby. Neither CJ, nor Adnan, could make out what was said, but the urgent tone in the American's voice said enough. He believed them.

"Okay, Reed. We'll have men on the ground at your coordinates ASAP—a couple hours at best. Is there anything else you can tell us?"

CJ thought back to what Logan had said about combating the Nach and relayed the same to the American. "Tell them," she answered, looking outside to the north gate as the Rhino passed through, not understanding what she saw, "to dress—"

It's then a black aberration leapt out from the shadows behind the Hummer. She screamed a warning into her earpiece, trying to warn Logan and the others, but it was too late. A creature easily the size of the Rhino struck.

* * * * *

"Logan!"

The voice was shrill, like nails on a chalk board, shrieking through their comms. The frantic manner in which his sister yelled, made him flinch, but it also spurred him into motion.

Seeing nothing in front of them, he grabbed for the door handle, but remembered it was gone. Instead, he jumped from the slow moving vehicle, and rolled, coming up with his FN SCAR ready to engage whatever had spooked his sister. But he had no idea what to do next as the monster emerged silently from the darkness.

He recognized it for what it *was*, a leopard, and it *was* most definitely one at one point. But not anymore. This was something much worse...and a shit ton bigger.

As the truck pulled past him and screeched to a halt, two things happened in what seemed like slow motion. First off, Dada, along with Kel, had both met the Rhino and its occupants at ground level, just inside the main gate. Each man was currently facing away from the opening, watching the Hummer. Big mistake. Next, the leopard, which was easily as large as a rhino—the living kind—went airborne, striking out at the two prone men. Neither of them saw, or heard, the silent killer attack. It was like looking into a living shadow.

Dada didn't stand a chance, having been the closest one to the entrance. The leopard just opened its jaws, unhinging them like a snake's. It engulfed the local man in one mouthful, stopping at his midsection. Then in one lightning fast motion it bit, severing the SDF member in half.

Logan watched as the beast threw its head back and swallowed its catch like a duck would its food. The loud gulping sound, spurred Logan into motion.

He pulled the trigger, firing, hitting the creature with everything he had. It took his rifle's rounds with nothing more than a shake of its head, more annoying than painful. But it worked. He had at least part of the thing's attention.

Kel dove away, somehow surviving the attack, and opened fire on the monster from its left. While his sniper rifle was much slower, it packed a stronger punch, making up for its limited rate of fire.

Damnit, Logan thought, seeing Kel from out of the corner of his eye. *He's still too close.*

Logan stepped left, away from Kel's direction, trying to draw the thing off. Unfortunately for him...it worked.

The behemoth-sized leopard snarled at Logan and turned its three blood-red eyes towards him, a look of hatred and irritation on its face. The crimson stain on its maw didn't help the situation any better, either. Logan knew exactly what it was, he had just witnessed another of his friends get slaughtered by one of these bastards.

A bullet found one of the creature's eyes—the one in the center—causing it to spasm and roar. It lashed out at the air in front of it, like a bee had stung it, but struck nothing. It obviously didn't understand that the bullets were what was producing its pain.

Until it blinked and turned towards Kel.

Shit.

"Kel!" Logan yelled, his aim never wavering. "Back up!"

Kel obeyed and slowly made his way further and further from the beast, taking pot shots at the side of its face, whenever he found a target. Logan knew he was almost out of ammo, having only the bolt-action weapon and a holstered Glock. The latter would be useless against a monster this size. Logan's hollow points might do the trick if he could score a direct hit into the thing's skull. The bullet would enter the brain and break apart, shredding grey matter, killing it.

Fat chance of that happening with as much as this thing is moving, he thought. The only other thing that could work was Kel's SR-98 sniper rifle.

The sniper rifle!

"Kel!" Logan shouted again, getting an idea. He fired off five more rounds, pulling the leopard's attention away from Kel. "Get farther away and aim for its eyes. Try to blind it!"

Kel dashed away, towards the front door of the Bullpen, giving himself more time to line up the shot needed.

Automatic gunfire erupted from behind Logan as Mo stepped up next to him, doing what he could to assist him.

"Where's Jan with the .50?" Logan yelled, slowly backpedaling. "We could use the heavier ammo right about now!"

"It was close to overheating after we finished out there." Logan saw Mo motion with his head to the plains outside the fencing, never looking away from his target. Logan had taught them to never, under any circumstance, take your eyes off the engaged target. "He was worried about damaging it long term."

Logan knew he was right. If that weapon went down they'd be royally screwed.

"Flash out!" a voice shouted, tinged with a German accent. It had come from behind the two men. They both instinctively, shut their eyes, and turned their heads away from the blast.

A *whump* and a light as bright as the sun could be seen through his eyelids, making Logan grit his teeth. His ears felt like someone had just stabbed them with an icepick, but he could deal with the following disorientation. The Nach on the other hand...

Cringing as he opened his eyes, he took in the scene. The leopard was on its side thrashing, roaring in pain, blinking its eyes rapidly. Jan was next to Mo, pumping slugs from his Mossberg into the monster.

Mo quickly recovered and joined in, doing the same.

Sit still you bastard, Logan thought, raising his rifle to his shoulder, taking aim at the monster's head.

"Logan!"

He quickly glanced back, away from the action, looking for the voice that had called his name. Within that split second, he saw who was yelling, causing him to sigh in relief.

"Get back!" He knew what was coming next. "Get behind the Rhino!"

Trusting their leader, Mo and Jan abided, sprinting behind the idling Hummer that sat twenty feet away. When they rounded the front of the vehicle, they leapt, just as a set of massive explosions rocked the concrete encompassing the command center.

35

"You alright?"

Logan didn't need to look at the speaker to know it was Fitz. The man had single-handedly saved them from an enemy that would have sooner or later bull rushed them, ending their valiant efforts. It had bitten Dada in half and swallowed his upper torso whole with little work. It wouldn't have had a problem with them.

We got lucky, Logan thought, laying on his back. He looked to his right, under the Rhino, and saw the carnage his former SAS teammate had brought upon the creature.

The leopard lay dead, smashed up against the outer fencing, smoking from the crater in its side. From this low vantage, Logan couldn't see the other wound, but what he could see was another cloud of smoke near where the thing's head should be. Apparently, Fitz had scored a direct hit.

"Ugh," Logan moaned, grabbing his head as he sat up. "One too many hits to the head for one day."

Fitz helped him up, slinging his XM25 around his back. They both circled the front of the Rhino, Mo and Jan circling around the rear. What they saw was both reassuring and downright depressing.

The leopard-creature was definitely dead, the left half of its face and skull missing. As Logan shambled closer, his vision waned from the after effects of the flashbang Jan threw. He shook his head and blinked heavily, slightly clearing up his sight.

He then looked to the fence, inspecting the damage. This is what gave him the feeling of dread.

The inner ring of the fifteen-foot high chain-link fencing was damaged beyond repair, a hole large enough to drive through, blown into the section the leopard now laid in. Thankfully, the outer ring of fencing, this one measuring ten feet in height, was still intact. The leopard's girth had been propelled through the inner, while laying up against the outer. *At least the razor wire at the top is still intact.* He knew it didn't really matter, but at least they knew where to concentrate their fire when the next attack came. And there would be another one. He knew that for a fact. They'd seen it on the some of the cameras.

A chink in the armor, he thought, recalling the weakness the monster Talos had in the classic, Jason and the Argonauts. It had a literal Achilles heel. He looked to the gate and relaxed his grip on the SCAR when he saw that it was still in good order, closed and locked.

"How's the M2?" Logan asked, turning to Jan.

The larger man shrugged. "It should be fine, but the constant firing almost cooked me alive." Jan said the last part laughing a little, soaked in sweat, but when Logan didn't join in he quickly stopped.

"Dada..."

Kel stepped up next to the others, looking at what was left of his friend. Mercifully, they could only see the bottoms of the dead man's boots. His lower half had fallen backwards, impeding their view of his insides.

"I'm sorry," Logan said, placing his hand on Kel's shoulder. "I know you were close."

Kel just closed his eyes and recited what Logan knew was a prayer in Swahili, asking God to protect Dada in the next world. Logan did the same, also in Swahili, but added that he would appreciate some help eradicating the curse that has been brought upon his park.

"Logan..." a solemn voice said in his ear. It was CJ. "We contacted Manda Bay..."

Logan spun and looked up towards the large windows of the Observation Deck. Between the late hour and the tinted glass, he couldn't see them, but he knew CJ and Adnan were standing there, looking down on the havoc.

"I'll be up in a second."

He turned to Mo and Jan. "Gas up the Rhino and reload the M2. I want it ready just in case we need to bug out and run for the hills."

Both men nodded and hurried to the Hummer. Before Logan marched off to the front door he stopped and turned back to his men. "And thank you," he said, looking to Mo and Jan. He then looked to Fitz, and then to Kel, who was still looking over to Dada's body. "All of you."

"Captain?"

Logan glanced to Kel. "What is it?"

"Are we just going to leave him there?"

Logan sighed, unsure of what to say. So instead of saying anything, he just walked over to Kel and placed a gentle hand on the man's shoulder.

"Come on Kel." Logan gently tried to turn him around. "There's nothing more we can do—"

Kel shrugged out of Logan's grasp and turned on him. "There *is* something we can do!"

"Like what?" Fitz asked, ready to step in if things went south between the two men. He knew Logan could kill the man before he felt the blow, but he also knew that Logan wouldn't necessarily *want* to fight back. Better he gets his hands dirty than the captain.

Kel turned to Fitz with a look of rage. "We can kill them all!"

The two Aussies watched as Kel pounded towards the front entrance of the Bullpen, seething with anger, ready to slaughter anything that got in his way. Logan knew that people did stupid things when they were angry and not thinking straight. This would absolutely qualify as one of those times.

"CJ?" He needed someone to calm him down before Kel did just that.

"I'll talk to him." she answered, hearing everything. "I'll talk him down from the proverbial ledge."

Logan gave the third floor window a half-hearted wave and followed in the direction Kel had just gone, Fitz in tow. They needed to regroup and re-up their ammo. This hellish night had only just begun, and inside he knew at this rate...they'll all most likely be dead by the time the Americans arrived.

He stopped, feeling the copper-filled breeze at his back. The overpowering smell of drying blood made him shiver. It was the first time he had ever doubted himself as a soldier—as a fighter. It was also the first time he had ever doubted his own survival.

36

"Hand me the torch, will you, Mo?" Jan asked, reaching out with his free hand. He had the thin sheet of metal propped up against the passenger side of the Rhino. Luckily for them, they had some scrap laying around, stacked in a corner of the garage. Dada was a whiz with this kind of stuff and always kept usable *junk* stocked.

The thought of Dada made Jan cringe. The man had just died a horrible death. *Although,* he thought, *better dead than one of those monsters.* He didn't believe these things to be the actual demons from his grandfather's stories—the Nachzehrer. Just the thought of it gave him goosebumps, though.

Could it? It was a question left unasked.

Mo sparked the welding torch, adjusting it to its appropriate temperature, and carefully handed it to Jan. He then leaned into the makeshift door covering, helping hold it in place. It wasn't the thickest piece they found, but it was the right size and light enough for them to lift. It wouldn't be as effective as the actual door, which was somewhere out in the demilitarized zone that had become the grounds just outside the Bullpen, but it would do.

"Just like the Duke boys," Jan said, commenting on the slight resemblance the sealed entry of the now un-opening door made to another vehicle he knew. "Have to climb in now."

He glanced up to Mo, whose confused look said it all.

"Really?" Jan asked, flabbergasted. "You don't know the Dukes—of Hazzard?"

Mo shook his head.

"The General Lee?" Jan asked, almost trying to coax the recognition out of the man.

"Who is he—this General Lee?" Mo asked, taking the legendary car's name literally.

"It's not a *who*... It's a *what*," Jan replied, shaking his head in disbelief. Even in Germany the General Lee was renowned and the Duke cousins beloved. Their antics were known throughout the globe.

Except Africa, apparently, he thought.

He went on to try and explain the concept of the famous T.V. show and the ever glorious Daisy Duke. The famed character was originally played by Catherine Bach on television and then again by the seductive Jessica Simpson on film. It had even coined the term, 'Daisy Dukes.' It's still used to this day when describing short denim shorts.

Mo shrugged.

"Unbelievable!" Jan blurted, half-laughing, half-frustrated. "You don't know who Daisy Mae Duke is?"

Mo didn't get to answer. Instead, they got a call in their earpieces.

"How's the Rhino?" Logan asked, from somewhere above their heads. Knowing him, he was probably flat on his back on the sofa in the living area, or at his station rechecking their weapons and ammo. The man either slept or worked on guns. He did what he could to stay occupied.

"Fine," Jan answered. "We just covered the hole in the right flank. You are going to have to climb in and out, but it could have been worse. The rest of the truck is in perfect working order."

"Right, mate," Logan said. "Luke Duke it is, thanks."

Jan looked up to Mo who was standing over his kneeling form and smiled, excited that Logan came up with the same reference as him. It didn't surprise him, though. He and Logan would routinely sit with Fitz and watch classic American action films like Die Hard, The Rock, and True Lies. They especially loved when the hero, or the hero's sidekick, would throw in some witty remarks and one-liners, adding just the right amount of humor into the movie. Hanging out in their down time was what first spurred Logan into *properly* introducing him to his sister.

CJ was an enigma to Jan. She was strong-willed and sassy, but compassionate and kind. She knew how to act when the situation called for it. It was a handy trick when stuck living with nine men out in the middle of nowhere for weeks—sometimes months at a time. They didn't exactly get out much—unless by out, you meant, *out* in the plains.

Their first 'date' was dinner and a movie, watching Zombieland of all things. CJ had that quirky sense of humor and Jan didn't mind. He actually really did enjoy it.

Thinking of a movie like that threw him out of his memory and back into the now of their situation. This was a *real life* movie, except more along the lines of a horror film. No witty one-liners. No cheeky sidekicks. There was only blood and death in this nightmare. He just hoped that everyone left—mainly CJ—would survive the night.

They all had jobs to do, but Jan would add keeping her alive to the top of it when the time came. He knew that between him and her brother, she would be fine. Logan was the best for a reason.

"Open the rear, please." Mo asked. "Let's have a look at the M2."

Jan nodded and stood, knocking on the grade school welding job he did on the sheet metal. He knew how to use a welding torch, but it wasn't exactly his forte. He was a retired demolitions expert—a field he rarely got to use out here in Africa. But he also knew one other thing...

He climbed into the open bed of the Hummer and inspected the .50 caliber machine gun. He knew heavy weapons very, very well. He had even recommended that Fitz try out the XM25, ordering it from a *dealer* he had known. Fitz was more like a kid with a new toy, where Jan was like a '*man and his truck*.' He loved the big guns, but he also respected them, knowing all too well of their danger.

He sat in the bolted down chair attached to the floor behind the weapon, and looked it over, seeing nothing wrong. He then slapped in a new cartridge, holding the belt-fed ammunition. "It's fine," he said, getting up and climbing down from the hatch. He slammed the bed's door and turned. "We just need to be careful with how long we run hot. We almost burned it up this last time out."

Mo agreed, mentally recalling the events of the last hour—really of the last *few* hours. The things they'd done and things they'd seen done were too much to comprehend.

He smiled, slapping the much bigger man on the shoulder. "Come... Let me buy you a drink so we can wash away all that we've been through tonight."

"*Es ist ein deal*," Jan replied, smiling.

Mo looked at him with a raised eyebrow.

"It's a deal," Jan said, translating his German for the Kenyan.

"Ah," Mo said with a grin. "Well then... *Mpango*—deal it is."

The two SDF men laughed, releasing some of the tension the night had brought, arguing over what type of scotch was the best. If either one of them would have looked twenty feet behind them, they would have noticed a small slender creature tucked in next to the garage door, doing its best to stay concealed in the shadows. Its recently acquired jet black fur helped in that regard. It, like everything else that had been infected, had attained the trait, proving useful in the low light.

The red-eyed Egyptian mongoose just watched, blinking against the large room's illumination, waiting for the right time to strike. It would be soon, it just needed one of the men to be alone, and then it would attack. It had witnessed firsthand how dangerous the people were when they killed the much larger predator outside. Its instinctual gifts of stealth and cunningness would be perfect to get close. And when it did...

DESOLATION

"*Frankenstein* was all about the idea that, through electricity and the destruction of night, man creating light and darkness, we took on god-like powers and then abused them like gods, and we are only men. That's a story about man making a man in his own image. The inversion of natural order."

~Benedict Cumberbatch

"Real victories are those that protect human life, not those that result from its destruction or emerge from its ashes."

~King Hussein I

37

Tanzania, 1946

Mengele knew his life was over. The beast that had once been the highly respected general had bitten him. It was only a nick—barely a scratch—but it would be enough. He could already see the skin on his hand darkening.

So he sat to write out a warning and explain what was happening. He would reveal to the world— whenever they found this—what the Wohn Tod was attempting... And why.

Sweat dripped from his scrunched brow as he sat, slumped over his typewriter. The pain wasn't just around the wound, it radiated through his entire body, like he had the worst illness on record.

It's not too far from the truth.

He pulled open a drawer in his desk and reached

in, trying desperately to find a single sheet of paper, but instead found something else. The relic that started it all, sat there, staring up at him. Its empty eye sockets, along with the fang-like teeth, emitted pure hatred.

I remember you, old friend.

A searing pain burned through his arm, stopping at his shoulder. He was just about to slip into unconsciousness, feeling as if his blood was boiling. Then, it released him from its deadly grasp.

Boom. Boom. Boom.

Banging erupted from his quarter's door, followed closely by screams of fright and of agony. It sounded like a battle was waging through the facility, but he knew better. True battles were fought between two opposing forces. This wasn't a battle... It was a slaughter. Something was loose.

Probably Dr. Albrecht, Mengele thought. He had been the first one to be bitten. They had been fools to think only simple ropes could contain the creature. Thankfully, the guards on hand secured a second, thicker set.

But Albrecht was done for. He had sustained a bite to his neck. It seemed the worse the bite and the closer it was to a major artery, the quicker it took effect.

Gunfire erupted in the hallway behind him, followed by a feral scream, and a wet splat. Two sets of footsteps came booming down the hall, stopping abruptly. Through the thin metal door, Mengele could hear one of the men muttering a series of curses.

Some were towards the creature they had just shot. Most were directed at the situation as a whole.

"*Doktor?*" one of the men asked, checking on Mengele. "*Bist du verletzt?*"

Am I injured? Mengele thought, mentally repeating the question with a laugh. *No, not injured. Dying maybe, but not injured.* Injury meant a possible cure.

He quickly dismissed the men, stating that he was fine and unharmed. It's not like they could get in. The heavy dresser in front of the door would see to that. He needed to be alone for what he was about to do.

Pushing the skull away, he resumed the task of writing his... *Memoir?* he thought. *No, not memoir... Confession.* He pulled his last sheet of blank paper out from underneath the skull's usual resting spot. He didn't have the nerve for it to be out in the open, glaring at him from across the room. So he kept it stored away in his desk's bottom drawer, hidden from his sight.

He slipped the sheet into the platen and rolled it into place. His fingers hovered over the keys, not really knowing where to start. So, he started at the obvious place—the beginning.

As he typed his finger nails slowly turned black and began to elongate. The virus, now starting, was carrying out *Phase One* of its invasion into his body. He had witnessed this dozens of times before—even on multiple human hosts, but never did he think he would end up like the countless test subjects buried above him. He had always figured that the Allied forces would eventually find him and put a bullet in his head.

The thought of death was actually a peaceful one. He wouldn't be caught and tortured by his enemies. He would be undone by his very creation.

A fitting end to the Angel of Death.

He knew his nickname around the world. He originally hated it, but as time had passed, he had begun to embrace it, using it to instill fear in those he sought to control.

Like the men here.

He flinched as he heard a moaning from the other side of the door. Apparently, Albrecht was still alive. *Alive...* The word wasn't right, but neither was *dead.*

More voices erupted from down the hall, yelling warnings to the others still here. They sounded desperate, unable to kill the creature that was once his colleague.

Once...but no longer, he thought, finishing the first paragraph. His grammar wasn't perfect—it's not like he was an author or anything. *Doesn't matter.* The message would be good enough to get across the everyday happenings here.

He kept typing, frantically, as the virus continued up his arm. The veins in his hand were already starting to glow a little and the skin was black as night. He needed to finish this letter before it fully took control of his mind. He *would not* become one of them.

Gritting his teeth against the blinding pain, Mengele pounded out the body of the warning. He wasn't trying to type out any one thing. He just wanted to convey the clearest of pictures. He even laughed a little as he typed the words.

Dr. Josef Mengele—the Angel of Death—writing a warning to those he set out to condemn. The sheer notion was utterly ridiculous, but he was the only one who knew the truth. The other scientists here knew *some* of what he did, but not everything.

It's then the screams gushed throughout the first level...along with blood from the sounds of it. He grinned. *If only they knew to aim for the head. They can't function without an intact brain.*

ARRRGH!

Mengele shouted his own blood-curdling scream, his entire arm black. The pain was immense, more than anything he had ever felt before. He felt as if his heart would burst. He had watched his *patients* go through the same, but he had never once felt sorry for them. But now...he completely understood what they endured. Then, his vision blurred and he felt his jaw tighten. He knew what was coming next.

Not if I can stop it first, he thought, content.

He raised his Luger to his right temple and pulled the trigger.

38

Tanzania, Present Day

Taking the elevator had never felt so right. He was bruised and battered physically...and the same could be said for his mental state too. Logan's knees ached from exertion and his feet were killing him. If he had any time, whatsoever, he would take another dip in the hot tub.

A shower and two soaks, he thought. *Would break my record.*

"Captain, we need you up top ASAP."

Damn. He sighed. The Jacuzzi tub would have to wait, but his aches and pains couldn't. He'd need to pop a few Advil before he got too engrossed with whatever Adnan needed him for.

Must be the Americans. He glanced down at his watch, estimating their time of arrival at just over an hour or so.

Hopefully less.

The lift smoothly slid by the second floor, passing the room where his heavenly immersion awaited him. The image of himself relaxing was quickly replaced with that of terror, as the memory of Dada being torn in half replayed in his head. Another of his men had been killed. Brutally.

As he continued up, he caught a glimpse of where Mo and Jan would undoubtedly be headed, sitting at the bar behind the sofa. They would then clink their low-ball glasses together, and say cheers to each other in their own native tongues. It was like clockwork for them.

The sofa...

He looked back to the couch, his body screaming for the cool leather and his mind weeping for just the basic sensation of lying down. He could even feel the relief—the tension leaving his lower back as he relaxed his muscles and gave into sleep.

As much as he loved leading his team, Logan understood that regardless of what his inner ego driven, testosterone imbued manhood believed, he was, in fact, human, and sooner or later his body and mind would shut down... He just didn't know which one would fail first. As a rule of thumb, he always assumed the body would relinquish itself before his will. As a former SAS soldier, he was trained to *never* give up.

"Never give up. Never give in," Logan said, mumbling the lyrics to an obscure punk band from

America. *Florida, I think.* He remembered showing Gray the band back when they were in the army—before joining the ranks in the SAS. *God... What was it, fourteen years ago?* He and then eventually Fitz were the only ones that he knew of who had heard of Middle Class Chaos in Australia, but they both liked them. Something about the simple, yet catchy rhythm, always appealed to the two men.

The elevator clunked to a stop, startling Logan's eyes open. He hadn't even realized he'd closed them. *Right,* he thought, *gunna' need some coffee too.*

He stepped out onto the third story landing, quickly and forcibly cocking his head to the side. The vertebrae audibly realigned in his neck, popping loudly, releasing only a fraction of the stress and pressure he felt. *Better than nothing.* He then breathed in deep and continued into the Observation Deck. He was as ready as he could be to do the whole leader-thing all over again.

As soon as he entered the room he had a voice yelling at him from across the spacious interior.

"Logan?" the voice asked. "That you, brother?"

"Yeah..." he replied, halfheartedly. "Give me a sec, will ya'?"

He headed straight for his desk and opened the small mini-fridge each of them had at their stations. They also had a large communal refrigerator in the living room of the second floor, but only had their smaller cousins on the top floor.

Logan opened a drawer and retrieved three pills, popping them into his mouth. He followed the chalky painkillers with half the ice-cold water bottle. He then took a breath and drained the rest, tossing the empty bottle in the garbage can next to his desk.

Next, Logan unslung his rifle and gently laid it on the work bench lining one of the many storage shelves. He then did the same with his Desert Eagle. Cleaning and reloading the guns would have to wait. He would first check on CJ and Adnan and see what the rush was, then he'd see to the weapons.

"Logan?"

He turned and found CJ leaning against a rack full of handguns, prepped and ready to go. It was where she *shopped* from most of the time.

"You okay?" she asked, noticing his dreary exterior.

"Fine, Cass," Logan said, lying. "Just spent is all." Before she could call him on his bluff, he continued. "What's going on?"

As she started the explanation about the initial conversation with the Americans at Manda Bay, Logan slid the SCAR to the side, foregoing the strict *clean and store* rule he had set in place years ago. He was going to do it after he talked to his sister, anyways. But now... He was too damn exhausted.

He then selected another identical rifle from a nearby rack, earning a reaction from his sister.

"Are you even listening to me?"

He half-turned, only letting her see his sly smirk. "With that voice?" He let the jab hang in the air, getting the textbook eye roll from CJ. "Loud and clear, Cass."

"What's their ETA?" he asked, wanting to double-check.

She looked at her watch. "Just over an hour...give-or-take."

He nodded at the confirmation.

"Anything on the cameras from around the park?" He had hoped they'd be clear, but if they weren't...

"Yes," CJ replied, deflating his hope. "Most of the Nach are moving away from us."

This wasn't what he thought he'd hear. He assumed another wave of the monsters would come banging down their door... And then another... And another.

"What do you mean?" Logan asked, shocked.

She shrugged. "Honestly, I have no idea, but I have a theory."

Logan just lifted his eyebrows, coaxing her to continue.

"You're not going to like it."

Now it was Logan's turn to shrug. "Do I really have a choice?"

She bobbed her head, agreeing.

"Fine," she said, trying to force the words from her lips. "I think they are attempting to spread the virus further into the park—build their numbers."

Logan's surprised expression wasn't lost on his sister who explained her hypothesis more.

"They aren't mindless monsters."

"Who aren't?" Logan asked, confused.

"The Nach."

He hopped up and sat on the table next to his discarded weapon, giving her his full attention.

"And you know that how?"

She fully entered his work space and propped

herself onto another of the workbenches, her legs dangling from the table like a child in a too-tall chair.

"The giant leopard that killed..." She couldn't say it. The wounds were still too fresh. "It stalked you back to the Pen. It *hunted* you and the others. It didn't give away its position and charge in guns blazing. It thought out its course of action and then it struck."

Logan understood where she was going with this, but he wanted to hear it from the animal expert's mouth. Especially someone who primarily focused their work on carnivores. He knew basic information on the more common of the creatures, but CJ knew *everything* there was to know about them.

"It showed intelligence and patience," she said. "I'm actually very curious to know what the virus does to the mind over a prolonged period of time. Does the subject's brain continue to deteriorate? Or does it eventually heal and become usable again?"

"Like... Does the thing gain back its self-control after a certain amount of time?"

She nodded.

"If so, then the leopard would have been infected a while ago, only now revealing itself as it changed, as were Saami and Pandu..." She choked back the words. "They didn't have time to redevelop their minds. They were only a few minutes into their reawakening."

Logan didn't want to accept it, but he understood her theory. What if these things were allowed to live long enough for the working parts of their brains to reform with the God Blood fully infused? Would they think of themselves as the same as before, or would they believe themselves a monster—or possibly a god? That much could be said for a human recipient, but what of an animal? What kind of change would their minds have? Would they gain a more human-like conscious?

Let's hope we don't have to find out.

39

She sat on her bed and wept, not being able to contain her fright and bottled-up grief any longer. CJ had always put on a good front, showing the boys that if a woman could handle the struggles of living out here, then they shouldn't have a problem either.

But that was before people started dying, she thought, looking to the picture she had of the *entire* team on her wall. It was a large panorama of the Serengeti sunset. The ten of them were standing in a line on the Bullpen's roof, backs to the horizon. It had been taken a couple years ago, but she remembered the moment like it was yesterday.

They had just taken down a large-scale poaching operation to the south. They didn't have Kipanga or the Rhino yet, so it was a huge deal to them...and their supporters.

A really big deal.

One of their benefactors had a chopper fly in a special dinner, complete with four cases of a VERY expensive champagne. The note had congratulated them on a job well done and said to take the weekend off and enjoy themselves.

So they did, which was completely out of character for the SDF—Logan especially. He wanted it to be a seven-day-a-week undertaking, with everyone rotating shifts, but he had quickly come to understand that not everyone was built like him. Not even Fitz. He was the first one to speak up against Logan's over-the-top schedules.

"Come on, mate," Fitz said. "We aren't the bloody *help*—we're your friends. You're gunna' burn out the others before they even realize they're burnt."

"We need to keep a tight grip on things out here," Logan countered. "One slip up and they'll get what they want."

Fitz shook his head. "You really think you can save them all?" Fitz stepped closer, but was still a few inches shorter than Logan. "Well, I got news for you Captain... It ain't gunna' happen!"

Fitz cut off Logan before he could respond. "Right now, as you and I are having our little scruff, dozens of them are dying out there—and there is *abso-fucking-lutely* nothing you or I or any of them," he pointed to the floor, meaning the team downstairs, "can do about it. So lay off!"

Logan sneered at Fitz, but gave in, dropping his head to his chin.

"Logan?"

He looked up to see CJ standing outside his room where he and Fitz were having their...discussion. Tears were streaming down her face. He'd seen her cry plenty of times before, but never like this.

"Please, Logan. Gray is right."

It was the last time she had ever seen Logan and Fitz stare each other down like that. Logan never realized how hard he was on them until he saw the emotion radiating from his sister's face. She was exhausted and mentally fried. It had reached a boiling point and it almost destroyed the SDF.

The next morning, they made 14 arrests and confiscated a truck load of illegally obtained goods. Some were caged, alive. Some weren't. The dead were properly catalogued and then respectfully incinerated. It was the only consistent way to destroy the poached. Burying them wouldn't do any good. More would just come to the graves and dig up the wares.

Like tonight, CJ thought. *If the Nazis had only burned the dead...*

She glanced back up to the picture. It showed all ten of them smiling ear-to-ear, as happy as ever. Logan and her. Fitz and Jan. Mo, Adnan, Kel...Dada...Saami...and Pandu. It's why she wept. Three of her friends were dead. All of them brutally killed by something they couldn't fight.

And she believed that.

Logan, Fitz, and even Jan were trained to battle a *human* enemy. This wasn't anything anyone could win against. She couldn't shake the feeling that they would all die out here. The red eyes would come for them and then—

"You okay?"

CJ flinched, the voice from her doorway scaring her. She looked up and saw Jan standing there, staring at her. His face—while normally a stoic, steadfast rock—was uncommonly...

He's worried, she thought, wiping away the tears.

"I'm..." CJ said, sniffing. "I'm..."

What—fine? Jolly? Just dandy?

"Scared..."

And she was.

Jan stepped forward, hand outstretched, inviting her into his embrace. They had stolen away a night together here and there, but had yet to really take their feelings for one another to the next level.

Was it love?

CJ didn't know, but damnit it felt right.

She let him guide her into his arms where they remained for what seemed like eternity. His arms were powerful, but gentle. His scent was rugged, but soft. Jan was her perfect ying to her yang. She made the giant laugh and he helped her keep her shit together.

They separated and CJ looked into Jan's crystal blue eyes. "What are we going to do?"

Jan's expression changed from worried to determined, all with the time it took her to ask the question. He stood tall and smiled.

"We fight," he replied, glancing to the panorama. He then looked back down to her. "We win." He nodded to the picture. "For them."

CJ nodded, another stream of tears falling down her cheeks. Then, a large finger lifted her chin up and another set of lips pushed up against hers.

The kiss only lasted a second, but it was enough. It was the reassurance she had desperately needed. CJ opened her heavy eyelids, meeting Jan's gaze.

"And for us."

"Ahem..."

They both spun at the sound of someone behind them.

It was Fitz.

Busted.

"Logan wants everyone upstairs for a briefing of what he wants to do next." He turned, but stopped. "Oh, and by the way..." He smiled. "You two can come out of the closet. We all know you've been banging each other for months now."

CJ's cheeks instantly flushed and Jan's eyebrows narrowed. He looked like he wanted to kill the much smaller man. But then Fitz started laughing.

"I'm just yankin' your crank!" he said, cracking up. "But seriously, I share a wall with *jumbo* over here." He motioned to Jan. "Logan doesn't know yet, but he'll eventually hear CJ's moaning all the way back to Melbourne."

Jan stepped forward, but Fitz turned and quickly scampered back down the hall, turning left when he hit the catwalk, heading back upstairs. CJ's faced flushed again, but she started to laugh too. Fitz had a way to cheer anyone up, even if he really wasn't trying to.

Placing a gentle, reassuring hand on her shoulder, Jan coaxed her to head in the direction Fitz did. They needed to put together a response, or at the very least, plan out a better defense until the Americans arrived.

CJ stopped after only a couple of steps and looked up to Jan. "Do I really moan?"

Now it was Jan's turn to blush.

He just shrugged. "I do good work."

She slugged him in the chest. "Jerk."

They both continued forward towards the staircase to the third level. As they moved off, a small, shadowy shape, long and low to the ground, slid through the hallway, entering CJ's room where it would wait until she returned. Its black nails made the quietest of clicking sounds on the hallway's hard floor.

CJ spun, but saw nothing, playing off the *obvious* paranoia on her overly emotional state and lack of sleep. *Delirium,* she thought. Most of them had been up for twenty-four hours by now. She turned back to Jan, and hand-in-hand they climbed the stairs to meet her brother.

The creature silently waited. It just needed to be patient. It would feed soon enough.

40

There were bodies everywhere. Pieces mostly. Shetani watched as his ancestor tore into another of the Nach—a zebra-hybrid—ripping a large chunk of meat from its neck, swallowing it whole. It had eaten parts of six now and had quickly regained its girth, standing a foot taller than Shetani. Its body, however, was something else.

It was maybe half the bulk as Shetani was, tall and slender, with a neck that was two times too long. It had four eyes that glowed...green.

That's what unnerved Shetani the most. The *green* eyes. They glowed like some alien lifeforms would. Like all his jumbled thoughts, Shetani couldn't remember why he knew what that looked like. But like those things, he just assumed it was right.

Its head was small in proportion to its size too, and it had no hair like him. Its bald head was covered with...scales, whereas his was skin. His ancestor lacked the pulsating veins as well.

The body of the Zebra sailed into the hallway, hitting the adjacent wall with a wet crunch of bone and viscous fluids. It was followed by a low growl as the much older beast emerged from its prison once more. But this time it was plenty strong enough to support itself.

Shetani watched as it stepped into full view, barely clearing the ten-foot ceiling as it stood. He looked over his ancestor, seeing the same veins he had, minus the red plasma. They weren't raised like Shetani's either. They were set into its body, glowing, illuminating the walls and ceiling around it.

It stretched its arms—all four of them—hitting either side of the corridor. Its wingspan was larger than it should have been as well—maybe fifteen feet. Shetani specifically watched its hands open, revealing the large three-clawed digits. Each one of the two *fingers* were over a foot long—half of it being claw. The third digit was something of a thumb, half the size, but having the ability to fully close.

Shetani regarded his own colossal hands. It would be able to grasp like he could, except his hands were thicker and contained five fingers. His fingers weren't as long either.

Regarding the older newcomer, Shetani snorted, acknowledging it, getting the attention of his taller relative. It looked down to him and returned the snort with a hiss. It ever so slightly opened its smaller, yet still undoubtedly deadly mouth, revealing its needlelike teeth.

While Shetani was brute strength, killing with sheer passion, desire, and muscle, his counterpart was leaner and would most certainly be quicker. It would strike with the same quickness as a serpent, and would be extremely efficient in the act. The fiendish look it had when its mouth hung open made it almost smile, like it knew something he didn't.

The way it stood also confused Shetani. While he stood, hands flexed, muscles taut, ready for a fight. This one stood with its arms to its side, relaxed, almost daring him to attack. He could sense its cunningness. He'd have to be careful.

Where?

Shetani stepped back. Had it spoken? Its mouth barely moved. It could speak?

Where!

It spoke again, demanding to know their location. It had obviously been in some sort of hibernation for some time. It probably didn't remember where it was.

Shetani looked into those menacing green eyes and thought the words carefully, forcing them to be vocalized.

Af-ri-ca, he said, concentrating, hearing himself annunciate the word carefully. Each syllable was long and drawn-out. It sounded like the voice in his head— the one that told him things—the one that explained the world around him. His ancestor's voice was higher and it spoke with an almost snake-like hiss mixed with a whisper.

Africa, it said, repeating Shetani's answer with what

sounded like a personal remembrance of the place. It definitely knew the land before it slept.

She-ta-ni, he said, carefully pronouncing his own name. He then held a clawed hand to his chest.

The four-armed creature did the same, speaking a language that Shetani had never heard before, but a language his mind had somehow translated.

Wustenfuchs, it said, standing taller at attention.

After a seventy-year slumber, the *Desert Fox* was awake.

* * * * *

Logan watched as CJ and Jan entered the Observation Deck. The two were becoming inseparable. He didn't mind though, especially now. CJ needed someone besides him. She wasn't a soldier. She was scared and needed a different voice whispering into her ear to stay calm. She would listen to Jan.

He regarded CJ, noticing the red, swollen skin around her eyes. She'd been crying. Thankfully, Jan was there. Logan would have felt terrible if he was up here working while she was off, falling apart, just under his feet. He respected the German even more now than he already had.

"What is it?" CJ asked, noticing Logan staring at her.

"We have a problem," he simply replied.

"Problem?" Jan asked, acknowledging Logan with a nod. "What kind of a problem?"

"Oh, about a six-ton problem."

CJ lifted her eyebrow at Fitz's comment.

"Irwin?" she asked, knowing it was *him*. He was the largest of the bulls in this region of the Serengeti, never straying too far from the Pen.

Logan nodded, a look of despair in his eyes.

"Is he..."

Logan shook his head no. "But he's been attacked. Half of his family is either dead or on the run, moving farther into the park." He breathed in, flexing his neck and back. "I think he's coming here for help."

Now it was Fitz's turn to lift his eyebrow. He and Logan had gone over the situation a few minutes ago, but his friend hadn't voiced this.

Thinking as he goes, Fitz thought, rubbing his beard. *His mind really does never stop.*

"Logan..." CJ said. Her tone was unbelieving, but then she stopped, thinking. "But... I guess it's possible?"

Jan looked down to CJ. "It is?"

CJ just shrugged. "Elephants—particularly Irwin— are amazing animals. They are extremely intelligent and Irwin has tested off the grid since I started studying him. He's truly one-of-a-kind."

"So," Fitz said, still not believing. "You think a twelve-*thousand*-pound pachyderm is coming to us for help?"

Logan looked at CJ for confirmation and then to Fitz. The Reeds just shrugged together.

"Whatever..." Fitz said, shaking his shaved head. "You're the experts." He then walked to the window, looking to the north where Irwin had last been tracked. "How do you want to help the big guy?"

This is why Logan loved Fitz. The man could have easily dismissed the idea of helping and maybe defending a bull from the Nach, but instead he just shrugged off the nonsense and got down to business. It really meant the world to Logan that his SAS mate trusted him *that* much.

"How about the Wraith?" The three Aussies along with Jan, turned, finding Mo standing behind them, arms crossed. "We could bring along Fitz's XM25 and make a mess. The Rhino's .50 needs to still cool some."

"We?" Logan asked.

Mo smiled. "Neither one of you can drive worth a damn, so yes, we."

Fitz looked at Logan and grabbed his grenade launcher. "I'm down for a cruise around the bush."

41

Logan was going over the plan with Fitz and Mo, figuring out exactly what they could do to help Irwin and whatever was left of his herd. Of all the animals that have been killed by this virus, the African elephant was definitely one they *needed* to protect at all costs. Its numbers were already dwindled down enough as it was. They didn't need any help from anything else.

Damn poachers are bad enough, CJ thought as she exited the Observation Deck. She sniffed her shirt, pinching the fabric, raising it to her nose. *Ugh. This body needs a rinse.*

Her plan was to take a quick shower and freshen up as best she could. It had been a full day of sweat and stink and she needed to clean up the lady bits. It's what she told Logan, making him blush. She just loved to tease him.

She unbuttoned the top of her shirt a little as she began the short climb down the stairs, letting in the much appreciated air conditioning. The wretched odor emanating from her sports bra was another thing all together. It was pressed so tightly against her skin that she could almost feel the small pond of sweat that had formed between her boobs.

She told Logan that too.

CJ smiled, laughing inwardly at how easy it was to make her kid brother squirm. It was a relationship that grew stronger as the years went by, but when he moved out to Tanzania, it had strengthened beyond description.

Logan never properly thanked her for saving his life, giving it purpose again, but she knew he understood what she did. He *was* thankful, she just knew he would never outwardly admit it.

Men and their pride.

Her boot found the second floor landing and she continued around the inner wall for another fifteen feet, arriving at the hallway that housed her living quarters. It held four rooms—two on each side— concluding at a dead-end that sported a window with a beautiful view of the park. The rooms belonged to Logan, Fitz, Mo, and herself, the four original SDF members. They had taken up residency in these rooms, wanting to be within a close proximity to one another, just in case. There was another similar hall further along the catwalk where the other six smaller rooms were. They were originally built to be guestrooms, not for full-time members.

She rounded the corner, turning right, and headed for the first door on the left. Logan's was the first door on the right, across the hall. He thought it only right that they be near each other. He jokingly said it was so he could keep a close eye on her when her door was open, but she knew he was just secretly lonely. He hadn't been with, or talked to, a single woman since coming to Africa, thinking it would only cause a distraction.

Funny enough, CJ half-agreed with him. Relationships *could* be a distraction if you cared for the other person enough that they were always on your mind, but they could also be a blessing—something to fight for. Either way, she was actually grateful for his steadfast belief in always being ready. They survived numerous encounters over the years because of his over-the-top preparedness.

Like the handgun holstered next to the front door just in case someone unexpectedly knocks and you need a weapon. CJ shook her head. *Just in case.* It became his motto. Like the bloody Boy Scouts of America—*Be Prepared.*

Then again... They never got visitors out here. If someone did knock, it was most likely trouble to begin with.

She entered her open door and sat on her bed. The only time they closed them was when someone was changing or sleeping. It was a house rule. If the door was closed... *Go Away.* She'd shut the door once she got her shirt off, until then there was nothing to be ashamed of.

Everyone had seen her in her bathing suits in the showers. Some had even seen her in the buff on accident. That was mostly her not giving a damn and stripping down before she got in the hot tub. There was nothing to hide out here. Especially, with her guard dog—slash—guardian angel, Logan, around. He would literally kill anyone that crossed her.

Except Jan.

She was still unsure of how to tell Logan about their relationship. Fitz had indeed heard them several times in his room. Jan had warned her several times about her moans.

Bloody walls, she thought taking off her shirt. She looked at herself in the mirror and smiled. Then she frowned, looking at her sports bra. *Not looking forward to the tug-of-war match with you.* Getting it off would prove troublesome for sure.

She then looked at her flat*ish* stomach. In her younger years she would have been self-conscious about it, but now...not so much. She wasn't as worried about her appearance anymore, not since being out here full-time. They were too damn busy and it was just too stifling hot to care. She hadn't even worn makeup in years.

Shutting the door to her room, CJ turned, sensing movement out of the corner of her eye. She looked to the foot of her bed, between it and her dresser, but saw nothing. She then bent to peek under her bed, but stopped and smiled.

Nervous twit, she thought, standing back up. She shut the door and removed her boots and socks. She was halfway done pulling down her pants when another skittering noise sounded from across her room, near her closet. She jumped at the sound, but again saw nothing.

Damnit, woman. Get a hold of yourself.

She continued stripping her black cargo pants down, stopping at her ankles—when something lean and furry launched itself from the open closet door. With a yelp, CJ fell back on her butt, kicking her feet out.

It's what saved her life.

A blur of jet black—an infected mongoose—dove headfirst into her pants, teeth bared, and got caught in the resistant fabric. They acted as the perfect net. She then quickly clasped her feet together, pinning it, and screamed.

"Looogannn!"

The thing bucked and squirmed, trying to free itself from the makeshift webbing, biting holes in the crotch of her pants.

"Logan! Jan! Anyone!"

Then, she heard them, the faint sound of pounding footsteps coming down the stairs, but when her door was thrown open it was Jan...and he was dressed in only a towel.

He lunged for the creature with his bare hands, just as it found its way around her improvised trap. Logan arrived a second later as the waterlogged Jan gripped the things neck and squeezed. CJ slid the rest of the way out of her pants and quickly crab walked back, slamming into her bed and watched as the German repeatedly pounded the mongoose's head into the floor. After the fifth strike, it stopped moving.

With a final twitch of its tail the Nach was gone, its skull crushed. Jan let go of the now *fully* dead creature and fell back on the floor into a sitting position, breathing heavily. His eyes were wide with fright and what looked like a massive adrenaline dump. He was wired for combat and would need a moment to come back down off his *high.*

"Cass?" Logan asked, stepping in. He helped her underwear clad form to her feet and held her, kissing the top of her head. She shook and then started crying again. This was the boiling point. She already shed so many tears for her friends, but this was her own life that almost ended. It was the first time she'd ever been in a true life-or-death situation.

"How the bloody hell did *that* get in?" Fitz asked from the doorway, Glock in hand. If Jan wasn't able to kill it, Fitz most definitely would have.

"Must have followed...the Rhino...in," Jan said, attempting to stand. Fitz bent down and helped the bigger man to his feet. Thankfully, Jan was strong in both body and mind and was already coming around.

CJ released herself from Logan's embrace and dove into Jan's arms, sobbing some more. Their feelings for each other were *officially* public and no one—not even Logan—said a word. He just looked up to Jan and nodded his thanks.

"Captain?" Logan looked out the door and saw Mo, keys in hand. "Everything okay?"

"It is now," he said, heading for the door.

He stopped and turned back to Jan. "Take care of her."

Jan stood straighter at the request and at the respect his captain—his boss—his friend—gave him.

"You know I will," he replied, nodding his thanks back to Logan. The two men were instantly bonded after what just happened—like brothers. Jan would do anything in his power to keep *both* the Reeds safe now, not just CJ.

"Let's go, Gray."

Fitz watched as Logan exited. He'd only seen a look of determination like this on Logan's face once before. *The day he almost killed our commander back home.* It was the day he decided to quit the army.

"Right then," Fitz said as chipper as ever, turning to Mo. "Shall we go for a ride?"

42

Mo eased the Wraith from the rear garage door, watching for anything that tried to make its way in. Jan and Kel were also there keeping watch. They didn't need a repeat of what just happened in CJ's room. She was in the showers, calming her nerves, taking a much needed break. She wasn't *alone* though. She brought a handgun too.

"Gentlemen, are we ready?" Mo asked his two passengers. Logan and Fitz presented their driver with identical thumbs up, giving Mo the okay to proceed.

The Wraith was Fitz's idea and something Mo had a hand in designing. It was, in essence, part ATV and part motorcycle. Mo was straddling the center of the odd looking vehicle, revving the engine. Logan and Fitz were strapped into dual sidecars, attached to either side.

The body of the off-roader looked like your typical

four-wheeler, except it was missing its rear wheels. Instead, there were two motorcycle sidecars attached. Logan in one, Fitz in the other.

They, in turn, sat on an extended rear axle, having the third and fourth tires on the outside of each car. Technically, it was still considered a four-wheeler, but its obvious modifications made it look like a scaled down death machine.

Its name, *Wraith,* was Fitz's idea too. Most of the time when naming things out here, they would use words that fit the bill or described things out in the plains, like Kipanga, Bullpen, and Rhino. They all meant something, but Fitz said Wraith just sounded '*badass.*'

Logan, armed with his trusted SCAR assault rifle, sat in the left-hand sidecar, while Fitz was in the right, armed with his new best friend, the XM25 grenade launcher. Normally, Logan would think the weapon to be overkill, but as of now, he wished they had another for him. He remembered what the thing did the last time they went for a drive.

As they neared, Adnan opened the gate from upstairs. The Wraith didn't have a button like the Rhino did. It just wasn't a good idea for the driver to take either of his, or her, hands off the steering column's crossbar to open it. Maybe with just him zipping around, it would be okay, but not with two other people's survival on the line.

Mo throttled up on the heavily modified Artic Cat: Thundercat, throttling its specially designed 1100cc engine. It had plenty of power to cruise around the grounds outside the Bullpen, even with three grown men bouncing around on it. The original 950cc engine block just wasn't *adequate* enough for what they needed. So with Logan's permission, Mo called in some help. He asked someone he knew from his previous life—someone who was a whiz with engines—come out for a week and put this thing together. They pre-ordered what was needed for the upgrade and eventually a man named Claude showed up one day.

"Claude," Logan asked. "Claude, *what?*"

"Just, Claude," the other man said. "Let's just say... I have some *discrepancies* against me that I'd like to keep under the radar."

Logan looked at Mo who just nodded, giving the newcomer his blessing. Logan backed off and let the two men work.

Four days later, the Wraith was all but done. They gave it their customary flat-black paint job, perfect for night recon, and took it for a spin.

"Can you hear me, Logan?"

Logan looked left, seeing a grouping of uninfected wildebeest off in the distance and smiled. He was really going to miss the serene view around here if the God Blood spread any further.

He keyed his earbud, yelling against the wind and roar of the Wraith's engine noise. "Logan here. Where's Irwin?"

"He's a couple miles northeast of your current position and heading straight for you."

"The question is..." Fitz added. "Is he still Irwin?"

There was silence over their comms. No one could

answer that now. They just needed to hope, and in some of their cases pray, that he was fine. It would devastate everyone beyond their current state if they lost the unofficial SDF mascot too.

"Keep us posted, Adnan," Logan said. "We're going in hot."

And with that, Mo throttled up even harder, accelerating to an absurd speed for this kind of vehicle.

The Wraith didn't have a standard display. Where the instrument panel—including the speedometer—was, was now a GPS system. It was the same software that Kipanga used, being able to track the known territories of the surrounding plains.

Please, please, please, Logan thought, biting his lip. He pleaded with God—if there was one—that Irwin would be spared. CJ believed in a higher power—not necessarily *religion*—but something bigger than just us lousy humans. That's what she called humanity as a whole. We were basically a virus that infected and killed a larger, greater, being—Earth.

"We are parasites to Mother Earth," CJ had quipped, beer in hand. She was already two in, and being an extreme lightweight, she was half in the bag. "We destroy for the sake of living until the host is dead and we ourselves die."

We ourselves die.

The words resonated in Logan's mind as Mo skirted around the previous battlefield. They didn't need to experience that again. There'd been enough blood spilled so far tonight, and traipsing through the still drying remnants of the grounds wasn't going to help anyone's attitude.

HRRRN!

Logan flinched, looking up at the sudden foghorn-like noise. It came from straight ahead, literally shaking his fillings loose. It sounded familiar, but there was no way it could have been that. It was just too damn loud.

Then his night vision picked up the faintest of things off in the distance. He saw a shape lumbering towards them—only—it was big...really big. Irwin was six-tons of nature's most dominating champion. No land animal was as big as an African bull.

But then he saw the red eyes. There had to be a dozen of them and they were all looking their way.

"The Nach?" Fitz asked, seeing them as well.

Logan shook his head, knowing what they were about to face. "No, mate. Not *the* Nach..." He breathed in heavy, holding back the tears he knew would soon begin to fall. "It's *a* Nach—it's Irwin... He's gone."

43

"Ho-ly shit," Fitz said, flabbergasted at the sight of the African elephant as it fully came into focus in his night vision device. It was like something out of a sci-fi flick.

The normally docile—almost playful at times—behemoth, was now the most screwed up, terrifying thing he'd ever seen.

Things just keep getting better and better...

He leaned back, around Mo, and watched Logan, seeing his friend's shoulders sag. Fitz felt for the guy. Logan had some weird bond with Irwin from before he ever stepped foot on the *Dark Continent*.

Dark... Fitting name under the circumstances, Fitz thought. Everything about this place represented evil now—down to the very creatures that inhabited it. Usually, he would only think of the poachers as the *dark side* of nature. The *Sith of Africa* he joked one night, watching Star Wars.

Fucking Jar Jar... He wasn't sure why he was cursing the floppy-eared moron's name. It just felt right to do so for some reason.

HRRRN!

Fitz covered his ears with his hands as Irwin bellowed again, causing them to ring. *Miracle ear, here I come.* He tried popping them like he was on a plane, but it didn't work. It felt like the flashbang from when he and Mo squared off against the lions.

"Why is it so loud?" Mo asked, having to yell. He gripped the brakes hard, sending the Wraith into a skidding stop. His hearing was also shot from the sounds of it, as was Logan's. Fitz watched as Mo shook his head, trying to clear the cobwebs. Then, Fitz saw why the decibel level of Irwin's trumpet was off the charts.

Not only did it have twelve eyes, but it also had twelve trunks. Plus, Irwin had to be another two—maybe three—feet taller and another couple thousand pounds heavier. His skin was also the same jet black as others who had become infected, including the red, pulsating veins just beneath the top few layers.

"You're kidding me, right?" Fitz said, dumbfounded. "It's a damn Woolly Cthulhu. His skin even looks tougher—like this." He knocked on his chest, hitting the Kevlar vest.

"Cthulhu?" Mo asked.

"He's right," CJ replied, cutting in over their earpieces. "Cthulhu was an alien entity—fictional of course—by legendary writer H.P. Lovecraft. It was said to have a humanoid body mixed with a dragon and a face that looked like an octopus. Irwin's naturally large skull and his prodigious trunk made for a perfect match once the God Blood took over."

Fitz appreciated CJ's straightforward information. In any other situation, the detached analysis would have been a little off-putting to him. He generally liked to keep things loose, but he understood why she was doing the zoologist thing right now. They had all grown attached to Irwin. Logan fought harder, CJ changed into an animal encyclopedia, and he cracked jokes. It's how each of them coped. But now, the candor helped him focus on what to do next.

The only problem was, that was Logan's gig. He wouldn't move on Irwin unless the captain gave the word. There were things Fitz was more than capable—and expected—to do on his own, but dealing with Irwin wasn't one of—

Bullets ripped into Irwin's face as Logan unloaded into the monster. Fitz expertly followed suit and unleashed one of his grenades. It soared, arching straight into Irwin's direction and detonated on his back.

The three men were shaken by the blast, causing Logan to stop firing. Losing some of his resolve, he lowered his rifle and watched. A cloud of smoke and dirt rolled around the Nach and was swept away by a light breeze. What they saw was horrifying.

Irwin was fine. The only sign of injury was a burnt spot on his back where the 25mm explosive hit. Other than that, he was just peachy. Pissed, but peachy. And to prove it, Irwin reared up on his hind legs and trumpeted again with all twelve of his full sized trunks, charging as soon as his tree trunk sized front legs hit the ground.

"Get us out of here, Mo!"

Fitz couldn't agree more. If his weapon couldn't put a ding in Irwin's new, more resilient skin, nothing could.

Unless I score a direct hit on its face and blow out a few of its eyes, Fitz thought as Mo spun the Wraith, doing a one-eighty, taking off back towards the Bullpen.

There has to be a chink in its armor. The problem with that strategy was obvious, though. They'd have to be directly in front of him again to get off that kind of shot.

The ground shook as the beast gave chase, catching up quickly. Fitz had no idea how fast they were going, but he estimated it to be around 40-mph.

It was huge, fast, and basically armor plated. If this thing got even close to the Pen it would rip through it like it was made of cardboard.

Fitz could see it in his head as Irwin smashed through the concrete and steel walls, collapsing the three story structure with ease. CJ, Jan, Adnan, and Kel would be killed without a doubt and then Irwin would chase them until they ran out of gas.

We need to change course.

Luckily, they didn't have to make that decision.

A cacophony of automatic fire rained down from the sky above, hitting Irwin from every direction as he ran. Most found their marks, and even more did nothing, but a few did find Irwin's eyes. He trumpeted again and slowed, thrashing about in every direction with his trunks.

Then it stopped and spun in circles, trying to grab anything that got close—but nothing did. The men landed all around the behemoth and unloaded again and again, never letting up.

The American military had arrived.

Just in time, Fitz thought, watching the skilled precision of the black-clad team of twelve. They formed a semicircle around the Nach and started to even push it back some, their parachutes dragging on the ground behind them.

Then as quick as a viper, each man quickly reached up to their chest and detached their harnesses, ditching said chutes. Then, with what Fitz knew to be meticulous training, each man reloaded and continued their barrage.

Fitz climbed out, as did Logan, and they joined in.

"Keep your men at a safe distance," Logan yelled to the closet, helmeted solider. "We can take it out if we hit it with our XM25." He knew these guys would understand the weapon and its capabilities.

Without acknowledging Logan's *suggestion*, the men—all twelve of them—began to quickly backpedal. Fitz and Logan climbed back into their sidecars as Mo threw the vehicle in reverse, backing them up another hundred feet.

He stopped and Fitz stood, yelling, "Fire in the hole!"

He opened up with everything he had, aiming

square into the center of Irwin's face. He let fly three quick *whumps*, connecting with each of his projectiles. Irwin bellowed again, but it sounded like there was rage mixed in with the pain.

As one, the twelve soldiers ceased firing, never lowering their weapons. They watched, fingers on triggers, waiting for the worst to happen.

"Damn," said one of the Americans.

Fitz agreed, the dust cloud was thick and swirling. They couldn't see through it and wouldn't be able to for a while. He looked around and noticed why... The wind had died down.

"Dionysus, Apollo, Hermes—move in," the man to Fitz's right said, giving the order. "I want confirmation that it's down."

Greek gods?

The three men moved in swiftly, disappearing into the haze. Silence filled the Serengeti for a beat.

Then, screams.

Then...nothing.

44

No one moved. Not a single member of the newly arrived force even flinched. They stayed rooted where they were and held their fire, patiently awaiting the outcome.

Logan watched as something sailed through the air towards another of the men encompassing the dust cloud. He tried to closely examine the projectile, but couldn't make out the object.

Until it landed.

"Ugh," Fitz said, leaping back.

It was a head.

Fitz stepped back again, giving the severed head a wider-berth.

"Now, what?" Fitz asked, looking to the American team's commander.

No answer.

Logan stayed silent as well. He knew the beast

would eventually emerge—or the dust cloud would dissipate and show it to them—whichever came first.

And then it did.

The extra-large Nach stepped forward, revealing its state.

A couple of the trunks were damaged and few were altogether missing. Logan also saw one hanging limply, barely connected by the thinnest of sinews.

The eyes were damaged too. Only five were still lit and presumably working, but he had a strong suspicion that the plagued Irwin could still see just fine. Twelve were obviously better than five, but five were still better than none. He'd also seen how these things fight injured. They would battle as brutally as they could until completely destroyed.

"Um... Captain?"

Logan looked to his left. Mo was still in the pilot's seat of the Wraith. The look of abject horror was plain to see.

It took three of Fitz's rounds to the face and lived...

Dread began to eat away at Logan's determination. He was beginning to believe that this was a lost cause and that they and the Americans were done for.

"Logan..." Fitz whispered. "You got any bright ideas?"

Bright...

Logan perked up at the thought. He then reached into one of the pockets of his combat vest and pulled out a flashbang.

He could see Fitz smiling as he did the same.

So did Mo.

"You sure that's going to work?" It was the American commander asking, looking over to the three SDF men. Logan just nodded.

"Tell your men to get ready," Logan said. "I'm assuming you carry these?"

He just cocked his head to the side saying, *duh,* and revealed an identical explosive. The American then whispered the orders to all his remaining men through their comms system.

Logan raised an eyebrow at how the man just mumbled his orders, never raising his voice enough to be understood, even from the distance he stood from him.

Sub-vocal communications—mostly likely throat mics, Logan thought. *Must be Delta.*

The United States finest were here, and *that,* Logan was grateful for. The problem was, they were still knee deep in a large pile of shit and there was no guarantee they would dig themselves out.

"On my mark," the American said. "Three...two...one...Mark!"

The remaining Americans, along with Logan, Fitz, and Mo, lobbed their respective flash grenades at the monster. They then all turned away and prepared for the concussive bang associated with the explosive.

The pressure wave knocked Logan off his feet, sending him sprawling to the dirt, but otherwise he was unharmed. He felt sick to his stomach and could feel what little food he'd eaten in the last day roil from the impact, but otherwise he would be okay. It felt like he'd just gotten off a bad amusement park ride, ready to vomit, but not. He didn't have to worry about the others either. They were all fully capable to continue fighting even while working through the flashbang's nauseating effects.

They'd better be able to.

The Nach on the other hand was *not* used to those same effects and it proved it by its behavior. It writhed on the ground, bucking and thrashing its prodigious head. Its trunks flailed and squirmed like a sea anemone getting tossed by an ocean wave.

"Fire!"

Logan complied with the American commander and let loose on the beast, pouring into the creatures already damaged face. The others just laid into whatever part of the beast was visible.

It's not enough.

"Bunch up!" Logan yelled, directing everyone. "Converge on my position and aim for its head!"

The American, who at first looked upset at the Aussie taking over his men, agreed, relaying the order. They continued firing, but promptly lined up with Logan, Fitz, and Mo—who was opening up with his Mossberg.

"It can't function without a brain," Fitz added. "Destroy it and we're clear."

And so they did.

The three SDF men and the nine remaining American Special Forces soldiers, added their collective might together, and let fly with everything they had.

Irwin's Nach form continued to thrash and squirm

under the heavy fire, it was still heavily disoriented and couldn't regain its footing.

Round after round pounded into the creature as Logan and the others reloaded, but still Irwin lived. He was using his ears as some sort of shield, half-covering his face from the abuse. It got one foot underneath itself and pushed, standing on wobbling limbs. Then it took a couple steps forward, advancing through the storm of gunfire.

"Keep firing!" Logan yelled, following his own advice. The only one not firing was Fitz, his XM25 was useless at this range, unless he wanted to kill everyone else too.

Armored skin flew as they began to rip apart the protective ears, but still Irwin advanced, trumpeting through the barrage. He dug his front limbs into the earth and pushed, advancing again.

"Logan?" Mo asked, having to yell over the noise. He stopped firing, taking position on the Wraith. His job was quickly changing from attacking pilot to getaway driver with every failed impact.

Then, Irwin reared up and charged, lowering its solid skull like a battering ram. It was still covering itself as well as it could, but now it was beyond angry. It would try to crush them and pound them into paste, using every ton it had in its rage-filled assault.

Two more of the Americans—those that weren't retreating quickly enough—were each grabbed by a trunk. They lashed out like a squid's tentacle, stretching to double its length, and snared the soldiers.

Irwin broke one of them in half, bending him backwards at the waist, tossing the American away like a ragdoll. The other man was slammed to the ground, getting his head stomped in. Irwin passed over the now flattened man like he had been an unseen ant.

"Run!"

Logan knew scattering was the best way to confuse the monster, but he also recognized that the Nach would not stop, and it wouldn't get tired. Eventually, they would all be found and killed and once they were gone, no one would be able to defend the Pen.

He turned and ran into the night and almost stopped in surprise. A set of headlights was coming in fast. Logan recognized the shape of the vehicle immediately.

The Rhino...

Help was coming.

45

CJ drove like a woman possessed. She floored the Hummer's pedal, burying it into the floorboards. She needed to get there faster.

She saw men running in every direction a hundred yards ahead and something massive moving behind them. It was hard to get a good look at the beast that used to be Irwin from where she sat. The Rhino was bucking violently, causing her line of sight to bounce along with it.

As she neared, something slammed into the windshield, glancing off the near-impervious bulletproof glass. A crack and a wet slap told her it was a body that had struck the vehicle, pinging off it like a bug on the highway. The smear of blood was another obvious sign. The monster had flung someone at them.

She reeled at the spreading crimson, but couldn't look away. She still needed to drive and looking through the windshield was kind of—sort of—important.

Pounding from behind and above, told her to stop. She complied as Jan opened up on the behemoth with the still cooling .50 caliber machine gun. He fired in aimed spurts, not wanting to render the weapon useless.

I'm sure we'll need it again, CJ thought, watching the massive thing in her headlights.

It still had the overall shape of an elephant, minus the face of course, but what Logan had failed to mention was its tusks. They were also longer—like a Woolly Mammoth's—and pointed like spears.

She watched as it impaled one of the Americans, punching a large hole through the man's back as he ran. He was then lifted off the ground, kicking and screaming. The soldier was carried away like a sick holiday ornament or a woman's dangling earring.

Jan scored a direct hit on Irwin's face, causing one of the eyes to explode in a gout of fluorescent plasma. The spray landed on another of the Americans, causing the man to flinch and fall. His face was coated in the viscus fluid and apparently it hurt like hell.

He didn't get up.

What the hell? CJ thought as she watched the black-clad soldier just lay there—then he sat up and looked her way. His eyes were red and glowing, just like the others.

"Oh my God!" she screamed. The infected soldier then ran straight at her brother.

"Logan!" she yelled. "Behind you!"

Logan spun as the soldier reached out for him. She could even see the man's fingernails rapidly elongating into claws. *Is the eye-goo an accelerated form of the God Blood?*

Her brother dodged the incoming attack, side stepping the newly turned Nach. He then turned his SCAR on the man and fired.

Click.

Out of ammo.

Logan dropped his empty rifle and drew his Desert Eagle, pumping a round into the back of the Nach's skull as it stumbled by, obliterating its brain...along with most of its head. He then quickly picked up his discarded weapon, slapped in a new magazine, and waved his thanks to CJ. Finally, like nothing had happened, he began his assault on Irwin again, sending another burst into the monster.

The best, CJ thought.

The ground rumbled as the beast fell—not dead— but definitely injured. It flailed some more, only having half of its original trunks left. The missing limbs revealed its blood covered teeth. It reminded CJ of a massive Piranha jaw. The teeth were small relative to Irwin's new girth, but no doubt razor sharp.

"Everyone back!" Logan shouted, limping towards the Rhino. He all but collapsed on the right quarter panel of the truck, leaning on it for support.

He's exhausted, CJ thought, watching him.

The surviving men adhered to the more experienced man, not even waiting for their commander's order. Logan's leadership and skill was obvious to the newcomers.

Five of the twelve Americans remained. They huddled around the Rhino, awaiting Logan's next order, but he didn't have to give it. Instead, Fitz fired another grenade from his XM25. It detonated on the bull's skull, blowing the weakened bone apart.

Irwin's once beautiful and majestic form fell still, as silent as the night. Only the soft breeze and heavy breathing of the men could be heard now.

"Logan Reed?" asked one of the men, wasting no time. He was holding his arm and was missing his weapon, but he carried himself like he was used to being in charge.

Must be the leader of the Americans? CJ thought as she slid out of the Rhino's driver's seat.

Jan appeared around the rear of the truck and joined her, watching the man approach her brother.

Logan straightened and turned to meet the American commander. He stopped a foot away, staring into Logan's hardened, unintimidatable face. They each just stood there, burning holes into one another, until the other man softened a pinch. He then stepped back and extended his hand.

"The name is Navarro." Logan accepted the American's hand. "But—" he continued, cutting off Logan's chance at introducing himself. "You can call me, Zeus."

Logan lifted an eyebrow. "Zeus?"

"Yep," the American said. "King of Olympus."

Logan nodded. "Well, Zeus. My name is Logan Reed...but you can call me..." he smiled, "Boss."

The American's face fell. "Boss? Do you know who I am?"

"I do," Logan said, getting a puzzled look out of everyone. "You're Delta—the best." Zeus stood taller, prouder. "But," Logan added, "you and your boys are way out of your league."

Logan then stepped forward, getting back into the man's face, sneering. Logan—not *his majesty* Zeus—was the *master* of intimidation. He lived and breathed self-assurance, even though he would sometimes admit the other. "You and what's left of your team work for me now." He stepped back again, beaming confidence. "Welcome to the SDF."

* * * * *

"We don't work for anyone," Zeus said. "Unless your name is Uncle Sam and you wear a top hat."

They sat in the Observation Deck of the Bullpen, gathered around Logan's desk. The leader, Zeus, was leaning on the table top staring down at the relaxed and very comfortable SDF captain.

Logan, feet propped on the edge of his desk, returned the glare, but added an amused look on his face. That didn't sit well with Zeus.

The Delta operator clinched his fists tighter as he leaned on them, causing his knuckles to audibly pop. It got a reaction...but not from Logan.

"Easy, mate," Fitz said from Logan's right. "You wouldn't want to go and do something stupid, now would you?"

Zeus looked over to Fitz. He was casually sitting on one of the workbenches, leaning back against a shelf full of shotguns. Then, he looked down to the Aussie's hands. Fitz had a Mossberg casually leveled at the soldier, finger hovering over the trigger. No one noticed he had even drawn it.

"You disrespect him," Fitz said, burning holes in the man, "then you disrespect me."

"And me," Jan said from behind Logan. He had no weapon, but just stood like a giant behind his seated friend, arms crossed. "You need to hear what's been happening before you say something you'll regret."

"Plus," Fitz added, "I thought you Yanks got along just fine with the SAS in the past? It's not like we Aussie's are warmongers or anything."

Zeus' eyes went wide for just second. "SAS?"

"Yep," Logan said, answering for Fitz. "Both of us served for a long time. Fitzy and I were on the same assault team for years."

"Okay, okay. Enough with the ego trips and pissing contests," CJ said from the corner of the room, stepping forward as she spoke.

All eyes were on her as the only woman in the room. She stepped inbetween Logan and Jan, placing both her hands on her brother's shoulders, feeling his tense muscles relax as she squeezed. Being between the two men gave her all the assurance in the world at the moment.

Zeus was about to open his mouth again, but CJ started first. "What do you know about Josef Mengele?"

This caught the American off guard. He stuttered a reply, but again CJ cut him off. "Well, we met his corpse a few hours ago and have been fighting to survive ever since. If you give me a moment to indulge you on the finer details, you'd understand why my little brother here is so adamant about doing things his way."

Ugh. Logan shook his head. *Thanks Cass...*

"Fine," Zeus said reluctantly, stepping back. He then crossed his own arms and waited for CJ to get the lecture underway. "Go ahead."

Logan smiled inwardly.

Hook, line...

He glanced up to the Delta man who was staring intently at CJ while she started her detailed explanation of what had transpired in the Serengeti so far. Her account sounded more like something from pure fiction than from real life.

...and sinker.

46

Zeus sat back, his bravado defused. He had nothing to say except, "What do you need from us?" He looked to Logan for an answer, committing him and his team to the cause without having to say as much. Logan wouldn't push it either. These men were proud warriors. Beating them into submission would only compromise their toughened exterior and their allegiance. He would need their full devotion to the SDF in order to survive the night.

And even then it's still a crapshoot.

Logan sat forward, all his animosity towards the team leader gone. "I need you and your men to trust us and fall in line. I don't want any rogue bullshit. You see something, you call it in. We have...experience...in this sort of thing."

"Experience?" one of the Delta men asked. "What kind?

"More than you, mate," Fitz answered biting one of his nails. He pulled the sliver loose, spitting it on the floor. "Believe me when I tell you, that *no one* on this planet has spent more time killing these things than us. And you can take that to the bank—or whatever the bloody hell you Yanks say."

The other man backed down with a glance from Zeus who was all in.

"So," he said, turning to Fitz. "It's true then... Zombies?"

Fitz just chuckled. "Not exactly. They're not really dead, but they aren't alive anymore either. It's a sci-fi purgatory type of state. They fight until you put a bullet in their head."

"The Nach," Logan added, "are creatures that will stop at nothing to kill you. Then, if you aren't ripped apart, you'll become one."

"Like your friends?" asked another of Zeus' men.

Logan just silently nodded.

"And yours," he said, reminding the men of the Delta soldier that had turned. The one Logan had shot.

"We saw them with our own eyes," Jan said, speaking up for the first time since his threat. "Saami and Pandu were family. Even more to some." He motioned to Logan and CJ. "The Reeds knew them for almost a decade. I've only known them for half as long," he then looked over to Mo, "and Mo over here for... How long?"

Mo perked up, but fell silent again, thinking of his deceased friends. "Fifteen years," he said in a whisper.

He then grinned at a memory—a happy one from his expression.

"We've lost three men in just a few hours," Logan said, glumly.

"We lost seven in ten minutes!" Zeus shouted. It wasn't directed at Logan, though. It was more of an outburst at the circumstances than at one person. Logan understood what it felt like to become unhinged out in the field. These guys were the best at what they did—like he was. They were used to doing things their way or no way, but the proverbial monkey wrench can sometimes come out of nowhere and make things wonky.

Like an infected elephant as big as a tank.

"Then you fully understand what kind of situation we are in?" Logan asked, getting back on task.

"Of course," Zeus replied, some of his tenacity returning. Logan also knew what that was like. Soldiers were taught and trained to heal quickly while out in the field—both physically and psychologically. They always need to be level-headed and thinking clearly. People dying—even teammates—was unfortunately a hazard that came with the job.

It doesn't always work, though, he thought to himself. He was still a train wreck after the Iraqi incident, but he wasn't a *complete* disaster anymore. Time truly heals *some* wounds, but not all of them.

Logan stood. "We need you and your men to defend this compound at all costs, but most of all we need reinforcements ASAP. We need as many feet on the ground as you can muster. Stopping the spread of the virus is our number one priority. Use whatever force necessary. If we fail, this turns global."

The finality of Logan's statement took everyone off guard. There was no '*could*' in his orders. There was only what *would* happen if they failed. He meant it too. He needed them to see the big picture. The plague would spread farther through Africa, heading south to more densely populated areas, infecting millions— hundreds of millions even.

Zeus stood, straightening. The steel that soldiers like this were known for was quickly returning to the man. "I'll make the call, but there's no guarantee that we can have people here any quicker than us. We volunteered to come out here because we were told the SDF was run by former military personnel. The brass back at Manda Bay were floored you hit the panic button to begin with. They said you guys never called for help unless Satan himself showed up on your doorstep."

"You may not be too far off," Fitz said, sliding off the table, grabbing his XM25. "What we are dealing with would make Lucifer himself wet the bed."

Logan laughed, not being able to hold it back. He was getting so loopy that Fitz's jokes were *actually* sounding funny now.

Zeus shook his head, trying not to smile at Fitz. He turned and spoke in whispers, no doubt talking to the powers that be back in Kenya.

"Reed," one of the men said, stepping forward. "What do you need us to do?"

He regarded the man. He was the same height as

Logan, but outweighed him by 20 pounds or so. *Probably a wrestler in school.*

"What's your name?" Logan asked.

"They call me Ares," the Delta operator replied, proudly smiling.

"The god of war?" Logan asked.

"The same," he said with a grin. "I make things quickly disappear."

Logan nodded, understanding. "Explosives then."

Now it was the other man's turn to nod.

"*Herr Gruber?*" Logan asked in his best German accent, calling over Jan.

He stomped over, stopping next to Logan. "Ares, this is, Jan Gruber. Once upon a time, Jan here was in the same line of work as you. Although... We have yet to need that exact expertise out here."

Surprisingly, Ares held out his hand to Jan. It was a show of respect to the senior demolitions expert. "You wouldn't happen to be the German called, *Zerstorer?*"

Jan's eyes flickered ever so slightly, recognizing the name. Logan didn't know what it meant, but Ares had clearly heard of Jan before.

"*Ja,*" Jan said, acknowledging the name. "I *was* once called, Zerstorer, but now I am just Jan Gruber of the SDF. I left that life behind when I retired."

Ares didn't continue questioning the larger man. It was pretty obvious that Jan didn't want to talk about his past any longer.

"Ares," Zeus said, calling over the man.

As the soldier walked away, Logan leaned into Jan and asked, "Zerstorer?"

Jan breathed in deeply, but answered. His voice was barely audible, but he simply said, "It means..." he met Logan's eyes. "It means, Destroyer."

47

While Logan and Zeus discussed what was next on the agenda, Fitz, Kel, Mo, and Ares—the Delta demolitions expert—walked the inner perimeter of the Bullpen's fencing. The operator wanted to check the surrounding defenses and see if he couldn't spice them up a little.

"This is your standard C4 plastic explosive and blasting cap set up," Ares explained, "and this," he held up a small black device, "is a remote trigger. All you have to do is push a button and, *boom*, see you in the afterlife."

Fitz and Mo watched as the man wadded up what looked like a small amount of clay. He then knelt down next to one of the gate's support posts, unsheathing his knife. Next, Ares dug a shallow hole into the dirt just off the concrete slab. It was just deep enough for him to bury most of the golf ball sized chunk. He moved on to the other post and did the same.

Ares forcibly shoved the plastique into the space, jamming it deeper with his thumb. Mo flinched, but Fitz knew it was actually pretty safe stuff. You could even shoot it and nothing would happen. It needed an electric shock to detonate.

"Why blow the gate?" Kel asked.

"What if you had one of those bastards follow you in here again like the leopard did?" Ares answered, lightly covering it with dirt. The Delta man wouldn't have believed it until he saw the body. He had said that it was, "the biggest damn cat he'd ever seen."

Kel's eyes furrowed in anger, but Mo placed a hand on his shoulder calming the man. Dada's death was still ripe in Kel's mind and he desperately wanted his revenge. Call it an archaic way of thinking if you want, but he was taught to stand up for something you believed in, or for those you believed in. He loved Dada like a brother and he had been wronged by his death.

"Good point," Kel replied. He stuck out his hand. "Why don't you give me the remote seeing that I'll be the one most likely staying here and keeping watch. It's not going to do you any good out in the field."

It would have generally been a good idea and no one would have said anything to the contrary, but Fitz knew of the mental state Kel was in. They had all watched Dada get bitten in half by the giant black specter. It was burned into everyone's memory for the rest of their lives.

"Kel," Fitz said. "I'm not sure if you're in the right—"

"I'm not suicidal, Gray," Kel said, actually offended that the Aussie didn't trust him. "I can't kill them if I kill myself."

Fitz nodded, shrugging, giving Ares the okay. The American then handed the remote to Kel and stood.

"Fine, but don't make me regret this," Fitz said sternly. He was in command of the men when Logan was busy after all, plus, Logan would have done the same. "I want the safety cover on at all times. This is a last ditch defense only. If we blow the gates at the wrong time, we will be giving the Nach a free ticket into the Pen."

"Yes, sir," Kel said with a mock salute. "I shall only blow it the next time you walk through."

That got a grin out of Fitz.

"Only if my eyes are glowing red and I have a raging appetite for man meat—"

"Okay, then," Ares said, interrupting the jibber-jabber. He looked around, spotting his next objective. He stopped at the sight of the two massive sentry towers. It would be a perfect trap if he could set them to fall into each other.

"Those are next," he said, pointing to the structures.

"Gray?"

Fitz keyed his earbud. "Yeah, boss?"

"When you're finished trying to destroy my property," Logan replied, "could you guys come back upstairs? We may have our next move."

"Oh, yeah?" Fitz asked, looking back up to the windows above. "Like what?"

"Just...come upstairs."

Fitz laughed, knowing how his friend thought. This wasn't the first time he'd sounded like this when going over a laughably crazy plan. "That bad, huh?"

He could hear Logan laugh on the other end. "Pretty much."

Fitz shook his head. "Just like old times."

"Yep," Logan agreed, "just like old times."

"Give us," Fitz looked at his watch, "another ten minutes or so and we'll be up."

"Ten it is. Out."

"Gray?"

Fitz looked at Mo and shrugged. "No idea, mate, but I'd go check on Kipanga and gas her up." He looked out to the plains around the compound. "Logan has a plan and I'm pretty sure none of us are going to like it." He then looked over to the rotting remains of the gigantic leopard still sitting half inside the inner fencing.

Even with the bright spotlights on around the Bullpen, the darkness of the night was foreboding. It had never bothered Fitz until now. It was pretty damn obvious why though.

What made it even more unnerving, was that the illumination stopped at the fencing. It didn't reach far enough to light the plains around it. No one had their night-vision tech with them on account of the lights, and it made Fitz feel insecure about their safety. There could be a horde of them just out of sight and they wouldn't even know. Not until someone upstairs warned them that is. They still had most of their sensors and cameras active around the compound, but being out here in the night was a different feeling altogether.

He thought back to the conversation he just had with Mo, recalling what he and Mo would think of it.

"Not one bit," he said to himself, turning his attention back to Ares.

Seeing the man prep this place for its potential demolition gave Fitz a horrible premonition of things to come. He was getting a sickening feeling that this would be the last night the SDF would call this place home.

Those of us who survive that is...

* * * * *

Climbing out through the metal hatch, *Wustenfuchs* now stood on the precipice of the koppie, looking out over his army. There was easily a thousand of them. All ready...all hungry. He grinned again, he himself prepared for what was to come. Like Shetani, he could sense the presence of something foreign. It smelled wretched, but at the same time it intrigued him. The freshness of the scent was intoxicating. It reminded him of nothing he saw before him.

Living death, he thought. *They smell like death.*

They tasted like it too. He needed fresh sustenance now. He wouldn't eat the dead again. The ones he ate were the newly turned, but some of these reeked like they'd been like this for some time.

Shetani had squeezed just enough blood out of the first few, kick-starting his body's healing properties. He was unsure why or how it worked, but he guessed it had something to do with his unique blood. The green plasma flowing through his system didn't match that of the others and by the ease of how they died and didn't regenerate, he figured it was the blood that made the difference.

Go, he said aloud, instinctively knowing they'd understand. He didn't question the beasts' comprehension for his speech. He just used it for their own benefit.

The massive gathering surrounding his pedestal moved as one, heading in the direction of the undefinable feeling. Something was calling him to that place. He could faintly feel their presence below too, but they had only been there a short while. They were responsible for some of the bodies beneath his feet.

Wustenfuchs blinked away a memory—the pain intense—something stabbing into his neck. It was long ago and hard to concentrate on the visual aspect of it. But the pain... It was real.

He shook his head and blinked his four eyes, refocusing his attention on the matters at hand. He brought up his hands, inspecting his blood covered fingers. These were new—like the rest of him. But it felt normal. It didn't *feel* new.

The scent.

He sniffed the air through the twin holes that acted as nostrils and smelled something else. There was something else in the distance to the west—away from his prey. *This* particular odor was far older than even he. It was beyond the borders of this land even.

Soon.

Once the inferior were dealt with, he would go west and see to this other threat. If it's what his senses were telling him, it was the only thing that would be able to stop him. The ancientness of the smell unnerved him the most. Whatever lay to the west had been there a long, *long* time.

48

"Logan, you can't be serious!"

Normally, CJ didn't argue with her brother when it came to his job. He was the warden for a reason. He was the boss and she learned to never cross the line. Yes, they were family, but that didn't give her the right to second guess him. He was her superior too and she needed to respect him like the others did.

Logan didn't react to her outburst. He just sat back down at his desk and looked over his SCAR. He had six extra clips and another six grenades in a satchel on the floor next to his chair. He already had four flashbangs secured in the pockets around his BDU's vest, easily accessible if needed. Sitting on the desk next to his rifle, was the Desert Eagle he used earlier in the night.

He looked up to his sister. "Not now, Cass."

CJ's face went from appalled horror, to downright pissed off. She stomped over, her face grim. "You're going to kill yourself—you know that, right?"

He looked up to her once again. CJ instantly saw the look of fright in his eyes and the bags that hung under them. It deflated her attack and brought understanding as well. He *knew* he may not come back.

"Just," CJ said, her words catching in her throat. "Just...come back to us, okay?"

Logan gave her the slightest of smiles, but there was doubt etched in it too. He was confident in his abilities to stay alive, but not in the situation itself. If there was ever a time for shit to hit the fan... It would be now.

Only Jan had fully agreed with Logan's plan to go back to the bunker and seek out more information about the God Blood. They needed to find a weakness or possibly a cure of some sort. The only way to do that was to find Mengele's research—which is why Logan wanted Jan to come along. It would most definitely be in German. He would need a translator for sure.

Let's just hope the Nach have lost interest in the place and moved on, he thought. It would be a waste of a trip if they hadn't.

"Right," Logan said, standing, getting everyone's attention. "Jan, Zeus, Mo, and I are going back to the bunker in Kipanga."

Fitz began to protest, his eyes wide, but Logan cut him off with a raised hand. "You," he said to Fitz, "Kel, CJ, Adnan, and the rest of the Olympians will remain here and prepare for anything that comes. I want this place locked down tight."

Fitz backed down, but wasn't happy.

"The *only* outdoor access is to be from above. No one is to step foot outside unless it's on the roof." He then looked at everyone, surveying the room...and the emotions of the people in it. "Is that clear?"

No one spoke. No one acknowledged his orders, accepting or refusing them. Then, being the good soldier and even better friend, Fitz stood at attention. "Got it, mate. You can count on us."

Logan patted Fitz on the shoulder, resting his hand on it. He then squeezed hard, locking eyes with his dear friend. "Be careful and be smart."

Fitz smiled. "You know me... *Always Mr. Careful.*"

"Seriously, Gray," Logan said, removing his hand, "I need you to be me while I'm gone. I need you to keep everyone here alive."

That sobered up Fitz, ejecting him from his normal jovial state. "Got it, but you should take your own advice."

"Will do," Logan said, smiling. "Be back soon."

He then turned to Zeus. "Tell your men that the armory is theirs. Have them restock and reload with whatever they need. I want them as geared up as they can be."

Logan turned to leave with Jan and Zeus, but stopped when Zeus put a hand to his ear, listening. Someone was contacting him via his team's radio.

He grinned.

"What?" Logan asked, as excited as his tired body would let him be.

"Support will be here within the hour," Zeus

replied. "But we still need more information about this...outbreak."

Logan nodded, thinking.

"How many?" Jan asked, sliding into an overstuffed, explosive filled backpack. He was bringing the *real* heavy hitting equipment this time.

Destroyer, Logan thought.

"Fifty regular troops incoming from Manda Bay—with another hundred or so coming from Djibouti by morning." Zeus said, checking one of Logan's SCAR assault weapons over. He liked the GL40 grenade launcher attachment, opting for the more volatile weapon.

Morning, Logan thought. He doubted it would be quick enough. *Well, better than nothing, I guess.*

"Good enough," Logan said, looking to Mo. "Get Kipanga prepped and ready to go. We'll be up in five minutes."

Mo nodded and headed for the door—not before grabbing a Mossberg shotgun from one of the racks and a box of shells. Even though he rarely ever stepped foot on the ground during these kinds of operations, Mo *always* went prepared.

He continued forward, exiting the Observation Deck's open double doors. He'd been meaning to remove the actual doors. They were never closed to begin with.

On any other day he would either use the lift or turn right and use the stairs to go down, but today was a different day. He opted for the third choice and headed left, following the metal catwalk around another twenty feet. It dead ended at a simple metal ladder, which went straight up for fifteen more feet before coming to a hatch similar to the one above the Nazi bunker.

His clanging footsteps echoed around the immense innards of the Bullpen, reverberating off every metallic surface like gunshots. Reaching out with a hand, he hoisted himself up and started his ascent.

A few seconds later he arrived at the combination lock keypad on the underside of the metal hatch, quickly punching in his personal code. Everyone had a different combo too. It was an easy way for them to keep track of things around here. Mo didn't think it was necessary though, just Logan being ultra-paranoid with his security measures.

The hatch popped open, swinging on a hydraulic hinge. Mo climbed out and stood on the roof, closing his eyes. He focused on the breeze coming in over the building, smelling the night sky.

After his second breath he opened his eyes and looked down at his hands. They were shaking. *Calm,* he thought, mentally directing the command to them. Mo was not normally a nervous person, especially when flying, but tonight had taught him something.

Even the strongest of us can get scared.

That was apparent with Logan, Fitz, and even Jan. They were hardened from war and all three of them were openly terrified at one point or another since the sun went down.

But Mo had stayed quiet, only voicing his opinion when he thought it relevant. He didn't like this plan—

not one bit—but Logan was the undeniable leader and Mo *never* openly questioned one of his decisions. He trusted the man fully.

"You good, Mo?"

Mo quickly turned, startled by the intruder. He thought he was still alone and didn't hear anyone climb up behind him. Logan was standing in front of the hatch, dressed for combat, with Jan climbing out right behind him.

Am I good?

Mo wasn't sure what to say. He had known Logan longer than anyone here beside CJ. If he was to argue the point and voice his concerns, Logan was bound to listen.

"Fine, Logan," he heard himself say on impulse. He truly did trust Logan to the fullest and wouldn't be expressing his apprehension tonight.

"Let's just get there and get back."

Mo watched as Logan laughed, relieved that his friend was apparently levelheaded. The last thing Logan needed right now was a shaky pilot manning a helicopter.

Logan slapped Mo on the shoulder as Zeus emerged behind Jan. They were all armed to the teeth and as ready as ever to take on whatever lay before them.

"Besides," Logan said, "we'll be in the air... It's not like any of these bastards can fly."

49

Shetani fed, regaining some of his strength. His body's continued evolution had sapped him of it, leaving him weaker. He was still a dominating presence even in his frailer state, but ever since the emergence of Wustenfuchs, he had felt something odd brewing in his mind. Doubt.

Doubt was a new emotion and it wasn't the only one he had experienced lately. He felt like something was clicking in his mind as time passed. He understood things better, like it was second nature. His speech with *Wustenfuchs* developed better too, speaking aloud with less pause. It still took him a great deal of concentration to think of the right words to use, but just a few short hours earlier, he didn't even know what speech was.

Intimidation was also a feeling Shetani was unsure of. In his time awake, he had considered himself the alpha and the omega. The beginning and the end. He was the one to be feared above everything else. But now?

If it came to it, he was confident in his abilities to retake the reign, but he still had his reservations. Wustenfuchs had yet to show his true capabilities, other than hunting and killing his next meal.

Shetani's prior evaluation to his elder being a quick and lethal killer had been correct. He watched as the four-armed beast sprang on a juvenile elephant like a cat would a mouse. He leapt high into the air and landed on the animal's back, startling it.

As the full-grown pachyderm thrashed, unsure of where the attack originated, Wustenfuchs slowly and methodically crawled towards its head, gripping its flesh. Once within range, it flipped so as to face the animal, driving its original set of hands into the elephant's hide. Then, with a firm grip, *Wustenfuchs* drove its secondary arms forward, using the long talons to pierce the animal's eyes.

The claws buried deep, finding something vital, causing the five-ton creature to pitch forward, dead on its feet. It was over in seconds, taking only one precise strike. Then, he fed.

The sound of tearing flesh pulled Shetani away from his meal as he felt something on his back pulling and twisting. He tried to look back, but his bulky neck and shoulder muscles wouldn't allow it. He just calmed and waited, feeling it out. The bones on his back were still too frail to do anything with, and he expected them to turn into a second set of arms like his ancestor had.

The pain stopped and another sensation overtook his body. It was a natural one, like using his legs to walk or run. There was no thought in the natural motion. It was involuntary, like breathing.

He willed the bones to move—and they did. He willed them to fold back down to his back—and they did, but they felt heavy. They had changed again. He spread them open again, still not being able to physically see them.

It's then he saw his shadow in the moonlight. There was a section that his massive form always blotted out, but now it looked different. It was broader—more widespread.

He flexed the new growths again, watching his shadow move in unison. It made him smile. He knew what had grown.

Moving them again, Shetani created a small breeze against his back. Some of the grass on the ground around him also bent with the invisible force.

He roared into the sky, loud enough for all of Africa to tremble, and beat the bone and membrane appendages, flapping them madly until his body rose off the ground ever so slightly. He was still too weak for them to be used to their fullest potential, but soon they would be ready. He needed to feed again.

He sniffed the air, looking for his next target, finding it a half a mile away. It wasn't in the direction they were currently traveling, but it also wasn't too far out of the way, either. He was confident he could make it there and then catch up.

Shetani dug into the turf and sprang into motion. That was something he knew he had on Wustenfuchs. He was much faster than his relative when out in open space, being able to run on all fours. He could feel his oversized muscles churning the dirt underneath him, gaining momentum, pumping harder and harder with every stride.

He grinned as he neared his next meal, knowing it should be enough to fully strengthen his new form.

Shetani... Devil.

He wouldn't only call himself one.

He would truly *become* one.

50

"We'll be as quick as we can!" Logan shouted over the swirling wind. "Pull up and wait here! I want a quick EVAC if all hell breaks loose."

Mo nodded and pulled up, lifting the aircraft higher into the sky. Logan watched from atop the koppie as the spectral form of Kipanga disappeared, camouflaging itself against the blackness of night.

They had arrived a few minutes before, relieved to find the bunker and pit virtually abandoned. They had only seen a few stragglers in the vicinity, but none of them paid them any attention. They just seemed disinterested with the large metal object hovering in the sky.

Confirming once more that they were undeniably alone, Logan gave the grounds around the rock formation one last glance. He then climbed into the vertical shaft, but stopped, looking at the open hatch.

He contemplated closing it, keeping out anything that may return and smell their fresh scents. He then quickly belayed the thought. Being locked down in this place gave him a horrible feeling. As a man driven by gut-instinct, Logan left it open, and descended after the rest of his team.

The clanging of his boots on the metal ladder stopped once he again reached the solid ground of the bunker's entrance. Jan and Zeus were already further down the hall, but waited for Logan before entering the next corridor.

"Alright," Logan said softly, "let's get this over with." He then stopped behind the other men. "Jan clear left. Zeus the right."

Both men confirmed with a silent nod and did their duties, clearing each side of the hall before stepping out. Zeus had loosened up a little since Logan took command of his men. He was a true soldier and hadn't argued about anything since. The loss of so many men when they arrived made it pretty clear that they were definitely out of their element.

Not that we're bloody experts, Logan thought, stepping into the hall. He looked at the door labeled, *Waschraum,* remembering Jan's comments about the seventy-year-old shitter it contained.

"Logan?"

He turned left, barely hearing Jan's whisper, and found the man staring at the floor between him and the first door—the barracks. Logan stepped up next to him and instantly realized what had given the big man pause.

Saami and Pandu's bodies were gone.

"Bugger," Logan mumbled.

"What?" Zeus asked, joining the two SDF men. Seeing it too, he pointed forward, confused. "Weren't your men supposed to be here?"

"They *were* here," Jan replied, leveling his shotgun down the hall. "Where they are now, I have no idea."

Neither did Logan. Either they were still alive— which Logan knew was impossible. He, CJ, and Jan, had shredded the dead form of Pandu and Logan himself had finished off Saami.

The other option gave him a sickening feeling.

"We're not alone down here."

Zeus spun and aimed his weapon—one of Logan's SCAR rifles—down the way they came, covering their rears. But there was nothing, just the emptiness of the hall that had greeted them upon their arrival.

"Do we abort?" Zeus asked, still scanning the dark hallway behind them.

"We cannot," Jan replied, looking to Logan for his approval.

"Jan's right," Logan said. "This may be our only shot at finding anything useful down here. If we run into anything unfriendly, we'll take it down with extreme prejudice."

Zeus laughed. "You sound like one of the bureaucrats back home—the tightwads *not* on the battlefields fighting, making decisions from the shadows."

Logan grinned. He was starting to like Zeus more and more. He was his kind of soldier.

"Okay, Jan," Logan said, "where to first?"

Jan pointed down the hall. "I think we should try Mengele's office again and see if we can find something. We didn't really know what to look for last time."

"We still don't," Logan said.

"True," Jan said, "but at least we have a *better* idea now."

Logan stepped forward, over the slick flooring where Pandu should have been. He could see a streak of fluids continuing down the corridor out of sight. Whatever had taken them, dragged the bodies deeper into the facility. The streak disappeared around the corner.

It could be waiting for us right there, Logan thought, aiming his rifle into the communal barracks, quickly rechecking to see if it was occupied. It was possible something was in one of the rooms they already cleared, waiting to spring a trap.

He took a step through the doorway, but stopped at Jan's request.

"Don't bother," Jan said. "I doubt they would leave anything pertinent in a public place, especially around the regular troops here. It would either be in Mengele's quarters or down in the labs."

Logan nodded, agreeing with him, and stepped back into the hallway.

They moved forward, careful not to slip in the twin streaks of blood. Whatever was down here had taken Pandu first, and then Saami, dragging them both together.

Still together, even in death.

"It's the next door on the left, correct?"

"Yes," Logan said, answering Zeus. "We searched it earlier, but didn't really think to turn the room completely inside out."

Logan entered first, weapon up, finger over the trigger. He gasped at what he saw.

"You're kidding me!" He lowered his SCAR. He stepped in so the other two men could follow. Their expressions were also those of confusion.

"Um," Zeus said, unsure, "I thought you said the doctor's body was sitting in a chair?"

Logan gawked at the empty office chair. Mengele's body was gone too. He kind of understood why Saami and Pandu's were taken—or *maybe* why. If something feral was down here and it was hungry, the bodies would at least supply it with a meal. But the Nazi scientist's corpse made *zero* sense. It was all bone and ragged, dried out skin.

Logan looked down at the floor and saw something that shouldn't have been there. Tracks. They were imbedded in the dust coating the room's floor. Something had been walking in Mengele's quarters between now and the first time they were here.

They were smaller than full grown humans, maybe the size of a child, and slightly shuffled forward, dragging its feet a little.

I swear, Logan thought, *if there are a group of undead zombie preteens down here...*

"Were those there last time?" He asked Jan, pointing to the floor.

Jan looked down at his feet and stepped to the side. "They were not," he said, his German accent sounding a little menacing considering their surroundings.

"That can't be right... Right?" Zeus asked.

Logan could only shrug, unsure. It was a common thing to do right now—shrug. No one understood much of what was going on. You could only shrug your shoulders and move on.

"Either the doctor's body still held some significance," Jan said, kneeling closer to the footprints, examining the closest, "or...he's alive."

51

"You're bullshitting me, right?" Zeus asked. "You said the guy put a bullet in his own head back in the 40's. No one—and I mean *no one*—can come back from that."

Under normal circumstances Logan would have agreed wholeheartedly with the American. Very few—if any—people survived a pointblank shot to the head. Even less when they'd been sitting in a concealed bunker for more than half a century. Mengele *was* dead. But now... He wasn't sure what to believe.

"At this point," Logan said, getting Jan and Zeus' attention, "we have no idea if the good doctor is alive or not and it doesn't really matter either way. We came here for one reason," he held up a finger, "research on the God Blood."

He turned his attention to the desk. "Start tearing this room apart. Look for anything you think might help. Jan can translate if it's needed."

The three men dug in, searching every nook-and-cranny of the room. Logan dove into the other loose papers on the corner desk, while Jan went through the titles of the various books again, primarily focusing on the German titles. Zeus opened the trunk that CJ originally went through and found nothing. He then kneeled down and looked under the bed, but again, saw nothing.

"Nothing over here," Zeus said, scratching his head.

"Over here," Jan said, waving him over. "Help me with these."

Zeus complied and joined Jan over at the large bookcase. There were hundreds of them in all different sizes, crammed into the wall-sized case. Two sets of eyes would definitely help.

Finding nothing of importance *on* the desk, Logan started his search *in* it. He opened the center drawer and found pens, pencils, and a few other kinds of nonessential office supplies. He then moved on to the top drawer on the right. He would then search the bottom one.

There were a few files, but none of them looked to be anything science related. He held them out. "Jan, a moment, please?"

His friend joined him, taking the offered documents, flipping them open quickly. Jan scanned them for any keywords pertaining to research done at the facility. Seeing nothing, he quickly closed the first file, and went to drop it to the floor. But he didn't. Instead he flipped the folder open again and reread the author of the letter inside.

"Can't be..." Jan said, his voice trailing off in thought.

"What?" Logan asked.

"The letter," Jan said. "It was written by Heinrich Himmler."

"Himmler?" Logan asked shocked. "The Commander of Hitler's SS?"

Jan nodded. "But from what I read, it didn't sound like he was giving Mengele orders. Himmler was giving Mengele progress reports from Germany and from other Nazi installations abroad."

"They were working together?" Zeus asked from behind, still scanning the bookshelf.

"Could have been," Jan replied, "but there is nothing said between the two men that undeniably linked them to this place—no hard evidence."

Was Himmler a member of the Wohn Tod? Logan thought. *Geez... This just keeps getting better and better.*

As Jan started on the second folder, Logan shut the top drawer hard, feeling his frustration getting the better of himself. He then grabbed the handle of the bottom drawer, forcibly yanking it open. The heavy wood stopped abruptly, going as far as it could.

CLUNK.

Something in the drawer rolled, hitting the front of it with a loud *thud.* Logan peered inside and froze. *The hell?* That was the *last* thing he expected to see.

"What did you find?" Jan asked, having heard the sound.

Zeus joined them as Logan reached a gloved hand into the opening. He gripped the bleach-white spherical object and carefully lifted it out.

"Is that a skull?" Zeus asked.

Logan didn't know what to say. It was obviously a skull, but he had no answer to *why* it would be in a desk drawer.

"Lights," Logan said, lifting his night vision goggles from his eyes. He waited a couple seconds for the others, then clicked on his small flashlight. The skull seemed to glow in his flashlight's beam, but he knew it was just his eyes getting used to the bright light. The others followed suit, clicking on their own lights, adding to Logan's.

As careful as a surgeon, Logan turned it over, stopping when he saw the teeth. They were razor sharp and looked like an animal's, perfect for tearing flesh. Whatever this thing was, it would have had a devastating bite.

"Was it human?" Zeus asked, leaning in for a closer look.

Logan examined it again, seeing nothing besides the teeth that would say otherwise. "Looks like it," he said. "The teeth aren't right for a human being though—even if they filed them to points like some cultures are known for doing. They're way too animalistic—like a carnivore's. Man has the best of both since we are inherently omnivores."

"K-9's and molars... Got it," Zeus said.

"It's not a man," Jan said, reading a newly found file. There had been a stack of them under the skull, "at least," he looked over to Logan, "not completely."

"I don't follow," Zeus said, adding his light to the papers in Jan's hands. "What are you talking about?"

"It's all here, Logan," Jan said. "They have information on the *origin* of the God Blood—where it came from."

"Came from?" Logan asked. "It's natural?"

"Seems to be," Jan said, reading, "but Mengele also explains that they..." he paused, thinking of the right word, "*tinkered*...with it, trying to expand on it. They tried to enhance the abilities of the *Verbraucher*."

"Verbraucher?" Logan asked.

"Yes," Jan said. "It means, *Consumer.*"

"Consumer?" Logan said, eyes wide. "Unbelievable!" He looked back down to the skull with a new mindset. "It means, Eaters—as in Dead Eaters?" He turned to Jan. "You're telling me the Nachzehrer—the German folklore—were real?"

Jan didn't get to answer.

Something tackled, Zeus to the ground, trying to bite him on the muscles between his neck and shoulder.

"Fuck off!" he yelled, thrusting his combat knife into the creature's eye. It fell from the protected Kevlar vest, having nearly struck his flesh. He rolled up and drew his pistol, ready for another attack. But none came. The only thing the three men could hear was frantic hooting coming from down the hall.

In what could have been viewed as a perfectly choreographed move, they all flipped down their night vision devices, once again reducing the world around them into shades of green.

"What the hell was that?" Zeus yelled, grabbing his rifle off the bed. He had dropped it when attacked.

"Baboon," Logan replied.

It looked like any other baboon too. It didn't have any of the obvious genetic modifications that some of the others had acquired. Only the eyes—or in this one's case, eye—was red. Definitely infected.

"You okay?" Logan asked, Zeus.

"Fine," Zeus replied, voice shaky. "Got me in the shoulder strap on my vest—no skin. Got lucky."

No shit, Logan thought.

"We must leave," Jan said, shoving the procured folders into his backpack. "There are more coming."

Logan heard the hooting too and couldn't agree more. Jan could finish translating the notes back at headquarters. First, they needed to get out of here alive.

"Let's move," he said, leading Jan and Zeus to the door.

CRACK!

Something smashed against the floor just outside the office. A chunk went flying farther down the corridor, but the rest stopped at Logan's feet. It was another skull, but this one still had decomposed flesh on it. It wasn't chemically cleaned like the Verbraucher skull was.

It was Mengele's head.

Well, that solves that, Logan thought. *100% dead—*

Damn. He forgot to give Jan the skull he'd found. CJ would want to examine it closer.

He raced back to the desk and found where he set it down, grabbing it. He then returned to the doorway and unzipped Jan's bag, sliding it in. Jan turned as Logan finished, about to question him.

"A gift for my sister," he said.

Jan smiled, slightly, but it disappeared quickly as the rest of Mengele's mangled corpse landed in front of them.

The hooting arose again, but this time it came from both directions. There was an army of these things down here with them and they were coming in fast.

"Move!" Logan shouted. "Don't stop until we're topside!"

Zeus exited the room, turning right. He led the way, firing down the hall as he ran. Logan could hear bodies falling in front of the Delta man as he followed Jan out.

The skittering of feet behind Logan told him he had company coming up on their six. He spun, still moving in the correct direction and saw the incoming force. There were four of them, one on every surface of the hall.

Bloody hell.

52

Logan squeezed off two quick three-round bursts, dislodging the baboon on the ceiling. Its limp body fell, tripping up the one on the floor. Logan calmly dispatched that one with another burst. He then turned his attention to the ones on the walls. He unloaded on the one closer to him—the one on the left. Two of the three shots ripped into it, knocking it off the wall—just as the one on the right leapt straight at him.

The thing's skull exploded as Jan's Mossberg blew its head apart. He then pumped a shot into the baboon Logan had maimed, leaving the four attacking Nach dead.

BOOM!

A concussive force shook the corridor as Logan and Jan turned, seeing a fireball down at the other end of the hallway. Bodies and pieces of bodies laid strewn about everywhere, some on fire. Zeus was just standing there loading another grenade into his rifle's launching attachment like it was just another day at the office.

Which it was, Logan thought. Stuff like this was a pretty normal thing for people like them—like what he used to be. *Except the bloodthirsty horde of demon monsters trying to eat you, of course.*

Zeus shrugged when he saw the two SDF men staring at him. "Seemed like the easier way to go."

Logan agreed, but his targets had been too close to use his identical GL40 accessory. One shot was always easier than more than one.

A chorus of hoots followed the men as they reentered the bunker's short entrance tunnel. They all walked backwards facing the incoming threat, ready to unload on the bastards.

And then they came.

A dozen of the baboons poured into the opening, gnashing their teeth, snapping at each other as they vied for position. The three men opened up on them, cutting down the first wave.

Logan reloaded, quickly slapping in a new magazine as Zeus did the same. He and Jan—who wouldn't need to reload any time soon because of the specially made high-capacity drum mag—continued their assault. He had at least another ten or so slugs left. Logan hoped they'd be up the ladder by then.

Bullets flew and bodies fell. They started to clog the entry, slowing down the mass of primates. With four left, Logan shouted for Zeus to get his ass up the shaft.

Not wanting to *disappoint* him and wanting nothing better than to get the hell out of there, Zeus obliged, racing up the metal rungs.

Logan dropped another of the monkeys as Jan's shotgun ran dry. The German went to reload it, but Logan waved him off. "Forget it!" he said, putting another two rounds into the second-to-last baboon. "Get up there with Zeus and get ready to close the lid!"

Jan nodded and started his ascent, leaving Logan to fend off against the last of the Nach. It jumped high over its fallen brethren, turned, and clung to the ceiling above. It smoothly continued forward, racing on all fours like it would have on the ground. He flinched when its head turned like an owl's, rotating nearly all the way around. It then bared its right-side up teeth, snarling.

Carefully, Logan aimed between its glowing eyes, taking his shot. The bullet zipped past the thing's head as the Nach dodged, imbedding itself into the beast's thick shoulder meat. Cursing himself for missing its head, he reacquired the target once more and pulled the trigger.

Click.

He was out of ammo and there was no way for him to reload in time. He dropped the SCAR and went to draw his Desert Eagle, but the creature was too fast. It let go and spun, landing on all fours, pouncing in mid-stride, reaching for Logan's throat.

He ducked and unsheathed his Bayonet, slicing the creature along its underside. The tough skin resisted for just a second, but soon it gave way, spilling the beast's innards all over Logan's shoulder and neck as it passed overhead.

Logan gagged as the rotting mass of organs slid off his back, smearing the thing's juices all over him. He swung around to meet his undoubtedly alive foe—and just in time. It sprang up and racked its claws against his chest.

He reeled back at the strike, inwardly thanking the inventor of Kevlar for protecting him. As a result of the aggressive strike, the creature overextended itself, leaving it open to retaliation.

And Logan did just that.

He swung his arm in a long underhanded arc, driving the blade through the baboon's chin and into its brain. It's how he killed the Saami infected Nach. The creature dropped and Logan quickly picked up his empty SCAR. He'd reload it when he got to the top of the koppie. Not *ever* forgetting his knife, he reached down and yanked it out of the baboon's chin.

He then stood, spun, and stepped on the bottom rung, freezing at the sound of more scraping behind him. Another wave of the things was on their way and he had no way of killing them all.

Logan scrambled up the ladder as the hooting of the next group of baboons entered the short passage. They'd be on him in seconds. He quickly reached the top as the ladder shook. Something was climbing it behind him.

Jan went to slam the hatch shut, but they had no way of locking it from the outside. The combined strength of who knows how many of the things could push it back open with no problem.

"Zeus, on me!" The two SCAR wielding soldiers aimed their rifles down the vertical shaft and gasped. There had to be two-dozen of the baboons this time...and they were seriously pissed.

"Get ready, Jan!"

Jan stepped up behind the lid and leaned into the heavy metal, getting prepared to shove it over.

"Fire!" Logan shouted. He and the American simultaneously pulled the secondary trigger controlling their grenade launchers, immediately diving down to the next level of rock as Jan shoved the lid shut with a bang. Jan followed closely behind Logan, leaping with the grace of a hippo, covering his ears.

The blast wasn't as loud as they thought it was going to be, but the SS engraved hatch went flying into the air, followed by a plume of fire. The lid sailed into the night, landing somewhere in the burial pit.

"Mo?" Logan asked, laying on his side, covered in sweat, dirt, and gore.

"Mo, here," the pilot replied from somewhere overhead.

"We need pick-up," Logan said, sniffing his sleeve, cringing, "and a shower."

He rolled onto his back and listened as the tell-tale *whup* of the Blackhawk's rotor blades chopped through the air. He couldn't yet see it, but he knew Mo was directly overhead and descending fast. They needed to get back to HQ and prepare for what was coming. The lack of Nach around the bunker disturbed him even more than the rot sticking to his skin. If he were the enemy, he would bring the fight to their front door. They needed to be there when it happened.

He groaned, standing. "Jan, Zeus... Get ready for EVAC—we're not done."

53

"I want the second .50 mounted here," Fitz said, pointing to the northern most section of the roof. It's the same spot he had been firing from before, but with his XM25. The ledge's central location would help add to the already natural choke point of the front gate.

"Hades," Ares said, keeping watch over the gate from above, "the gun is yours." He then turned to face his teammate. "Be ready."

The plan was to wait for the incoming force to get a little closer, and lead them to the gate. Most of the frontline was made up of smaller, less menacing species, but Fitz knew they would still be a threat. Once the larger of the Nach arrived they would blow the gate, obliterating them, and hopefully confusing the rest. Hades would pour into them with the M2A1 and him his XM25.

The Aussie looked down to his feet, seeing the

boxes of explosive 25mm shells. He brought every single one he had left up from the armory around Logan's workstation—about four-dozen of the powerful little bastards. He then looked around the .50 cal and saw the boxes of ammo for it. They lugged up as many as they could spare without completely disarming the heavy machine gun in the Rhino.

It'll have to do, Fitz thought, itching his beard. He instantly decided to shave it if they got out of this mess alive.

He looked back to his left, seeing another of the Delta men setting up one of Logan's M82 sniper rifles. Logan had suggested they bring the two he had out of retirement, and set them up on the roof too. It was an extreme upgrade over Kel and Dada's cover fire from before. They would be able to take limbs off with those things, not just put holes in them. The second M82 would be set up twenty feet to the right of the machine gun.

Operation Overkill, Fitz thought. *Nothing could get through this.* His shoulders sagged. *Nothing human...* But they weren't fighting a human enemy. They were fighting something straight from the depths of Hell itself.

"Fitz, this is Mo, over."

He keyed his earbud. "Go ahead, Mo."

"We are incoming. Prepare the roof for landing in ten minutes."

"Roger that, mate," Fitz replied, watching the others clear the landing pad of boxes and loose garbage. "Any luck?"

"Some," Mo replied, "but it can wait. I'm assuming you've seen the sensors?"

"We have," he said. "We're just about done setting up here... Why?"

Fitz waited for a reply. It eventually came, but not from Mo.

"Gray, it's Logan."

"Yeah, boss?" Fitz asked, concerned with his friend's tone.

"We found some info on the Nach in Mengele's office. Jan is going through it now, but..."

The pause in Logan's voice sounded solemn, like he was defeated.

"Logan?"

"Sorry, Fitz, but it doesn't look good."

* * * * *

"What doesn't look good," Fitz asked, his comms crackling for a second.

Logan found it hard to explain what Jan had read, unsure of how to properly convey the information. "Hang on... Jan?"

Jan looked up and spoke. "The God Blood is an altered version of a natural genetic deformity from somewhere to the west—in the jungles of the Congo, I believe. The SS found it while searching for some relic for Hitler." He flipped to the next page. "Mengele heard of the news of a tribe with a feral and monstrous disposition, requesting to study the body of the one they had killed. It was the first time he had come to Africa—"

"But not the last," Fitz said, getting the point.

"Correct," Jan said, continuing. "The tribe reacted like any normal off-the-radar tribe would when conflicted with an unknown invader."

"Right," Fitz said. "They let the SS waltz in and slaughter their people." He shook his head. *Like the bloody Aztec. They had let Cortez and the Spanish march right into the heart of their kingdom and take control. Thought they were bloody gods and—*

"Not exactly..." Jan said.

"Huh?" Fitz replied, thrown off.

"The Nazi report says the *Verbraucher*—the tribe— *did,* in fact, allow them safe passage into their village, but they weren't permitted to leave."

"The indigenous people turned on the Nazis, surrounding and slaughtering eight men in a matter of seconds," Logan added, cutting in. He and Jan had quickly gone over the find before contacting Fitz back home. "They were said to instantly grow lion's teeth and eagle's talons, and they used them to decimate the soldiers' ranks before disappearing back into the jungle, taking most of the dead with them."

"Hang on, mate," Fitz said. "You're telling me the bastards could control the virus?"

"Yes," Jan replied. "But it wasn't a virus to them. Mengele's research showed that the one they killed may have been born with it. It was a natural evolutionary trait among the *Verbraucher*. They may have even *evolved* into a different species of homosapien."

"Verbraucher?" Fitz asked, hearing the name again.

"Fitz," Logan said, "it means *eaters*. The Nachzehrer are real and I think this is where the legend originated. The folklore even says you must take their head in order to kill them. Sound familiar?"

Logan looked up to Jan for confirmation. The German nodded. He was thinking the same thing.

"But I thought the legend was older than the Nazis...and German, not African?" Fitz asked.

"It is," Jan said, "but who's to say this wasn't the first time the tribe had been visited—or maybe the Verbraucher traveled across the continent and were seen by early explorers. Karl Mauch was a well-known traveler who found some ruins in Zimbabwe in the 1870's. Who's to say he himself didn't run into the tribe. We don't know how far their territory reached back then—or if it even still exists today. Plus, Mauch reportedly *fell* from a balcony and died. Some say it was an accident, but what if he saw something that haunted him until the day he jumped?" Jan breathed. "Does it honestly matter?"

Logan agreed. It didn't matter how the legend of the Nachzehrer was started. What really mattered was that it was real and had been altered.

And it was spreading.

If he had been Mauch and not a soldier accustomed to death, he may have done the same and ended it before it drove him mad.

PTSD be damned, he thought, looking out the window of the Blackhawk. *These nightmares are going to be much worse.*

54

"Good God, Logan! You smell like a shithouse!"

Logan laughed as CJ approached, helping him from the rear of Kipanga. They had just set down and were now unloading, getting ready for the next phase... The attack and hopeful defense of the SDF headquarters.

"Thanks, Cass," Logan said. "You wouldn't happen to have a wet nap handy, would you?"

She grinned.

Logan knew if it were her covered in the fluids of a Nach, she'd get ripped for it too. It was not only their personal relationship, but that of former military. Joking around was an easy way to break the nervous tension before, or in this case after, a battle.

She led him to the stairwell hatch on the roof, but he stopped and turned, surveying the current set up. He saw three of the Olympian Delta team members manning weapons—his two sniper rifles and the second of the .50 caliber machine guns they had on hand.

He watched as Fitz finished a conversation with Ares. Then, his friend turned and made his way over to him and CJ a grim look on his face. Logan wasn't sure what upset Fitz since they couldn't hear any of the exchange between the two men over the noise of Kipanga winding down.

"What's wrong?" Logan asked, concerned.

Fitz stopped. "You smell like zombie dung. We could smell you from over there. I told Ares I needed to come over here and get the hose."

Logan looked over and saw Ares smiling just before he turned around to man his post. Seems that Fitz was definitely helping the newcomers fit in. He had a way of loosening up even the most uptight people—like a group of highly-skilled no-nonsense soldiers.

"Thanks," Logan said, trying to scrape off what looked like a piece of skin with black fur.

"The hell is that?" Fitz asked, his nose turned up in disgust.

"Baboon, I think," Logan replied, peeling off the sliver of flesh. He then quickly flung it at Fitz and watched the man lunge to the side, barely avoiding the flap.

He turned and headed for the stairs, but not before seeing a look of hate coming from Fitz. "Try that shit again," Fitz said, doing his best not to laugh, "and I will end your stanky ass."

Logan climbed into the hatch. "Speaking of stank," he said, "I need a shower. I'll be out in ten. If something happens, come get me, will you?"

Fitz's eyes narrowed, but CJ cut in before Fitz had a chance to sling his empty threats again. "I'll come find you, brother. Go and wash up. You're seriously making my hair go white right now."

He smiled slightly and clopped down the ladder back into the relative safety of the Bullpen. Kel had taken care of the dead mongoose while they were gone and CJ temporarily moved in with Jan now that their relationship was out in the open. Her room was a biohazard for now. No one wanted to be in there and Logan didn't want anyone inside it—let alone his sister of all people.

As soon as his boots hit the catwalk of the second floor, someone came banging up behind him. He turned and found Adnan who looked like he saw a ghost.

"What?" Logan asked, instantly knowing he wasn't getting his rinse. Adnan was one of the few who hadn't been out in the fray of things. He'd kept himself fairly composed throughout the entire incident so far. He, like Logan, always kept himself busy, never giving himself time to reflect on the things happening around him.

"The Nach," he said. "They are headed this way."

"I know, but how many—"

"All of them," Adnan quickly said.

"All of them?" Logan asked.

"Yes," Adnan replied. "There must be over a thousand of the creatures coming straight here. He looked down at his watch. "At their current pace, they'll be here in thirty minutes."

Yep, Logan thought, *definitely no shower.*

He skirted around Adnan and entered the command center, stripping his armor and most of his clothes along the way. He grabbed a fresh set from a row of hangers behind his desk. There was always a spare set handy. Just in case.

Be prepared...

"What are we going do?" Adnan asked, following him. "How can we stop that many?"

Logan paused and looked up to Adnan, his eyes giving away his feelings. Logan had no idea what to do. "We fight and hold out as long as we can until the next wave from Manda Bay gets here."

"Lock down?" Adnan asked.

Logan stood, shirt in hand, weary of the question.

Lock Down, was a failsafe that was discussed as a last resort act if an enemy large enough ever presented itself.

This counts.

He rubbed his forehead, but answered quickly.

"Yes," he said. "Lock us down tight. Let everyone know to get downstairs ASAP. I want only essential personal topside when the Nach arrive."

"Cassidy?"

Logan paused again, about to slip the clean shirt over his head. CJ would not hear of hiding from the incoming threat, but Logan knew she'd get herself killed if she stayed.

"Kicking and screaming, Adnan. She does not stay here."

Adnan nodded. He would respect Logan's wishes and make sure his sister was safe.

Logan watched as Adnan walked away, thinking to himself. Everyone had that look. The internal battle was definitely raging in the software engineer's head.

Two sets of feet came up quickly from behind Logan. By the sounds of the short, quick strides and the slower, heavier strides, Logan knew it was Fitz and Jan.

He slid his shirt on, but not before giving his chest hair a quick baby wipe bath, and dousing himself in a fresh coat of cologne and deodorant. He had to mask the scent coming from his body any way he could. His headache was raging now and the smell was aggravating it further. The last thing he needed was full-blown migraine right now.

They both came around the corner quickly, standing before Logan in all his half naked glory. Each man looked utterly exhausted like how he felt now, but neither man complained. They had all been through hell before, at one time or another... But not like this.

"We just heard," Fitz said, all business. "What's the call?"

"Lock Down," Logan simply said, stepping into a fresh pair of pants.

"Damnit," Fitz said under his breath. It was their worst and last case scenario.

"You sure?" he asked.

Logan nodded. "If it gets to a certain point, we'll need to take action on a larger scale. Bullets only do so much damage against an army this size."

No one agreed with the ultimate result of *Lock Down*, but in this instance, it may be the only viable way to stop the Nach. If they could get the concentration of them near or at least around the compound, then it was possible, but it would be Logan's call. He would have to press the proverbial—and in this case—literal button.

"Jan," Logan said, "get *everyone* downstairs that doesn't need to be here." He emphasized "everyone," making sure he understood that he primarily meant CJ.

He got it.

"Logan," Fitz said, "Jan found out something else about the Nach you should hear."

Eyebrow raised, Logan waited for Jan to begin.

"I may have a way of stopping them, without obliterating the Bullpen and everything in it."

"Tell me," Logan said, desperately needing a little good news.

"The Nach—they are ultrasensitive to light, yes? But I thought it was just a sensitivity based on what we've seen—their extreme nocturnal nature, I mean," he waved to the outer windows, "like now."

"Okay?" Logan said, unsure of where this was going.

"Mengele's notes went on to explain a side effect of the blood in the Nach. Remember the veins—how we could see them just under the skin on some of the creatures?"

Logan nodded, recalling the red pulsating veins on the rhinoceroses' and Irwin's bodies. The rest of the animals had fur covering them, but Logan had no reason not to believe they also weren't present on those species too.

"What about them?" Logan asked.

"The light sensitivity is their downfall. It messes with their blood on a biochemical scale. For whatever reason, direct light can literally fry them. The can burn to death from the inside out."

"It's why the flashbangs hurt them so badly," Fitz added. "We just need a steadier source of illumination. The flashbangs are too short and sweet for it to kill them."

"What of the fur?" Logan asked. "Does it protect them from the light?"

Jan's face fell a little. "I'm afraid it doesn't say."

Damn, Logan thought. *Let's hope it still works.*

Either way, he perked up at hearing the news. There was a way to actually kill them without the use of their quickly diminishing firepower. Even the *ever prepared* Logan Reed didn't have *that* much ammo on hand. They'd need more than just bullets and explosions. They needed—

Logan looked down at his watch, but realized he took it off to change. "What time is it?"

Fitz and Jan both looked down at their own watches and said together, "Five o'clock."

Logan slipped on another pair of socks, followed by his boots. He then started to put his other Kevlar vest on, but Fitz stopped him.

"Why?"

Logan looked up. "We need to delay them anyway

we can. In an hour, all our troubles will disappear... Literally"

"What happens in an hour?" Fitz asked.

Jan whispered something in German, most likely a curse, but the look on his face told Logan he understood. "The sun, Gray." He smiled. "The sun will begin to rise in one hour."

55

"The sun? That's your plan? You want to use the sun to overheat the enemy."

Logan could hear the disbelief in Zeus' voice, *but* he didn't argue against it. He may not fully believe that the ultraviolent rays of the sun could do such damage, but again, he didn't dispute the notion.

"Yes," Logan said. "We have two courses of action left. We can either hunker down in the basement beneath the garage, and light this place up with enough packed explosives to turn it into one of the moon's craters..." He paused to breathe. "*Or* we can stand and fight. I for one, would like to save this place. It stands for a lot more than just our home. It's a beacon of hope to those who believe in our cause."

Everyone was gathered around Logan's desk now, minus the men manning the rooftop defenses. They were listening in over the communications set up between both teams, though. Logan wanted everyone accounted for during the conversation. Their safety was on the line and Logan wanted any and all opinions. Ares was also present, having given up his place behind the .50 cal. He elected to be in the thick-of-it with the rest of the team—SDF and Delta working together against humanity's greatest enemy.

What could be mankind's last stand would happen here, in the middle of nowhere, in southern Africa. Not in New York or Washington D.C. Not in London or Moscow or Tokyo—but in the Serengeti. If they didn't defeat the Nach, it would spread, consuming the continent, killing millions. Then, once Africa was decimated, it wouldn't take much for one or two of them to make it across the water into Europe and Asia. The Americas were truly the only land that *might* survive the devastation, but more than half the world's population would be gone, turned into death itself.

"We fight," Zeus said. "Plain and simple. It's what we do—it's what you *used* to do."

"I'm in," Fitz said, stepping forward even though he didn't have to say a word. Logan knew his friend would be by his side until the end. "You think we can make it thirty minutes?"

"We'll have too," Logan said, not overly believing his own words. "Regardless, if we do nothing, we lose. We might as well try and stomp this bugger out before it comes to that conclusion."

Turning to CJ and Adnan, Logan spoke. "You two, however, are *not* going to be here for this."

Adnan's look was one of relief, but CJ looked

pissed. "Don't even—"

"Cassidy!" Logan shouted, emotionally spent. The last thing he needed was for her to argue with him. "I need you and Adnan to wait for us downstairs. We need to keep a line of communication open with the Americans. You are the only two that can do that."

"He can," CJ said, defiantly, "but I'm coming."

"If we all die, you're willing to leave him alone down there? Could you live with that? Because I sure as hell couldn't. Under any other circumstance I wouldn't argue this, but this is not one of those times."

She was cut off before she could give her two cents. "Please, CJ," Adnan said, pushing his thick glasses up, glancing at Logan. He realized this is what Logan *wanted* him to do when he asked him to make sure she stayed safe. "I may be a lot of things, but a fighter is not one of them. Plus, I could really use the help with the camera feeds too."

Logan watched as she looked to Adnan who was half-acting and half-serious. He doubted the man actually needed help with any of it. He helped design the damn system after all. Adnan was just doing what he had asked of him. Soon it would be Jan's turn.

Logan needed to end this before it got out of hand. "Consider it an order."

He could actually see her skin redden, before she stormed out of the room, fuming. Not a second after she left did Jan follow her. His job was to appeal to her emotionally.

It'll work, he thought, turning back to the others.

"Okay," Logan said, calming a little, "Mo, Jan and I

are in the Rhino like before, except I'll be in the back
with him this time." He then turned to Kel, Zeus, and
Ares. "You three are in the Wraith. We do like before
and draw off the Nach. Then, we let the boys upstairs
rain down their own personal brand of hellfire."

Everyone nodded. Mo was their best pilot/driver,
but Kel was the second best, having logged more time
on the Wraith than anyone else besides Mo. It was the
best options they had. If things went south—which
they most certainly would—they'd haul ass back to the
Bullpen and join CJ and Adnan in the basement. They
had plenty of supplies and layer after layer of concrete
and steel over their heads. Their own personal bomb
shelter. If the situation got severely out of control,
then Logan would blow the compound, taking
everything within the perimeter fencing—and then
some—with it.

Lock Down, Logan thought, dreading even the idea
of it let alone the act.

"Shall we..." Logan nodded at Fitz who stuck out his
hand. "It's been a pleasure, Captain."

Logan shook the outstretched hand, pulling his
friend in close. The two embraced in a hearty hug,
unashamed of their affection for each other. CJ was
biologically his sister, but Fitz was his family too—his
best friend.

Logan let go and looked at everyone else. He heard
footsteps behind him and found Jan and CJ reentering
the room. Her eyes were red from crying again, but
there was no malice in them. Only sorrow.

She marched over to him and threw herself into his

arms. The Reeds held each other, squeezing the life out of one another.

"Come back to me, Logan."

Logan squeezed back, harder. "I always do."

He stepped back, a tear running down his face. There had been a few moments in his life where he questioned whether or not he'd come home, mostly in the army, and once in SDF, but none of them involved his sister. The thought of losing her was more than he could handle.

Logan turned, gaining some of his composure, not having to see CJ's tear streaked face anymore. "Mount up and move out. Let's show these bastards who the fuck they're dealing with."

56

The Rhino roared to life once more. Mo floored the accelerator, spinning the tires a little as they peeled out of the garage. They turned, taking the same route as before, but this time no one was in the sentry tower giving them the customary thumbs up. It was empty and gave Logan a terrible foreboding feeling. They would surely lose more men.

The wind whipped through his hair as he stood in the open rear of the Hummer. Jan's seat was gone, giving him the ability to swing the M2A1 heavy machine gun in a full three-sixty. Logan would be dodging the red hot barrel, coordinating with the German so he wouldn't get burned...or shot.

A higher pitched purr echoed off the concrete surroundings as the Wraith, piloted by Kel, closely followed its larger brother. They would stay together for as long as they could, giving each other support.

The real danger came from Fitz.

He would direct them from above like an Offensive Coordinator would his football team. When Fitz saw a pattern he wanted to exploit, he would quickly tell Mo or Kel where to go. Then, he'd unleash what he called the *Power of God*.

Steering around the northwest tower, Logan watched the eastern horizon as they moved, impatiently waiting for just the slightest of evidence that the sunrise was near. But there was nothing. Not yet, anyways. They would have to wait a little bit longer.

"Everyone ready?" Logan asked. Everyone quickly confirmed and they sped off towards the front gate.

BOOM!

A massive form landed inside the compound, crushing the concrete below its girth. It was easily ten feet tall and who knows how heavy. Its six eyes were menacing and its jet black hairless skin covered in glowing veins was petrifying. But the wings...

"What is that?" One man yelled from above. The fear was evident in his jittering voice.

"Reed?" he heard Zeus ask.

"Oh, my God," Mo said from inside the Rhino. "It is the Devil... *Shetani.*"

Logan had no doubt this thing could have been Satan himself. Its black talons and teeth were a dead giveaway—along with its humanoid shape.

"Our missing poacher." It was a match to what attacked them next to the pit, but much larger, having some other nifty upgrades too.

Mo slammed on the brakes and threw the truck into reverse.

"Fire!" Logan yelled.

Then everything happened in slow motion. Jan got off a few rounds, as did everyone else. The monster flexed its massive legs and leapt into the sky, taking a large portion of the bullets in its chest and stomach areas. It flapped its large bat-like wings hard and shot up into the darkness above. More gunfire erupted as the rooftop team added their own fire power to Logan and the rest of the assault team.

Shetani, as Mo called it, was raked with barrage after barrage as it climbed higher into the night. They would soon lose sight of it and it would be able to again surprise them.

"Fitz!" Logan looked up as he yelled, watching a fireball of orange and red erupt on the demon's chest. It flailed from the impact, but quickly regained some of its in-air equilibrium. The second .50 cal roared to life too, joining in the constant sniper rifle fire. They didn't do the same type of damage as Fitz, but at least they were hitting the bastard.

Then, it angled *towards* the roof.

"Incoming!" Logan shouted, watching the winged Nach, land on the circular roof of the Bullpen. His men—Fitz—were done for.

* * * * *

"Move!" Fitz shouted. The creature landed with a crunch, cracking the concrete floor of the roof.

"Scatter!" he yelled, over the ear-shattering noise. He and the three Delta men quickly abandoned their posts, running in separate directions.

It turned and swiped one of its horrible clawed hands at the nearest man, catching him in the back. The man was flung from the roof like a rag doll, screaming the entire way down.

Fitz didn't need to watch the man land to know he was dead. *One down and three to go,* he thought as the beast turned towards him.

As soon as it looked at him Fitz fired another round. It hit the Nach's shoulder, detonating on impact, stumbling the thing only a little backwards.

The kick of the XM25 being fired from the hip threw off his aim as he tried to let loose another round. He quickly shouldered the weapon and went to reacquire it, but it was gone.

The hell?

"Roll right!"

Fitz did as instructed and threw himself into a less than graceful roll—just as the monster landed where he'd been standing. He quickly got to his feet and ran. Hades and the other Delta man, raked it with round after round, most of them barely missing Fitz as he sprinted forward.

He was about to turn and help—when he saw both men's eyes go wide. Instinctively, Fitz dove to the roof, sliding forward on his chest. A huge set of claws shot forward, impaling one of the men through his chest. Fitz continued sliding, passing right between the man's legs as he was lifted off the ground.

There was nothing Fitz could do for him except survive and avenge him. So, he jumped into the open hatch of the roof access, reached out, catching one of the metal rungs halfway down the ladder. He looked up as he dangled, his left shoulder protesting from the stress. The weight of his XM25 almost pulled him free, yanking on his other shoulder.

"Run!"

Fitz caught a glimpse of the last man, Hades, get yanked from the opening. His screams followed, but were cut off by a wet gurgling sound.

There was nothing he could do. Fitz needed to regroup and reload. *Damnit,* he thought racing down the ladder. All of his XM25 ammo was still on the roof and he was out. He needed another plan.

The thing roared, making Fitz fall the last couple of steps. He landed hard on his back with an audible *oof.* He looked straight up and saw the worst thing yet. Six demonic glowing eyes looked down at him with what felt like all the hate the world had to offer. He scurried back on all fours, scared out of his mind.

Then, the beast reached a clawed hand in after Fitz, its weight cracking the roof around the rim of the opening with its heavy body. The *'Devil of the Serengeti'* was forcing its way inside, forcing its way to Fitz. This was the first time Fitz had ever pissed himself, and if this thing got a hold of him...it would be the last.

Standing, he was about to flee down the stairs, but he saw something that gave him hope. He dashed into the Observation Deck, ditching his empty grenade launcher on the floor. The rear section of one of the weapons racks held what he needed. He grabbed the already prepped satchel and a shotgun from the rack next to it, formulating the dumbest, most idiotic plan of his life as he went.

Bolting for the doorway, Fitz looked up and saw that the creature was halfway in, getting stuck around its hips and wings. He turned and pounded down the stairs, passing the living quarters, rounding the catwalk at a speed he never thought possible—especially in his current condition. The chances of it paying off were slim to none, but Fitz could guarantee one thing... Staying put would all but guarantee it.

Not a chance, he thought, waving his hand overhead. *I'm going to kick the shit out of this thing and then kill its kids and grandmother too!*

"Come on you steroid-induced jackoff—follow me! Come get the bath of a lifetime!"

57

Jan watched as Mo barely had time to stop the Rhino before Logan leapt out of its bed, dashing back towards the garage. He was no doubt going to try and help Fitz and the others.

If they're still alive.

Unfortunately, from the sounds of the initial destruction and of the resulting screams, Jan guessed that the beast may have slaughtered everyone.

Probably trying to force its way in through the roof access.

He was about to ask what to do next but—

"Same plan as before," Jan heard Logan say in his ear. He was panting, still running at a sprint. "Do what you can to protect this building. I'll be back as soon I as can."

Okay, Jan thought, turning and getting a glimpse of Logan rounding the rear of the building, closing in on the south entrance.

"Move out," Jan said, "and—"

He was cut off giving orders to the remaining team—when the front gate exploded from its hinges. It was thrown thirty feet, landing with a bang, sliding and stopping inbetween the sentry tower structures.

"Um..." Jan had nothing to say—no feelings to express. Another monster entered the compound, this one more menacing than even the living devil from before. It stood at least twelve feet tall, but was built like an insect. Lean, but no doubt strong muscles rippled through it.

"Damn, damn, damn," Ares said, shifting in one of the Wraith's sidecars. "Looks like a bug from Mars or something!"

Jan agreed with the apt description, but he also knew without the shadow of a doubt, that a bug from Mars wouldn't be this bad.

The first thing everyone saw was the four arms tipped with talons the size of Mick Dundee's bowie knife. The arms themselves all had what looked to be razor sharp spines running down the inside, like a praying mantis.

Its body was humanoid in build, but elongated like an insect's, or like your typical Hollywood grey alien.

But the face is what gave Jan the biggest start. It was so horrifying that he couldn't look away. The four eyes didn't blink. They just stared like a shark's, sizing up its prey. The color was another thing altogether. Its eyes—and its visible veins—glowed a fluorescent green. It's like the fiend had some kind of toxic chemical flowing through its body.

It stepped into the illumination of the overhead floodlights and showed its oddest trait. Its skin was completely translucent, revealing its bones and organs like a fish tank would fish. Jan watched the thing's massive heart pump and its stomach flex, no doubt digesting its most recent meal.

The creature stretched its long arms out to its side, hooking its talons, ready to strike.

Arms... Four arms? He remembered where he'd seen it before. *No!*

"It's the Verbraucher from the bunker!" Jan said, shouting his dismay. "It's alive!"

The monster turned to Jan, tilting its head to the side like it was internally processing the words he had just spoken.

Then, *it* talked back.

"*No...*" it said audibly, "*not...Verbraucher... Wustenfuchs.*"

Jan's face went white. Not only did it speak back to him, but it spoke in German, calling itself, *Wustenfuchs.*

Wustenfuchs? The only reason it would call itself that is if it knew of Rommel or—Jan retched over the side of the Rhino at the *real* implications. It didn't know about the general. It *was* the general.

Jan wiped his face with his sleeve, and spoke. "*Guten morgen, Generalfeldmarschall.*" Jan said, wishing the creature good morning.

"It can't be..." Ares said. "That...can't be."

"It is," Jan said. "It is General Rommel."

"Wustenfuchs," Ares said, repeating the name. "My grandfather is from Germany and I picked up on some of the language. He had fought *against* the Nazi's, helping German Jews escape Hitler's wrath. Everyone knows who the *Desert Fox* was."

Is, Jan thought. *Who he still is.*

Jan stomped on the bed yelling, "Fire!"

Mo floored the Rhino, straight at the monster that was once the Nazi's greatest champion, never wavering in his aim. He was intent on ramming the beast, plowing him back into the razor wired topped fencing. Jan depressed the trigger sending wave after wave of .50 caliber ammunition into the creature's chest.

They were only ten feet away when the general leapt into the air, avoiding the collision. As it passed over head, one of Wustenfuchs' wounds dripped the luminescent blood onto Jan's shoulder, causing his clothes to steam.

Acid, Jan thought, desperately trying to shake out of his BDU's upper, but the Kevlar vest strapped tightly to his body made that feat impossible.

He screamed as the fluid made contact with his skin, eating away at the top layers of his left shoulder, melting away some of the muscle. Before he passed out, the pain ebbed some, releasing him from the torment.

Trying to look down, but having no time, he heard the beast shriek. He looked up and watched as Wustenfuchs spread its fifteen-foot-plus wingspan again. If the arms were frills, it would have looked like the spitting dinosaur from Jurassic Park. It even bent forward like one of the raptors from the movie, about to charge.

Mo spun the vehicle to a sliding stop, allowing Jan to reacquire it with the machine gun. His shoulder cried in agony, and the smell of his own roasted flesh caused him to gag back another round of vomit. He instead used the pain as fuel to his already adrenaline spiked nerves. He gave his own battle cry and crammed down the trigger, releasing another destructive salvo.

It bit hard, punching into the four armed behemoth. Wustenfuchs staggered back and prepared to jump again, but the Wraith came flying into view, opening up with its own barrage of gunfire. Zeus and Ares poured on the assault aiming for its legs, causing the thing to stumble again.

"Get it close to the towers and I'll blow them!" Kel yelled, holding up the detonator in one hand.

No one argued against it, never letting up.

Wustenfuchs stepped back under the steady stream of bullets, closing in on the trap.

Now within range, Kel held up the remote and thumbed the first of two buttons—the second being attached to the gate posts. The explosion rocked the compound hard, throwing Jan and the Americans from their stations. The only ones not affected, was Kel who was holding onto the handle bars of the modified four-wheeler, and Mo, who was safely inside the armored truck.

Jan rolled to his feet and looked for the creature,

but didn't see it. He then heard a resounding crunch as it landed back towards the empty gate, almost being thrown clear through the ravaged opening.

Kel sputtered a curse and Jan saw why.

One of the Nach's talons, ripped off by the explosion, was lodged in Kel's chest, protruding through his back. The man was calmly sitting, hands on the crossbar, slowly dying. With a peaceful smile, he looked to Jan, whispering the words, "For Dada."

Jan nodded and watched as Kel gingerly turned the Wraith around, and sped off into what would finally be his revenge. He let out a gurgled cry as he approached the mortally injured Wustenfuchs. Then, Kel and the creature were gone, replaced by another ball of light and a thunder clap.

Jan was thrown against the rear of the truck. He bashed his head, against the bed's door, blacking out.

58

As soon as Logan entered the garage he could hear all hell breaking loose outside. There was no doubt that his team was engaging some sort of hostile force. It sounded extremely close too.

Did they even make it outside the gates?

Leaving the others was a move he'd normally be against, but the enemy was trying to make its way inside. It was exactly what they were trying to avoid. It's why they were going back out into the thick of it to begin with.

He slung open the door to the stairs and took them two at a time, quickly ascending the two flights. Then, slowly, he cracked open the door leading into the second floor and heard the roar. It sounded like a bear, but was as loud as a freight train whistle, reverberating through his head.

"Fitz," Logan said quietly, "you read me?"

No answer.

With a bang and a crunch, a section of the roof caved in, followed by the demon from outside. Logan dove behind a small wall that separated the entry walkway attached to the stairs from the second floor catwalk.

Generally, he wouldn't have hidden, but fighting this giant by himself wasn't an option.

"Damnit, Gray," Logan whispered again. "Where are you?"

His ear bud crackled to life.

"Be out in a second, mate. I'm going for a shower."

Shower?

But then Logan saw the beast whirl around, almost finding him. He could hear it sniffing, testing the air. Logan was still caked in grime and dried out Nach guts, but also had on easily recognizable fragrances. Only a human wore cologne and deodorant after all.

He went to stand, readying his only grenade, but heard a clanging of metal on metal emanating from inside the bathrooms. Gray had said he was taking a shower, so Logan assumed he was hiding in them. But the clanging was coming from there? Fitz was baiting the beast to enter.

Why? Logan thought. *Did he have a plan?*

"Come on you bastard!" a voice yelled. "I just dropped the soap and am open for business!"

Logan raised an eyebrow. While Fitz's humor was usually a relief for most, right now, it was a little uncalled for and downright confusing considering the circumstances.

Peeking out again, he watched the large, winged Nach sniff the air. Its six hellish red eyes settled on the direction of the bathrooms and it leapt, straight at the wall between. Behind it was the showers and presumably Fitz.

It landed on the catwalk hard, causing the sturdy metal to groan in protest under the monster's considerable weight. Then, it struck the wall with its meaty fists. One after the other, it struck the concrete and steel partition, quickly cracking and destroying it. Logan didn't even think a grenade could get through it if he had tried.

He looked down at the SCAR, deciding if now was as good a time to use it, but Fitz told him otherwise.

"Logan, you may want to get to cover and shut your peepers in about ten seconds. I have your pack in here with me."

"My pack?" Logan said to himself. Then, realization dawned on him. He had packed a satchel *full* of flashbangs which he took on the last trip in Kipanga. They didn't need them, however, and he never put them away. Fitz had ten of them and obviously planned on doing something big with them.

Logan searched for a place to hole up. He had no idea what would happen if someone set off ten of those things at once in such a small space. Whoever—or whatever—would be guaranteed to be blinded forever. The flash would be like looking into the sun while having your night vision on.

The only place he could get to in time without being detected, was back into the stairwell. The door would offer him some relief from the cannon blast of light they were about to experience.

He pushed through the door just as the monster smashed its way through the wall, fully entering the showers.

I hope you know what you're doing, Gray.

* * * * *

"I hope you know what you're doing, mate," Fitz said to himself as he watched the creature obliterate the wall between him and it. It kicked at the remaining pieces, sending chunks of concrete flying into the tiled room almost hitting Fitz where he stood.

He needed the thing to see him and attack before what he was about to do worked.

If it works, he thought, watching from the center of the room.

He stood knee deep in one of the boiling hot Jacuzzi tubs. Normally, he would have enjoyed a quick dip, soaking his beat body while reading a Bishop novel. They were his favorite. He especially loved the perky no-nonsense Raven chick. She was a sassy thing, Fitz's type.

He and the monster made eye contact, causing it to sneer. Fitz did his best not to piss himself again, but since he was severely dehydrated he knew it wasn't possible. Even the excessive heat in the bathroom was causing his eyes to dance and his brain to swim.

He shook his head and got ready, clearing his blurring vision some.

Then, the devil attacked, lunging headlong. He came to an abrupt stop, hitting the ceiling.

It was the delay Fitz needed to do what he planned.

He hefted the duct tape wrapped ten-pack of flashbangs and yanked a zip tie he had attached to all ten pins. They sprang into the air in unison as he lobbed the light bomb straight at the bastard's head.

With the form of a drunk party guest, Fitz jumped, cannonballing into the churning waters of the hot tub. He hoped the water would muffle the light and sound.

As soon as his knees hit the bottom, he curled into a ball and blew the air from his lungs. Then, he got punched in the stomach by an unseen force. The flash wasn't too bad for him, but he was guessing it must have been for the beast. He could hear its cries, even from under the agitated water.

With little time to waste, and no air, Fitz pushed off from the bottom of the tub, climbing out. He grabbed his Mossberg from under a large pile of towels. He wasn't sure if it would identify the weapon, so he decided to play it safe and hide it.

The giant writhed in agony, bashing into anything it could, swiping at whatever it could find. Its six eyes were black and smoldered like lit coals. There was no way this thing could see.

Can probably still smell me though.

Cautiously, Fitz edged the left hand wall and fled down the main entrance of the bathrooms, passing the sinks, mirrors, and stalls, readying himself to initiate *phase two* of his plan.

It's time to light this bastard up.

59

Logan was about to charge out of the stairwell rifle up, ready to engage the monster, but the disheveled forms of Jan, Mo, Zeus, and Ares arrived halting his attack. They had all retreated to the garage, rolling down the door, and locking it. Once the front gate was gone, they had no choice but to fall back and regroup. Plus, their main fire power was down. The roof team had been wiped out.

Except Fitz.

Logan watched as Jan, who was dazed and badly wounded, brought up the rear, dragging himself up by nothing but pure will. He was worse off than all of them now, having lost a considerable amount of blood from his shoulder wound. Zeus had looked it over and compared it to a bad chemical burn. It would hurt like a bitch for a while, but it wouldn't kill him.

"Jan," Logan said, "fall back to the basement and

wait it out with CJ and Adnan. They can look after that injury better than we can."

The German was about to argue, but he nearly doubled over in pain. He relented and nodded his head in agreement. He then slowly limped back down the stairs. The hatch to the basement was in a false closet. It only contained a ladder that descended three stories. Jan would need to take his time and grit his teeth, but Logan knew he'd make it.

"Okay," Logan said to Mo, Zeus, Ares, and...

"Where's Kel?"

Mo just looked to the ground and shook his head. "He got his revenge."

Biting his lip, Logan breathed in and out, slowing his pulse.

Another man down.

"Let's move."

He flung open the door and spied a bottle flying through the air. It struck the beast and burst into flames, coating the thing in the flammable alcohol. The fire quickly enveloped the creature, causing it to roar.

Logan saw Fitz behind the bar about to light another Molotov cocktail. He smiled at the man's ingenuity. First the flash bomb, now this. Fitz was truly a fighter who thought on his feet.

The four men stepped in and let loose with a staccato of gunfire. It echoed horribly through the round room, bouncing off the concrete walls and steel catwalks.

No wonder we don't allow gunfire in here, Logan thought. The real reason was safety, but the way the room amplified the sound was excruciating.

Fitz paused from lighting his next fire bomb and joined in on the assault, but the Nach was far from overwhelmed. It leapt into the air, buffeting them with a strong gale of wind, knocking them to the ground. The pause in the men's attack was all it needed to recover.

Though blinded by the light of the massive flashbang, it still had its other senses—primarily scent. Its ears were probably shot from the concussion too. At least Logan *hoped* it affected the monster's hearing like any other living thing.

"Split up!" Logan yelled, running right, towards Fitz. As he ran, his friend unloaded a couple of slugs into the creature's torso, before ducking and leaping away from a wing as it spun to meet his advance.

Logan followed suit, rolling, feeling the membrane of the bat wing drag across his back. If it had been one of its foot long claws he may have been cut in half. Either way, it threw off his maneuver and caused him to roll towards the edge of the catwalk.

Unable to stop his forward momentum, Logan banged into the railing and flipped over it. He reached out and grabbed the middle bar as he fell, halting the plunge beneath the elevator's platform.

Ugh, he thought, feeling what had to be a broken rib. The metal rail was the final bump his body needed for something to finally give. Fitz's hands appeared a moment later as he started dragging Logan back over the rail.

The brutish Nach turned towards them, hearing

Logan's body clang off the metal. It stepped forward tilting its head back and forth like a dog would. Then, it sniffed, finding the two men immediately, looking blindly at them.

It raised one of its large hands, preparing to strike. They would die together if it connected. Logan knew Fitz wouldn't let go, and he knew if the roles were reversed, he would've done the same too. It would've been like condemning your brother to death. Neither man would be the one to do it.

The blow never came though. The monster paused at the sounds of gunfire, twitching as the rounds found its back. The shotgun booms echoed around the room and Logan knew they connected with something vital because the giant flailed and turned, meeting the more dangerous enemy head on.

Mo was halfway up the stairs between the second and third levels, firing from a higher position, shotgun in hand. He was the one apparently causing the most damage.

"Go," he yelled at the Americans, but pointing to Logan and Fitz. "Help them!"

Mo then turned his attention back to the demon. "Shetani! Follow me you devil!"

The Nach stopped mid-roar at the word. Logan wasn't sure if it understood the name. He really didn't care about anything right now, other than surviving, and it was the break they needed. Zeus and Ares came to his rescue, helping Fitz haul him up and over the rail. He crumpled on top of the three men in a pile of tangled limbs. The landing was awkward, increasing the pressure on his already busted ribs.

"Up here, Shetani!"

Logan looked up and found Mo on the third floor just in front of the Observation Deck doorway. The Nach was right behind him, climbing the walls. He watched as the creature stabbed the solid concrete, claw first, burying them in deep enough to gain purchase on the smooth surface. Then, like an insect-monkey hybrid, it climbed, pursuing the foe that taunted it.

Damnit, Mo, Logan thought, getting to his feet.

He keyed his radio. "What the hell are you doing?"

"I will lead it outside and take Kipanga. There is no way it can fly as fast as our bird can, but I will need time to get her started."

Logan looked at Fitz who shrugged.

Damnit.

"Alright, we're coming up behind you. Haul ass and get in the air." Logan turned to Fitz. "Grab a few more bottles of booze. We need to distract it long enough for Mo to get airborne."

Fitz dashed into the living area, grabbing three more bottles. Logan, Zeus, and Ares, quickly made for the stairs, firing as they went. The beast slowed, but didn't stop, swatting blindly at the bullets. Logan doubted they were doing any real harm, like King Kong on top of the Empire State Building, but at least they appeared to be annoying it enough for it to temper its pursuit of their friend. Mo easily climbed through the large hole that once held the roof access hatch, scrambling over the loose rubble.

As Mo's foot pushed off the top step, the ladder dislodged and bent away from the opening, weakened from the demon's entry. Logan knew that any kind of retreat for Mo was now impossible. He *needed* to get in the air immediately.

They reached the third and final platform just as the Nach attempted to climb out. Logan aimed, but stopped when Fitz yelled for them to scatter. They listened and watched a bottle sail over their heads and smash into the creatures back, setting its wings alight.

It roared in anger and almost extricated its claws from the wall, but the ceaseless fire from the Delta men gave it pause. They may have actually given it a reason to flee.

Logan couldn't let it go. Even if Mo's plan worked, it would be loose and he had no idea if these things could heal. Maybe in time it would fully recover and they would have to fight it all over again.

"Back!" Logan yelled. He heard the telltale sound of the Blackhawk's rotors kicking in. All Mo would need is a few more seconds. Logan needed to hit it with something harder.

He pulled the trigger of his GL40 grenade launcher mounted under the main firing barrel of his SCAR rifle. It bucked and sent his last explosive straight into the creature's back. It detonated, removing one of the wings and shredding the other. It wouldn't be flying anywhere, anytime soon.

It was catapulted into the air, just barely clearing the edge of the cracking roof. Concrete came loose and started slipping into the open roof of the Bullpen.

A few of the larger pieces dropped like bombs, landing right next to Fitz. He yelped and backed away as the roof access ladder tore away, landing with a clang on the level below.

"Shit!" Logan cried, watching the Nach flip ass-over-teakettle, landing with a boom above them. "Back outside. We need to give Mo whatever support we can from the ground."

Logan led the charge seeing Jan, CJ, and Adnan waiting for them below.

"What are you doing here?" he yelled from above as he ran.

"We were watching from the live feeds around the compound," CJ replied, Glock ready. Adnan was also armed with an identical pistol, but Jan was unarmed looking like he was fighting a fever. "The Nach outside ceased their assault once the other big one was killed."

Other big one? Logan thought. *Must have missed that one.*

"Fine—whatever—just move!"

They all ran like world-class sprinters, through the stairwell door, down the stairs, and out the previous locked front door. They quickly exited, bulling through the northern entrance, looking to the sky for Mo and Kipanga.

Whup. Whup. Whup.

The helicopter was off the ground, angling north straight over their heads. Mo had made it.

What of the creature?

60

Logan watched as Mo and Kipanga glided away from the decimated roof. He wished his friend luck and prayed he would see him again.

A roar echoed through the night sky, chilling Logan's sweat soaked body. The monstrous form of, *Shetani*, the name Mo gave it, leapt into the sky, towards Kipanga and subsequently Mo.

Logan reached for his earbud and tried to signal him to climb higher, but the creature was too fast. It lashed out blindly, miraculously grabbing the right landing strut, making the chopper list horribly to the side. Thankfully, Mo was a damned fine pilot.

Kipanga's engines revved harder, compensating for the extra weight, and leveled out as well as it could. It then, indeed, climbed higher, straining at the effort. It looked like he had the aircraft under control, until the Nach started trying to make its way inside the rear hold.

It punctured the sliding door with its free hand, gripped it, and pulled, snapping the heavy metal from its hinges like it was a twig. It sailed into the sky and arched...straight at Logan and the others.

They dove back towards the building, but Logan went the other way, being farther out into the open. It landed with a reverberating *GONG,* just behind him, nearly clipping his boots where he now lay. Logan sprang to his feet and watched as the monster climbed in.

* * * * *

It roared, making Mo flinch and lose the stick. Kipanga, like a Mustang with no reins, flailed and danced to a song that Mo couldn't hear. He snagged it, though, and did his best to keep the aircraft from falling out of the sky.

"Mo... It... Inside..." Mo could barely hear Logan over the wind and whine of the failing engine. They were just too heavy for what the helicopter had left in it. It needed gas and a complete overhaul when they were done—

Gas, Mo thought—as a massive clawed hand burst through his chest. Blood sprayed, coating the windshield and instrument panel.

Mo looked down at the four inches of talons protruding from his chest as they slowly retracted and slid out of his chest and then his back with a slurp. His eyesight fluttered and his breathing stopped. Both lungs were punctured and getting anything except the smallest of breaths was impossible now. He'd be dead in a matter of seconds, but he still had a job to do.

Except, he thought, *that was on the slightest of chances that I survived.*

Now, he didn't have to worry about leading the monster away. He was able to do what needed to be done and damn the consequences. He was already dead.

He grabbed the throttle and looked back into the cargo hold, seeing the demon for the first time up close and personal.

Its six dead eyes stared back at him. Even though they didn't function anymore, they still had all the hatred of hell itself burning through them. The blood covered maw of the creature hung open, unable to close like a proper mouth should. The teeth had grown so long that the lower jaw couldn't shut completely.

Mo smiled and then grinned at what he was about to do, seeing the beast lodged into Kipanga's rear cabin.

"*Kuona wewe Kuzimu, Shetani,*" Mo said in his native Swahili. *See you in Hell, Devil.*

The demon tilted its head like it recognized the language, but Mo didn't give it time to think it over. He yanked back on the throttle, cutting all power to the overhead turbine, making Kipanga drop like a stone. Mo looked out of his window, watching as the sun just began to peek out from behind the horizon. As his mind and body faded, Mo could hear his passenger shriek in recognition of what was about to happen.

Then, Mo was gone, sacrificing himself for the greater good. He protected the animals of this region with fiery passion, but he knew that wasn't his greatest feat. His ultimate accomplishment was saving his friends. Logan would see to the rest. He believed in the Aussie with every fiber of his being. Even though Logan wasn't the most passionate of animal lovers, he still respected them. That was enough.

61

As the Blackhawk fell from the sky, Logan turned and ran, rounding the last of the two northern sentry towers. One was a crumbled mess, but this one had miraculously survived Ares' charges. The others, being closer to the building, would be able to flee inside, but he was too far. This would have to do. Kipanga was about hundred feet up when it started to fall, enough to destroy the aircraft and its occupants, but close enough for him to have to find secondary shelter other than what was left of the Bullpen.

He ducked and covered his ears as the helicopter struck. It detonated on impact, the fuel left inside the tank creating the perfect large scale Molotov. Fitz would be proud. The concussive force, paired with the heat and shrapnel, should definitely be enough to kill the monster.

Should.

A fireball burst past either side of the sentry tower, scorching some of Logan's hair as it passed. He would probably have some minor burns, but it could have been worse. It could wait.

Thank God the tower held up—

SNAP!

Logan peered through stinging, smoke-filled eyes and gasped. The base had originally cracked and started to fall apart from the C4, causing the inner metal framework to bend and break. The explosion produced by the crashing helicopter must have caused the weakened structure to buckle under its immense weight. The thirty-foot concrete and steel tower was about to fall.

He scrambled back and then to the side—and then back again, unsure what direction the thing would actually fall. It was like an undecided Redwood, teetering whichever way the wind blew it. If he chose the wrong way, he'd be paste.

Another roar erupted from the twisted, ruined Blackhawk, as something large and black emerged from the wreckage.

No...

The beast was alive—completely and utterly broken—but alive. Its left arm was missing at the shoulder, as was its lower jaw.

POP!

Logan watched as the Shetani shambled forward, on what looked like, two broken legs, but then turned his attention skyward. The tower leaned, ever so slightly, eventually tipping beyond its breaking point, and fell. It collapsed faster than Logan thought anything that solid and big could. He closed his eyes and hoped the end would come soon.

And it did.

It's over, he thought, waiting.

Shetani lunged forward and was crushed by thousands of pounds of modern engineering. Logan even caught a glimpse of an iron rebar pierce its skull, making it implode.

He fell onto his back and laughed as the dust plume settled over his body, making him cough in spurts. It was over, but unfortunately for him, a good portion of his beloved Bullpen was wrecked. The monster had really done a number on it.

Still got my hot tub, though.

"You alright, mate?"

Logan didn't answer. He just held up a hand, giving Fitz the finger, laughing again. They had survived. And so did—

"Come now, brother. Show some manners."

Logan lifted his head and smiled. CJ had made it. She was a mess of cuts and blood like the rest of them, but otherwise, she was fine.

"So," Fitz said, offering a hand to Logan. "Does this mean we're out of a job?"

He pulled Logan to his feet, both men grunting from exertion and the results of various injuries. Patting Fitz on the shoulder, Logan laughed, when his friend winced in pain.

"You're really starting to soften up there—"

GRRRNNN.

It came from behind them, back towards the Bullpen's open front door. The guttural moan repeated from just inside the north entrance.

A scream erupted from the doorway as something attacked, latching itself onto Adnan's neck. It bit and tore at the man until all that was left was a garbled whimper. Then, just like that, Adnan was dead, killed by—

"Jan?" Logan softly asked himself, stepping towards the mayhem. He meant to check on him and make sure he didn't need immediate medical attention—

It's then the big German dropped the deceased Adnan, covered in the man's blood. Logan saw the eyes... The *green* eyes. They stared back through the smoky haze swirling around them. Jan wouldn't be needing any medical attention... He was already dead.

"NO!"

Logan had to catch CJ as she tried to run to Jan's aid. "Don't, Cass. He's gone." He wrapped his hands around her waist as she kicked and clawed to get free.

"Um, mates?"

CJ stopped just long enough to see the worried look on Fitz's face. She stopped fighting and Logan released her, but he kept a firm grip on her shirt collar, keeping her from running off again.

"No..." CJ repeated. Tears streamed down her face for what must have been the tenth time since the sun set. But these were the worst set yet. The man she came to love...was gone.

She stepped forward.

"Cass?" Logan asked, not letting go of her.

"It's fine Logan. I'll handle it." She then turned and faced him. "He'd want me to."

He looked down and saw that she had her Glock. He and Fitz had both lost their weapons in the latest fight and the two Delta men were waiting for them to move first. They lowered the barrels of their weapons upon seeing CJ grip hers. It was up to her to finally finish this nightmare.

The Nach that had just been their good friend—the gentle German giant—stalked forward. It then barred its black fangs, stretched out its newly formed claws, and charged.

CJ began to cry again, but lifted her weapon. She watched as Jan's eyes—the same eyes that had made her insides squirm just a few hours ago—buried into her soul for the last time.

She noticed the wound. It was pulsating with green blood, enveloping the whole of the shoulder, easily seen from this distance. He'd been infected by the four armed demon, when it dripped some of its blood on him. She'd seen it live on the security feed from down in the basement, but thought nothing of it.

At first Jan wanted her love.

Now, he wanted her life—to take it.

"I'm sorry," she said, sniffing back a sob.

She pulled the trigger.

EPILOGUE

One Week Later

Bodies littered the Serengeti for miles, stretching out from a central point. The bunker. Until further notice, the SDF and the American military labeled the park a hot zone. No one in and no one out. It was something that even the poachers wouldn't mess with. They wanted nothing to do with the disease that ran rampant through the area overnight a week ago.

But it was gone now. When the sun came up, anything infected with the Nazi's *Gott Blut* burned from the inside out. It was an exact match to the description in Mengele's notes. Something about the UV rays not agreeing with the chemical makeup of the plasma coursing through their veins.

Logan was surprised and relieved when the country's government *officially* allowed the U.S. Army to have boots on the ground. They had seen the reports. It was public knowledge that something horrific had happened, but they weren't told everything—the exact cause.

It had been labeled as a *plague*, which wasn't technically lying. A virus of some sort had, indeed, broken out, infecting over a thousand animals and a few unlucky people.

Zeus and Ares, the only surviving members of the twelve-man Delta outfit, offered to stay on and help oversee the cleanup efforts. They had lost a lot of men and wanted to see it through.

Logan, CJ, and Fitz were all the SDF had left too, losing seven other members. The Bullpen still stood and was currently under heavy renovations. Logan had thought about tearing it down and rebuilding it from scratch, but there were too many good memories of the people they had lost in those walls. Plus, the only real hiccup the building had was the hole in the roof. That was almost completely fixed as of today. By Monday morning they could theoretically get back to work if they wanted too.

"No frickin' way," Fitz laughed, looking up at the tarp covered ceiling. "I need a damn vacation."

Logan slapped him on the back, causing his friend to wince. It was good to see Fitz's sense of humor was still alive and kicking under the circumstances.

"Logan?" Logan turned and found Zeus standing a few feet away. He had a phone to his ear and looked deadly serious as he listened to whoever was on the other line.

"What is it, Navarro?" Logan asked. Zeus—David Navarro—had insisted on him calling him by his less formal last name while in private. But once they were back out in the field, it was Zeus. Calling the man by his first name was still off limits. Something about getting to close to people in this line of business.

"Samson put in a call," Navarro said, mentioning Ares by his own last name. *No wonder he likes Ares,* Logan had thought when properly introduced to the demo expert. "He got a hold of someone who now works with an old friend of mine."

Logan raised an eyebrow. "Who?"

Navarro handed the phone to Logan.

"His name is Jenkins and he works for a former colleague of mine from when I was a Ranger. He has some high-tech program working on the rest of Mengele's paperwork."

Jenkins?

Logan took the phone.

"This is Logan Reed. Is this Jenkins?"

The man on the other end chuckled. "The name is Todd. You soldiers and your last name mumbo-jumbo... But yes, I'm Jenkins."

Logan was confused with Todd Jenkins. He didn't sound military at all.

"Who are you and who do you work for?" Logan asked, getting down to business.

"Who am I? Well, I'm a software engineer, who likes to dabble in some of the other forms of online art, and as far as who I work for... Well, I'm not really allowed to tell you that."

Great... A government hacker spook.

"Fine, Todd, but why you?"

"Well," Todd said, "your friend here called in a favor to my boss and asked me to look into something."

Logan looked back over to Navarro whose face was stone. He had, indeed, been in the Army Rangers before becoming a Delta operator. He even told Logan a candid story about an old Ranger friend of his. He was a mountain of a man with a loudmouth and a goofy sense of humor. Logan knew Navarro wouldn't have asked for outside assistance unless he knew it would help.

"And?" Logan asked, sick of the chit-chat.

"I've come up with two things. First... We found some more information on the *Verbraucher* that Mengele spoke of."

Logan's eyes widened as the spy continued.

"We can confirm that they are most definitely in the Congo."

Logan suspected as much.

"One of the most unexplored ecosystems in the world," Logan added.

"Yes," Todd agreed. "Quite so."

"And?" Logan asked again, waiting for the other thing Todd had mentioned.

"Secondly, they need to be stopped at all costs."

Tilting his head in confusion, Logan asked the obvious question. "What do you mean, *stopped?*"

Todd cleared his throat and continued. "I've come to the conclusion that they will be even more dangerous than we expected. Think about it, Logan. Mengele said they could turn it on and off—the virus I mean. Who's to say they aren't already infiltrating the modern world?"

"Sounds like a lot of speculation, Todd." Logan said. "You need to give me more than this."

A voice spoke in the background and Todd mumbled something incoherently back. "Fine. Fine... Okay, look. All I can say is that we need you to go to the Congo and at least give it a look. We'll finance everything in Serengeti and rebuild your base of operations with everything I can come up with. It'll be better than ever and ten-times as safe and defendable. We'll triple your original staff and train and arm them. You'll get a brand new Blackhawk and a small convoy of vehicles."

"Todd, I—"

The I.T. man cut him off. "We need this Logan. You can have Zeus and Ares, too. Until this threat is over, that is. They're yours until then. No one on the planet is more suited to look into these... *Verbraucher*...as you and your current team. We will help you all but eliminate poaching in your park."

That sobered Logan up a little. Not only was there a potential threat to take care of, but his ultimate goal of protecting the species of the Serengeti was coming true. Manpower had always been their limitation, but not now. The SDF would truly be feared by everyone illegally hunting in *his* park.

He looked at Navarro who nodded. It seemed the soldier would definitely be accompanying them.

Samson stepped up next to Navarro and crossed his arms. The look of determination in the shorter bulldog's eyes confirmed his involvement.

He looked to the rest of his crew. CJ and Fitz apparently heard the conversation as well. His sister's face was filled with glee. The prospect of saving the animals was her lifelong dream. Fitz's expression was as indifferent as ever. He would be by Logan's side either way.

"Okay, Mr. Jenkins. Tell me everything."

A MESSAGE FROM THE AUTHOR

Thank you for supporting me and purchasing this book. I truly hope you enjoyed it. I was extremely nervous when I started on *Plague* as it was my first story outside of the *Hank Boyd* series. But man it was fun! I had planned on writing something else truthfully, but then got the idea for this novel and ran with it.

Also, if you have a spare moment, could you please leave a review on the website you purchased this from and/or on Goodreads.com? It would be very much appreciated. As an indie author, I rely heavily on word-of-mouth and social media, and every little bit counts. I don't have some big name publisher driving sales for me. So, it's all you, the readers, and the more interest I get...the more books I can write.

Thanks again, Matt

ABOUT THE AUTHOR

Matthew James is the author of the critically acclaimed Hank Boyd Adventure series, *Blood and Sand* and *Mayan Darkness*. He was born in West Palm Beach, Florida and still lives in his hometown with his family.

*Look for his next novel, *Dead Moon*, coming soon in 2016.

You can visit Matthew at:

www.Facebook.com/MatthewJamesAuthor
www.Jamestownbooks.Wordpress.com
Twitter: @MJames_Books

Made in the USA
Lexington, KY
22 June 2016